LOVE, CAMERA, ACTION

LOVE, CAMERA, ACTION

A Novel

NOËL STARK

alcove
press

This is a work of fiction. All of the names, characters, organizations, places and events portrayed in this novel are either products of the author's imagination or are used fictitiously. Any resemblance to real or actual events, locales, or persons, living or dead, is entirely coincidental.

Copyright © 2025 by Debra Felstead

All rights reserved.

Published in the United States by Alcove Press, an imprint of The Quick Brown Fox & Company LLC.

Alcove Press and its logo are trademarks of The Quick Brown Fox & Company LLC.

Library of Congress Catalog-in-Publication data available upon request.

ISBN (hardcover): 979-8-89242-040-2
ISBN (paperback): 979-8-89242-235-2
ISBN (ebook): 979-8-89242-041-9

Cover design by Kristen Solecki

Printed in the United States.

www.alcovepress.com

Alcove Press
34 West 27th St., 10th Floor
New York, NY 10001

First Edition: April 2025

10 9 8 7 6 5 4 3 2 1

For Jude

CHAPTER ONE

Sex was a tricky thing. A powerful amount of discipline went into making sex effortless yet magical.

No, not magical. "Magical" was too cliché, and Calliope Daniels knew that cliché was the death knell of good sex. Saying it was good didn't make it so. It had to *be* good.

Making good sex was Cali's job. Well, not exactly making *sex*, but making the most fake, awkward, and public sex choreography look intimate and real. That was why the hotly anticipated network TV series *The Demon* had hired her to direct THE hookup. The mid-season, two-part episode where the titular demon and her human prey, after burning for each other over the entire season like supernova suns, finally *got it on*. And who did they want to direct that pivotal moment in the story?

Calliope Daniels.

Because she was good at sex.

Well, that and the tiny fact that the original—male— director had stated on social media that the industry had overcompensated for the #metoo movement, and "thankfully the pendulum had swung back to where it should be." That pendulum fired his ass, and *The Demon* production team needed a female replacement for him, fast. With no women directors on their slate to help clean up the PR mess, the producers on *The Demon* reached out to the bush leagues. There, they found Cali—an up-and-comer, a pro, and, well . . . a woman who was available.

Cali flung open the door to the Atlanta studio and raced through its sets, her mind scouring through the script she'd all but memorized for clues on how to make the sex scene sing. She knew whatever she came up with would have to be more than good. It was an unspoken reality that a male director had the first day of a shoot to win the trust of the cast and crew, while a female director had the first scene. As a relative unknown in the American television market, Cali knew this was a make-or-break moment in her career.

She couldn't just direct this sex scene—she had to direct it *flawlessly*. This was her chance to prove she was a director to be reckoned with, a director who should be ranked among the best.

This will work. I will make this work. Can I make this work? Oh God, it's not going to work. It's really not going to work.

Cali told her inner voice to fuck off, and strode onto the bedroom set that would be the location of her first scene, just as someone boomed out, "Watch your back!"

Cali turned to see a bundle of two-by-fours headed for her face. She froze, unable to move, part of her hoping that her nose bone would get rammed into her brain by a piece of wood, and all her fears and doubts would blissfully vanish.

Love, Camera, Action

Two hands closed around her shoulders and yanked her back as a burly carpenter shouldering the planks barreled through. "Eyes up, sweetheart!"

A deep voice rumbled behind her in weary irritation, "What did I say about calling people 'sweetheart,' man? It's not 2018."

"Sorry, sweetheart." The carpenter blew a kiss to whoever owned the voice that vibrated through her like grandma's neck massager. Cali followed the trajectory of that floating kiss and came face-to-face with a vision that made her chest seize.

He was a bit taller than Cali—a rarity since she was usually the tall one (her mother's cackle filled her mind: *"They're all the same height lying down, honey"*)—and built in that manly-man kind of way crafted by the brutal pace of a busy TV set rather than a vanity project. The intensity of his crystalline blue eyes and sandy-blond hair hearkened noble warriors primed to take a tumble into hell just for kicks. The sheer magnetism was discombobulating. You know—if you were into dangerous men who could lead a Roman legion.

Cali backed up a step to remind herself how to breathe.

He had no problems breathing, practically huffing out beleaguered irritation. "You here from PR? Today is a closed set, so you'll have to go over to the offices."

Cali blinked in confusion. "Oh no, I'm Cali Daniels."

"And I'm Jory Blair. But you're still going to have to leave. Just go back the way you came . . ."

Cali stopped listening as excitement, mortification, and dread burbled up at once.

This was Jory Blair, director of photography.

The DP's purview was the look of the show—the style, the lighting, the composition—and Jory Blair was considered

3

the next great visionary, changing how everyone saw the world. He brought an unflinching gaze to every moment he shot, whether it was the delicate love between parent and child or the chaotic terror of the battlefield. His precision; his choice of angle, frame, and light; his dedication to detail made everything unerringly *real*. He was alternately referred to as a true genius and a control freak.

Cali was firmly out of her league. She'd lucked into this gig because the few low-rent, racy TV shows up in Canada she'd directed had suckered the executives into believing she was the woman for this exceptional job. A job working with Jory Fucking Blair. A Real Artist. A Real Innovator. The Real Deal.

On top of all that, he was inconveniently, illogically, and devastatingly hot. She could barely look at him for Pete's sake. And when she cast her gaze to the sensually lit environment, where trendy art hung on ecru walls above a very male, oak bedroom suite dressed with a chiffon blue duvet and ten-thousand-thread-count cotton sheets as though it had floated out of *Elle's* tribute to "virile bed sets," a girl was bound to get some ideas.

She ground her imagination to a halt. She didn't consider guys on set as potential flings. Not only was it bad for her reputation as a director, but she'd witnessed others on set getting into relationships, and they always went south, making the long, intense workdays unbearable. For both the people involved and the crew around them. Still, as she took in Jory's strong, tanned forearm gesturing to the door, she remembered there was nothing wrong with a little appreciation.

". . . and then another left past the mermaid fountain," he finished, sighing as though it was all too much. "You

Love, Camera, Action

know what? It doesn't matter. Go that way, and I'm sure someone will direct you."

Pushing aside her panic and fascination while swearing an oath to the gods of "fake it till you make it," she tried again. "I'm Cali Daniels."

His face flattened but for the tiniest smile that lifted his lips. His beautiful, sensuous, Chris Pine lips. "You said that."

"Hi there! Hey! Hi! Can I help you? This is a closed set."

Past Jory, a stunning woman in her mid-thirties, with black hair, violet eyes, and a don't-fuck-with-me-or-I-will-destroy-you vibe stepped blithely toward them over multitudinous cables, in five-inch Fluevog pumps.

Melanie Reiter was the co-executive producer on *The Demon*. Second only to the showrunner, she did everything from finalizing scripts and approving wardrobe looks, to championing directors no one had heard of to take over lynchpin episodes. Melanie was *the* reason Cali was here.

"Hi, Melanie, I'm—"

"Oh my God, Cali." Melanie's hands flew to her cheeks. "I'm sorry, I didn't recognize you. What took you so long? Did your driver come via Savannah?"

"Yes, sorry, the traffic—"

"Isn't it unreal? I thought LA was bad. Ryan!" Melanie's gaze snapped to a wiry man precariously hanging off a ladder. "Did you get your electrician's license in the last five minutes? You are *not* authorized to rewire that light, and I do *not* have time for an insurance claim if you get electrocuted." Ryan reluctantly descended the ladder as Melanie returned her focus to Cali with a clap of her hands. "So! Big scene today, right off the top."

Cali felt Jory's attention shift in curiosity, but she kept her eyes on Melanie. Barely. "Absolutely. In my mind this scene is as important as the ultimate love scene since it's got to build their tension to the breaking point."

"So true," Melanie agreed. "I'm glad you think that. That's great. Really great. Well, I can't wait to see what you've got planned. You have something planned, right? I know it's been a whirlwind."

"I have some ideas that will really make this scene pop." Cali hoped the lie would eventually become true.

"Great. Great. Remember I'm here to encourage, to support, to cheer. I'm *just* here to observe."

Melanie fidgeted in her stance and flicked her eyes at Jory, probably to gauge his reaction. As much as Melanie had fought for her, Cali knew she must be nervous about sticking her neck out for someone most people saw as a rookie.

Jory turned to Melanie. "So this is . . . ?"

"Oh my God!" Melanie gasped. "You haven't met. I'm so sorry! It's been such a hectic time with the switchover in directors and getting you here and . . . well . . . never mind. Cali is Robert's replacement and is beyond fabulous. You're going to love her."

Cali turned to Jory with a confident, mildly accusatory smile, squeezing herself into the upper hand with all her might. He was still implacable, but Cali swore she saw the tiniest hint of a blush.

"I'm Jory Blair." He put his hand out.

She mimicked his tiny smile. "You said that."

Yep. That was a blush. She took his hand and felt his warmth soak into her, the pressure of his grip strong but not forceful, as though he had nothing to prove.

Love, Camera, Action

Melanie's attention snagged on a set dresser prepping the bed, already on the move. "No, no, no. That's too many pillows. No man has that many pillows."

"That's sexist, Mel," Jory called after her. "Men can have pillows."

"You're absolutely right, Jory, and I feel terrible for being so judgmental." Then Melanie lit into the set dresser, who quickly gathered the excess pillows in her arms.

Left alone, Cali forced her attention back to Jory with Herculean effort. "It's a pleasure to meet you. I've always admired your work."

"Thanks." The blush disappeared, his features snapping into full neutral.

She'd said the wrong thing. Maybe he wasn't the type who liked compliments. "I mean, it's hard to avoid your work since it seems to be everywhere."

The tension eased in his jaw. "That's my secret plan, to flood the market with only me."

"Smart. That way even your mistakes look like art."

"Oh, I don't make mistakes. Don't you read the trades?" He leaned in. "I'm a genius." His brows were all austere seriousness, but that slight smile returned.

Hot and humble? *Mon Dieu.*

Cali couldn't help but smile back. Which made his smile falter. And then hers faltered. Was smiling wrong too?

"Good flight?" He straightened away from her.

Cali grasped at the change in subject. "The flight was fine, but when I got off the plane, I felt like I'd been hit with a boiled washcloth. Is it always so humid here?"

"It's called Hotlanta for a reason. Wait until you see the afternoon storms—they're like a four PM alarm of thunder, lightning, and wind."

"Do they break the humidity?" she asked hopefully.

"Not even a little."

"Gross."

"Very."

A slightly easier silence descended. Maybe Cali could do this. If Jory was half as good as his reputation, he could be the ally she needed. "Well, we've had the compulsory weather chat—I guess we should move on to work. Did you get my shot list?"

"I did." His tone took on the vocal quality of Switzerland. "Looks good."

Did he hate it? He must hate it. She shifted to self-deprecation mode. "It's a bit boring—smooth, sexy shots to show off the actors' bodies. Meh."

Jory's eyebrows shot up. "I don't think I've experienced a director who dissed their own ideas before. The shot list is fine."

"I think that might be the trouble." Cali shook her head. "I didn't have a ton of time to come up with something better since I only got the call three days ago."

"One director's stupid, sexist move is another's lucky break." A cloud crossed Jory's face. "There is zero tolerance for that kind of behavior on my set." Cali noted the— probably subconscious—claim that the set was his. He continued: "But three days prep isn't a lot. I would've preferred to discuss the look of the show with you, the protocols, but here we are and your ideas are fine."

Cali grimaced. "Fine" wouldn't get her where the scene needed to be. Where *she* needed to be. "There's that word again. I'm sure you've never settled for 'fine.'"

"Sometimes 'fine' is all I can hope for." The cloud darkened, and he quickly glanced away, as if he'd startled himself with the admission.

Love, Camera, Action

Cali experienced a curious wave of protectiveness, which was ridiculous. Men could take care of themselves. "Okay. Well, I was hoping for something a bit better than that. And to that end, there are a few moments that I think we should explore."

"What do you mean by 'explore?'" Cali felt rather than saw Jory square his shoulders.

"Well, there's a deeper meaning to this scene. Something we can tease out if we risk being a bit more *avant-garde.*"

Jory glanced off to the side with a thoughtful look on his face. His body had gone still, as though he needed all his considerable energy to weigh the idea.

Cali brightened. This was what she had hoped for, a collaboration between two like minds working toward an unforgettable moment in *The Demon* universe. Excitement roiled up, snuffing out her doubt.

Jory turned his excessive blue eyes back to hers. "Can I give you some advice?"

Cali nodded eagerly, breath bated.

"I get it's your first day and you're keen to do a good job, to put your creative stamp on things. It's a tough gig, and I get that. But if you just get the shots we need and do it in a reasonable time, that will make everyone, including me, really happy."

Cali frowned. She must be misunderstanding him—it sounded like he *wanted* to keep everything rote, simple, boring. This wasn't the Jory Blair she had read about, had studied. "I think the scene has more potential, but it hasn't revealed itself yet. I'm sure we can find it together once we see it on its feet." She pressed on. "And when we do find it, we'd be making the story happy rather than people."

"Making people happy is ninety percent of my job."

"And the other ten?"

"Making sure directors don't overstep their bounds. Stick with 'fine,'" he said.

Then he winked at her.

A twenty-something blond woman holding two camera lenses cleared her throat. Jory took them from her and stepped away, dismissing the conversation and leaving Cali alone in a pool of shock.

He winked at me. He winked at me! Who does that?

Cali had never been made to feel like she was twelve—even when she *was* twelve. A girl who had singlehandedly brought up her little sister and herself, while keeping their mom under control so they weren't put into the system, didn't often get looked down on for lack of seriousness. She'd been condescended to before, sure—what woman hadn't? Mostly she'd always been, rightfully, assessed as a mature adult with confidence and brains.

With one eyelid, Jory had brought the curtain down on her idea, relegating Cali to a peon barely worth his regard.

A honeyed male voice interrupted her furious thoughts. "So, who's on top?"

Cali shifted her gaze to take in a ridiculously beautiful man.

Melanie swooped in beside him, her tone tolerant. "Cali, this is Paolo Ramirez, our male lead. Paolo, Cali directed *Suddenly, Hot Summer*."

Suddenly, Hot Summer was a low-budget, ill-advised cross between Tennessee Williams's *Suddenly, Last Summer* and *Cannonball Run*. While the producers had thought they were making a masterpiece, mixing a cross-country

Love, Camera, Action

race with a commentary on mental illness, Cali saw the train wreck for what it was, and shot the film, and the multiple sex scenes in various vehicles, like a comedy. As a result it had become a cult hit.

Paolo seemed impressed for a nanosecond, then returned to what was probably his base face—chill with a serving of pout. "That Segway scene was fire."

"Thank you," she offered humbly.

Paolo played Rafe—the object of the Demon's annihilations and affections—in his first acting gig after being plucked from a model photo shoot. He was perfectly cast with his dark angelic features: wavy chestnut hair, green eyes, and full dusky lips. He vibrated with charisma.

He was also naked.

Well, almost. Naked but for the open robe carelessly hung off his shoulders and the flesh-tone banana hammock thong that may have been made of rice paper. Cali couldn't tell if Paolo was über-comfortable with his body because of the various states of undress required of a model, or flaunting the hours spent at the gym instead of, say, in front of a book. He wasn't known for his smarts.

Squashing her feelings of disappointment and general unworthiness, and looking forward to the moment the intimacy coordinator arrived on set, Cali gestured to Paolo's hammock. "Can you move around in that?"

Without warning, Paolo dipped into a deep squat followed by a full burpee that ended with a roundhouse kick. The move would have been impressive if his foot hadn't connected with a passing production assistant's ear, knocking her headset off.

Boyish embarrassment slid over him as he rushed to help the horrified PA. "Sorry, sorry."

Fumbling for her headset, she wound up eye level with Paolo's protruding manhood. With a gasp, she squeezed her lids shut. "I'm okay. I'm okay," she squeaked while Melanie hurried her off set.

"Smooth move, Ramirez."

Cali turned to see Thalia Bautista, the female lead. While Paolo was pure ethereal beauty, Thalia was nothing but earth. Her tan skin, black hair, and amber eyes only enhanced her fiery sensuality that seemed to have its own atmosphere. Thalia had a reputation for being a solid, thoughtful actress who was deeply committed to her craft, if a bit uptight.

Paolo's features covered the full spectrum from mortification to arrogance. *Interesting,* Cali thought. On screen, Paolo showed an alarming lack of emotional range, but in person, he demonstrated a rainbow of expression. If she could pull that out in front of the camera, the show had the making of a star on its hands.

Cali turned her attention to Thalia and the leather bustier–jumpsuit concoction she wore. "How are you feeling in this?"

Thalia gave Cali a practiced smile. "It's comfortable enough, but I feel like I'm wearing a parka next to Paolo. I mean, I'm good with losing it . . ."

Suddenly Melanie was back. "I was wondering about that choice myself. The network loves Thalia and, if anything, would like to see more of her."

"Yeah. Whatever you need." The slightest tension crept into Thalia's shoulders, even though her voice was all silky acquiescence. A disquiet thrumming under all that leather and confidence.

Love, Camera, Action

Cali loved actors. They were gushy balls of feeling who were full of surprises and charm and energy. Lots of directors didn't understand how actors worked their magic, so they fearfully hid behind the technical aspects of the camera. Cali was all about figuring out the language of a shot or how to create a mood with light, but knew that was only part of the puzzle. Recognizing and drawing out hidden emotional nuance from these complicated beings was her jam.

And Thalia was nervous. Cali didn't know if it was the sex scene or her costar or whatever she'd had for breakfast, but if Cali didn't give Thalia a safe and secure environment in which to perform, the scene would fall flat. This was Cali's true super power—to make others feel safe. Maybe because she'd had so little opportunity to feel safe herself.

"I get the network wants to see more of Thalia—she's gorgeous and talented." Cali kept her tone breezy. "But we don't want to cheapen her status as a badass demon. This isn't a booty call, it's the slow assassination of someone she's come to care for. Besides, Thalia can convey more sexual energy covered in burlap than another actress in pasties."

"Oh yeah, I totally agree." Melanie nodded a bit too vigorously. "I'm just passing along a compliment." Melanie's head snapped to the left. "Cesare! That budget? Do we honestly need all those 4K lights?" And she was gone again.

Thalia let out a long breath. She glanced over at Paolo, who was doing quad stretches, seemingly oblivious to the conversation taking place. Thalia didn't hide her disgust as she took in the man she was about to get down and dirty with. "How long is this going to take? I don't mean to be pushy, but the less time I have to be in this particular scenario the better."

Paolo's eyebrows drew down in annoyance, but he quickly smoothed them, pout back in place. "Yeah, I've got a press call later."

Cali took note of the obvious animosity between her leads and tucked it away for later—she never knew when she'd need to use an actor's real feelings in a scene.

Thalia unclenched her hands to hitch up her bustier as if to cover more skin.

"I'll try to get you out as fast as I can." On a hunch, Cali motioned to the bustier. "Do you mind if I test your wardrobe?"

Thalia swung her gaze back to Cali in surprise. "Sure."

Using the touch of a scientist, Cali pulled and twisted the leather that hugged Thalia's body, while Paolo pretended to ignore them. "This is well made. Good seams, strong leather. It's like a suit of armor." Thalia's eyes searched her face, perhaps for sincerity, and Cali returned the regard with one of open support. "There's no getting through this thing."

Thalia nodded and blew out a small breath, relaxing her shoulders.

Cali turned to Paolo with an easy smile. "Get in there. You're on the bottom."

Paolo brushed by Thalia with a sex shimmy, eliciting an eye roll from the petite actress. He smirked, then took his place on the bed, turning toward the on-set makeup artist like a flower finding the sun.

Attention still on Paolo, Thalia's volume dropped. "Nice to have a female director. It's a different vibe."

"Blocking!" A gruff man with an afterthought of a haircut and fraying jeans two washes away from the garbage barked orders across the studio. "This is a closed set due to the sensitive nature of the scene, so if you don't need to be here, get out."

Thalia murmured, "Don't let them bully you."

Cali leaned back to gauge the warning sent her way, but Thalia was already walking to the bed with a military air. She matter-of-factly crawled over a prone Paolo, placed two hands on either side of his head as she straddled him, and stilled to await further instructions.

Melanie's curvy frame moved back into Cali's path, forcing her to hold back a yelp of surprise. "We're not going to see that much of Paolo, are we?"

"Uh, no. It's just to make sure he has the freedom to move without being bound by clothes."

"Because there are firm network rules about nudity—what can and can't be seen."

Cali crinkled her brow. "The network wants to see more of Thalia but less of Paolo?"

"Of course. This show isn't streaming," Melanie snorted.

"Right." Cali recalibrated her approach to the puritanical rules of broadcast TV rather than the free-for-all of streamers. "What do I need to avoid?"

Melanie counted off on her fingers. "Tops of butts are fine, but no balls, penises, or vulvas, obviously, and no Thalia nipples but Paolo's are fine."

"I got you covered, Mel." Jory's toe-curling voice rumbled across the set.

Cali cursed herself. Her toes were not curling. They were perfectly straight.

"For sure keep Paolo covered," Thalia chimed in.

"True. You might be blinded by my manliness," Paolo drawled.

Thalia brought back an encore performance of the eye roll and accompanied it with an "Ugh."

To the untrained ear, Jory was helping Melanie out. To Cali, who had become attuned to the subtle art of men stealing authority, his casual remark was meant to control. And it needed to be nipped in the bud.

Cali responded a titch louder than necessary, "I think it's best to shoot the actors as intimately as possible so the tone stays solid. If they're worried about covering up, they won't give you the performances you need."

"As long as his package isn't in the middle of my frame. I can't adjust for that," Jory growled from behind the camera.

"We'll get lots of different angles so that won't be a problem." Cali smiled at Melanie, ignoring him.

Melanie threw up placating hands. "Oh absolutely, I get it. I'm just here to observe." And she was gone.

"Rehearsal's up!" Crappy-hair guy bellowed.

The crew and cast quietened. This was it. Cali surveyed the sea of carefully blank faces waiting for her first move that would set the tone for the next six weeks. She risked a glance at Jory, who stood by the camera with the air of a general protecting his troops, arms tightly crossed, legs akimbo, gaze heavy with judgment.

She felt as though she were balancing on the edge of a moment . . . the moment that marked either the next stage or the end of her career.

No pressure. No pressure at all.

"Hi, everyone. I'm Cali Daniels. And I will be your director."

CHAPTER TWO

I winked at her. I never wink. Who does that?
 Jory half listened to Cali's opening day speech, wondering what latent misogynist energy had bubbled that wink to the surface.
 Maybe it was because he'd barely made it to set—hell, barely made it out of bed—confronted with the thought of another tedious day on a show that should be fueling his drive but only engulfed him in a bleakness he couldn't find the energy to define.
 Maybe it was the cumulative stress from ignoring his test for so long, existing in the purgatorial state between health and sickness that had become his base line.
 Or maybe it was because Cali Daniels's smile had pinpricked his monochromatic existence with a stream of color. From her aura or some shit. Which was stupid. He didn't believe in auras. He barely believed in color anymore. And he refused to believe in the electricity shooting straight from her—what color were they? Hazel? Green?—hazel-green eyes

that were level with his. A strange perspective since he looked down on most people, in more ways than one.

The wink was most likely an unconscious defense to keep her away, he reasoned. His "little" health scare last year had rearranged his social life to a more hermit-like existence. Even though he was probably in the clear, the possibility of living on borrowed time had him abandoning his casual search for a life partner and pointedly avoiding any entanglements. Which might explain the attraction to someone who was off limits. Jory never dated anyone he worked with, even before the #metoo movement blew up the predators who pressured, stalked, and abused—mainly women—on set. His personal mandate was nonnegotiable, not only because it was wrong to take advantage of his position, but any whiff of harassment could destroy his career. The beginnings of a flirtation with the director had to be shut down, no matter how much color she exuded.

The Demon was his calling card to gain creative control and segue into directing himself. He was sick of watching directors who didn't know what they were doing destroy his vision. And he certainly wouldn't risk that vision for a newbie director who wanted to "explore" the scene in order to be "*avant-garde.*" It was better she knew her place off the top: beneath him.

Not in a sexy way, obviously.

Confidence restored, he planted himself next to Dan, the first assistant director and manager of the set. "Your daughter cut your hair again?"

Dan scowled. He worked hard to appear like an asshole in order to keep the production running on time, but really he was a big teddy bear. "Excuse me, but I'm trying to listen to our new director. And I think my hair looks great."

"Your daughter has an eye for images, not hair."

Dan blew out a defeated breath. "I know." He glanced at Jory. "Thanks for writing her that recommendation. She's over the moon about film school."

"She's talented. I didn't do much." Jory wasn't into throwing his weight around, but if he could get more women into the camera department, that was good for everybody. "What's our day?"

"Nothing too intense." Dan returned his attention to Cali and kept his voice low. "This sex scene, a couple in the office, a short action sequence."

"You going soft on her isn't going to help her game." Jory noted Cali's easy smile and amiable air while addressing the crew.

Dan raised his eyebrows. "Those scenes are trickier than you think. She's going to make you work."

"I haven't worked for a director in years. I'm not about to start now."

Jory left Dan to his sigh and quietly positioned himself behind Cali's left shoulder. It was a move he pulled to unnerve directors, to let them unconsciously know who's turf they were on.

As she broke down the scene to the crew, Jory watched the natural wave of Cali's auburn hair skim across her back. He wondered what it would look like cascading down in slow motion after being set free from a tie. His mind skittered to another curtain of hair released from its bounds, this time blond and on a bride standing barefoot on the beach, the sun setting behind her. The wind whipped her loose tendrils, tickling the groom, making them laugh as she tried to tame it in place. Jory remembered the hot sand under his feet and how safe he felt. Then what came after— the sadness, the loss.

Cali clapped her hands, breaking him from his reverie. "So! The scene has Anna working her demon magic on a sleeping Rafe. Rafe opens his eyes, and instead of screaming bloody murder, he takes her mouth in the long-awaited kiss. We'll do a master shot first and then dolly alongside with the second camera. Where's sound?"

"Brandon!" Jory boomed, as much to shock himself into the present as to rattle Cali.

Cali jumped and swung around to lock eyes with him. Any delight over his petty move quickly died when her intense energy crashed against him in a wave of tsunami proportions. He fought the urge to sway.

Cali put a hand to her chest in mock dismay. "Oof. You're stealthy."

The golden retriever who was Brandon bounded up with a boom microphone bouncing on his shoulder. Cali withdrew her gaze from Jory, and he felt an odd deprivation, like he'd been unplugged from a socket.

"Brandon, we're going to need some love on this. Good sex is all about the sounds," Cali explained.

Brandon guffawed with boyish eagerness.

"A boom wasn't in the original lighting plan. The mic will create a shadow. Dan!" Jory called over his shoulder while keeping his eyes on Cali. "How long would we need to switch the lighting?"

"An hour."

Jory shook his head. "Seems like a lot for a few sighs and moans that will be covered with music in the end."

"I'm not sure if I want music or not," Cali told Brandon. "Can you mic from under the bed?"

"Yeah, for sure!"

Cali turned a sharp smile on Jory. "Work for you?"

He wasn't sure if he felt angry or impressed. He definitely felt annoyed, because whatever *it* was, he felt *something*. He begrudgingly nodded while catching a droll smirk from Dan, à la *"Told you so."*

Cali moved on to Melanie. "Where's the intimacy coach?"

Melanie cleared her throat. "Uh . . . We don't have one."

Jory frowned. "We don't have an intimacy coach?"

Cali's eyes flicked to his in surprise before returning to Melanie's. "I thought all sex scenes were required to have an intimacy coach in order to protect the actors."

"It was deemed this scene didn't have the level of sexuality necessary to garner one."

That meant the higher-ups didn't want to spend the money. Jory suspected Melanie had fought hard against the decision, but voices above hers valued profits over decency. People who felt uncomfortable around sex scenes didn't get a vote when budget was on the line. Just another frustrating aspect of the business Jory couldn't control, and his apathy descended like a familiar blanket.

Cali gave Melanie a troubled nod, then sank down on her haunches beside the bed to get eye-to-eye with the actors. "Paolo, I'm going to be indelicate here."

A cloud of confusion crossed his face. "Indelicate?"

"I'm going to talk sex," Cali clarified.

"Oh, cool." Paolo eagerly propped himself up on his elbows, forcing Thalia back on her haunches.

"You're sure you're good to talk about this?" Cali's question had a solemn tone.

"Absolutely." Paolo nodded.

"What's your favorite sound when you're with someone?"

Paolo scrunched his flawless brow in deep contemplation. "I like that dope sound of surprise when I sink in."

Paolo turned a conceited grin on Thalia. He opened his eyes wide and sucked in a high-pitched feminine sounding breath. "That gasp of shock. I hear it every time."

"Ugh," Thalia muttered.

"And the wet slapping. I like the sound of the wet slapping," Paolo matter-of-factly added.

Jory seconded the *ugh*. He didn't have a lot of time for Paolo. His looks had landed him this role, and Jory spent a lot of valuable time pulling out camera tricks to cover Paolo's bad acting. He was a boy hiding his insecurity with crass jokes and bravado that no one was buying, least of all his costar.

Thalia sniggered. "Figures you'd only like the business part. All force and no finesse. Gross."

Thalia on the other hand was a delight to shoot—focused and professional, even if she was a touch aloof.

"Can you plant a mic in the pillow?" Cali asked Brandon.

"Oh yeah, definitely!"

"Not too close to the headboard," Thalia said sweetly. "It might pick up me ramming Paolo's skull into the wood as I ride him." Despite her treacly smile, it was clear Thalia would like nothing better than to smash Paolo's pretty head into the dense oak.

Cali rose to whisper to Brandon, "No, we need that sound. Make sure you get that sound."

"For sure."

Jory's irritation rose. This woman was changing the plan on the *first setup,* while corrupting his unsuspecting crew members. If he didn't do something soon, her influence could tumble the whole day out of control.

Love, Camera, Action

Melanie stepped between Cali and the two actors, all embarrassment forgotten. "No swearing, and keep the 'Oh gods' to a minimum please."

Paolo lowered his eyes in deference. "Yes, ma'am."

"This is a waste of time!" Jory threw up his hands. "It's never going to make the cut."

Cali turned to him with a feral smile. "Ah, the quiet man, I see. What do *you* like to hear?"

"I like to hear, 'Camera's up.'"

Cali put a finger to her lips in faux confusion and gestured to the front of his jeans. "Huh, I've never heard it called that. Whatever floats your boat."

A guffaw shot out of Dan as Cali turned to give her full attention to Thalia and Paolo. Jory stood gaping for a moment too long and then fumbled out his light meter just so he had something to do.

"So, Thalia, you're using your demon powers to influence Paolo's dreams and give him the worst nightmare of his life. You need to impress your demon overlord, Abigor, so you can get that promotion. But your prey wakes up. Where are you?"

"I'm caught. But too surprised to move."

"Are you angry?"

"No. I've been secretly wanting it." The tension in Thalia's shoulders dropped a fraction and she leaned into Paolo.

"Good." Cali shifted to Paolo. "Where are you?"

"I'm scared. But there's this super-hot chick above me so . . . yeah."

"But isn't this the woman who's been tormenting you? Aren't you tired of feeling helpless? Don't you want some control?"

Jory stole a glance at Paolo, who stared blankly at Cali. Suddenly, Thalia was upended as Paolo rolled her beneath him, pinning her down as she squeaked.

"You okay with that move?" Cali asked Thalia. Thalia nodded, looking everywhere but at Paolo.

Cali's voice deepened, seducing. "You lower down to kiss her because that's better than throwing her out, right?"

Paolo's body stilled over Thalia's. "Right."

"And Thalia, despite the fact you could incinerate him, you allow the kiss."

Thalia's eyes met Paolo's, shining with challenge. "Yeah."

"Great." Cali's tone turned businesslike. "Paolo can I see you grind your hips into her?"

Paolo ground his hips. Thalia yelped and Paolo flinched back.

"Not so much," Cali said lightly.

He moved forward and softened his grind. Cali turned to Thalia, "Better?"

Thalia assessed their bodies, adjusted her hips and then nodded, satisfied.

"Nice. And Thalia can you raise your leg that's nearest to camera to hug his flank?"

Thalia checked the angle of the camera, shifted her outside leg, and wrapped it around Paolo's butt so it was perfectly in frame.

"Thank you. Then, Thalia, you come to your senses, disappear, and we're out. Good?"

Thalia nodded.

"Good, Paolo?"

Paolo nodded.

Love, Camera, Action

Cali turned her gaze on Jory, all the warmth she'd shown to the actors withdrawn, barricaded behind a cool shield of professionalism. "Good, Jory?"

No. I'd like that warmth back.

Jory almost stuttered at the thought, wondering where it had come from. He quickly squashed it and gave her his cold assent.

"Okay, let's shoot."

Paolo sprang off Thalia, who scrambled from the bed.

"Places, people!" Dan roared out.

Jory followed Cali to Video Village, the area where crew members could watch what they were shooting on the monitors. Directors' chairs were set up in front of them, where the director, the DP, and the producer traditionally sat in the front row. He carefully made his way to the quiet space, gingerly stepping over cables that snaked across the concrete floor, and took his place beside Cali. He was suddenly struck by how soft the light was spilling over the set flats, the area's only source of illumination, and irrationally hoped Melanie would join them in her producer's chair. He'd never noticed how intimate a setting Video Village could be.

Molly, from Wardrobe, stood off to the side, scanning the actors' costumes for flaws. Umber, in Continuity, had her binder open, intently marking the scene in her script so no line was missed, no pillow misplaced. Others buzzed in and out, doing their final checks before cameras rolled.

Jory kept himself still and apart, watching Cali in his periphery. She was intensely focused on Paolo and Thalia's images on the small screen, furrowing her brow while clicking the pen in her hand. *Click, click, click.*

Noël Stark

The rigidity in her body made his soften. In the hush before the scene started, he could understand that maybe he'd been too hard on her. It was her first day, and she was probably excited over her big break. The message had been delivered that this was his ship to run, so he could lighten up a little and still maintain the control necessary for the shoot to go well. Plus, flies, honey, et cetera.

Leaning in, Jory nodded at the monitor where Thalia and Paolo were getting their makeup touched up, and murmured. "They don't like each other much."

Cali quickly glanced around to make sure they had some privacy and, satisfied, returned her focus to the screen. She matched his volume. "I'm getting that. Why?"

"Paolo's a poser and Thalia knows it. And he knows she knows it."

Cali turned her direct gaze on him, and he forgot what he was getting at, drawn in by her eyes that were now shining green. He'd seen that color at his family beach house in early summer when the ocean began to warm. A color he'd been cocooned in as he swam, safe and quiet.

"It must be hard," Cali said, "for someone who's new to the craft to realize everyone's judging them. That they have to come up to speed on something that's taken others years to perfect. Paulo feeling like a fraud would be a natural response." Her tone was strong even though her voice was barely above a whisper.

Jory straightened, annoyed at the tickle of guilt he felt over the possibility of having read Paolo wrong. "Maybe Paolo should listen to people with experience instead of thinking he knows everything."

"He shouldn't get too big for his britches?" Cali's smile was cynical.

Love, Camera, Action

"There's a reason for that saying."

She raised a brow. "As every white man knows."

Jory reared back. He wasn't that guy. "That's not what I—"

Cali cut him off with a wave of her hand. "Oh gosh, I didn't mean you, of course," she soothed. Even though Jory thought she very much meant him. She dropped her volume further, checking those around them again to make sure they were still in a cone of silence. "I was speaking to a greater idea of male privilege. I just think maybe Paolo needs a bit of a break. Weren't you scared when you started out?"

"God, no. I was too arrogant to be scared." Jory almost blushed over his early days on set. An honors graduate at AFI, he had maybe spent a year doing student films and small indie projects before he got his first gig. He remembered walking on set that day and barely talking to anyone because he knew the director was a hack. People had thought Jory was mysterious and taciturn, but really he'd just been an ass. "What about you?"

"Oh, I'm just scared." Her eyes held challenge in them, as though admitting she was afraid was a sign of strength.

Most directors would strangle themselves with the nearest cable before admitting to vulnerability, especially to the DP. But Cali was waving it like a badge of honor. "You say that like it's a good thing."

Cali shrugged. "Fear can work for you, give you an edge. Fear will make you hone in on a look or a nervous tic, or sense if something's out of whack. It can help you understand that maybe the reason Paolo's difficult is because no one's taken the time to find out who he can be. It's not uncommon for people to hide behind the projections others put on them."

Jory peered through the door of the set, where Paolo was demanding a different lip gloss. "He *wants* people to think he's an arrogant douche?"

"It might be easier than revealing who he really is."

"There's nothing to see, nothing to find." He turned to her again, judgment final, but he suddenly had the idea Cali wasn't talking about Paolo anymore. He could feel the gray edging its way back in, and suddenly he wasn't sure he was talking about Paolo either.

Cali silently took him in, her expression softening into something suspiciously resembling sympathy.

Jory shuttered himself from her pointed gaze. "Or maybe they're just in love with each other."

Cali's eyes shot to the screen. "Do you believe that? That animosity is a cover for love?"

"I've seen it happen."

"It's a dangerous argument that's kept a lot of women in unhealthy relationships." Cali's tone flattened.

Jory couldn't let the one-sided argument slide. "Unhealthy relationships affect men too."

She turned back to him, parted her lips to speak, and then seemed to think better of it. Closing them, she murmured a tactful "hmm."

Jory narrowed his eyes. "Did you just 'hmm' me?"

Cali narrowed her eyes to mirror his but couldn't hide the spark of intrigue that lit them. "I did." Her lips tipped at the corners.

Jory felt like he'd scored a point.

"Scene's up!" Dan's voice rose over the flats, settling the crew as they waited.

Jory looked over at his team and got the nod. "Camera speed," he said.

Love, Camera, Action

Cali straightened to the monitor, her focus honing in like a peregrine on the hunt. She took a breath and stilled her pen. "Action."

On the small screen, Thalia switched on immediately, seething and gyrating over Paolo in demonic fashion, who in turn twisted cartoonishly and grimaced, deep in his "nightmare." Jory lost interest and checked his frame. It was balanced, had good depth, well lit, but . . . something was off. There it was—a light cut across Thalia's shoulder too sharply. He made a mental note to fix it, when a movement caught his eye.

Cali was bouncing her knee. Bouncing her knee and hating on the monitor as if it had just cut her off on the freeway while giving her the finger.

Paolo opened his eyes as he "woke" and reached for Thalia as Cali shouted, "Cut!", blasting out of her chair before the echo had a chance to trail off.

What had she seen? Jory rose to search out the offending light while zeroing his peripheral focus on Cali and the actors.

Pissy anger stowed, Cali crouched by the bed, one knee on the floor, hands together in a prayer pose as though in supplication. "Paolo, I like what you're doing. It's got a lot of energy, and it's clear that you are dreaming and it's bad."

Jory could practically hear Paolo puff out his chest. "Great. So why stop?"

"Can you try—and this is just an exercise." Cali sounded almost apologetic. "Can you pretend, with your eyes closed, that you have a concrete block on your chest and you're desperate to get it off, but it won't budge? Push with everything you have, but you can't move."

Jory stole a glance at Paolo, who blinked up at Cali in confusion. "I . . . guess."

"Great. Thanks."

Cali bounced up to pull Thalia off the bed and to the side. Jory spotted his quarry and gently, gently adjusted the diffuser to soften where the light landed on the bed, while keeping an ear on Cali and Thalia.

"You are a demon. You *are* Power." Cali's intonation was all steel, a mile away from how she spoke to Paolo. "You don't have to prove you're powerful. Yes?"

Jory peered over to catch understanding flow over Thalia's features. "Yes."

Cali gave her a curt nod, and both women strode back to their positions, Cali calling over her shoulder to the crew, "Let's go again."

"Going again!" Dan echoed.

Jory drifted back to his chair, the tension in his shoulders kindling a headache. Why the unnecessary stop? Sure it had given him the opportunity to fix his light, but what did Cali think she was going to accomplish by giving those directions? They didn't even make sense. Ten minutes had just been wasted because Paolo and Thalia were going to do whatever they wanted.

In her chair, Cali's leg was back to bouncing, her eyes boring into the monitor. "Action."

The scene started again, but this time it took on a completely different tone. Thalia barely moved, while a dark energy vibrated through her, eyes burning as though she was sucking out Paolo's very soul. Jory shuddered. It was somehow creepy *and* sexy. How was that even a thing? Jory had only seen occasional glimpses of Thalia's real acting skill before today, but now she personified dangerous charisma.

Love, Camera, Action

Meanwhile, Paolo was . . . acting. He grimaced as he tried to move, the weight of the imaginary block testing him beyond his capability. Fury and futility crossed his features as Paolo lost himself to a heartbreaking struggle that made him appear so defenseless Jory felt compelled to rush in and wake him from his torment.

Jory dragged his attention away to stare at Cali, who was immobile, face alight, completely immersed in the scene—no bouncing leg, no clicking pen. She looked like a little kid watching her favorite show, heart bursting from wonder and magic.

She smiled, and Jory looked back to see Paolo open his eyes, the imaginary weight gone as if he were freed by the beautiful woman above him while Thalia froze in fear and shock. Jory involuntarily gasped at the contrast, unable to look away.

"Cut! Thank you. Moving on." Cali's clear voice dragged Jory out of the scene like he'd been in the depths of the ocean. She was already out of her chair, leaving him in her wake.

She turned back mid-stride. "Thanks for fixing that light," she said.

And then, she winked.

CHAPTER THREE

Something was missing. Something vital. The last shot of the scene was about to wrap up, and it was smooth and sexy and passionate and . . . fine.

It made Cali's skin itch.

She looked at her watch, then at her script, then back at her watch. She snuck her umpteenth glance at Jory. Returned to the monitor. Snuck another glance.

He was so *still*. She could never be that still. It was like he was meditating, gathering the tendrils of images from the monitor on an inhale, circulating them through his body to root out flaws that threatened his delicate wizardry, then disseminating them on an exhale, all while in complete stasis.

It was distracting. All his concentration and breathing and stillness produced a roiling heat that was scrambling her brain. Some guys were like that. They had an intense sexual vibe that was difficult to ignore. Cali usually steered clear of them because, while they were fun to get to the

Love, Camera, Action

sack, they weren't fun in it. Too wrapped up in performance. She preferred a guy who had something to prove and then didn't balk when she walked away. Those guys were great for letting off steam—grateful for the hookup—but wouldn't push for more. Cali wasn't into *more*.

She grunted out her frustration. She shouldn't be focusing on her steam; she should be focused on the steam on set which was more liquid than gas. She furiously fanned away the clouds of pheromones Jory exuded with the flimsy pages of her script. He stole his own glance, implying her fanning impinged on his airspace.

"Sorry," Cali muttered.

He returned his eyes to the screen, dismissing her.

A buzz emanated from the side pocket of her chair, and Cali fished out her phone with all the gravitas of a very busy and important person.

The name "Patsy" glowed at her from the screen, and Cali glowered back, her chest filling with the familiar concoction of annoyance and guilt only her sister could foment. Patsy knew Cali was at work. She wasn't usually this thoughtless. Or was this the dreaded call?

The older of the two, Cali had practically raised Patsy while their mother was either holed up in her room or out on a manic spree. Cali had helped Patsy with her homework until it got too advanced for Cali to do much good, had collected neighborhood beer bottles to buy Patsy the increasingly rare books the library didn't have, weaseled invitations to other people's houses where the heat hadn't been shut off. And that was before their mom's most disastrous relationship with Rick.

Cali had always struggled balancing her career with the financial and emotional responsibilities of her mother and sister. Now that Patsy had a job and Cali had set up their mother with an untouchable nest egg to pay for her bills and meds, Cali was in the clear for the first time. Financially anyway. Emotionally, even though Cali steered clear of their mother as best she could, there was still Patsy, who was no less exhausting.

Cali forced herself to swipe left and typed out a quick text.

Working. Call you back?

NP! ☺

Cali frowned at the response. Patsy didn't do text slang. Her job as a translator of ancient Greek at the university meant she found the millennial use of acronyms an insulting bastardization of language. If Patsy sent an *NP* there was clearly a *P*.

Cali squeezed her eyes shut and blindly tapped out a response against her better judgment.

You sure?

Cali waited for a reply.

Colin wants to take me to his cottage this weekend . . .

That ellipsis was alarming. Patsy attached herself like a barnacle to every passing male ship, turning him into The One within weeks. When the guy inevitably dumped her, Patsy went on a destructive bender that shut down everything in her and Cali's life. Colin was new so, by Cali's estimate, that gave her about eight weeks before the meltdown. *Please let this one be different,* she prayed.

As Cali composed a response in her head, another text came in.

What am I doing? You're shooting! Ignore me. And she finished it off with a sparkly heart emoji.

Cali had no point of reference for an acronym and two emojis.

Love, Camera, Action

She forced her attention back to the monitor, realizing she was furiously fanning herself, most likely in the improbable hope the paper would waft away her unease. It also wafted the script Jory clenched in exasperation.

Cali ignored him, captivated by the undulating sheets.

That's it. *That's it.*

On set, Dan bellowed, "Moving on with—"

"Hold, please," Cali interrupted.

Dan stiffened. Cali winced. It wasn't great to cut off the first AD, but to his credit, Dan schooled his features into a neutral mask and awaited further instruction.

Cali turned to Jory. "Can you join Dan and me for a moment?"

Jory graced her with a stony stare, and her omniscient doubt rose. Cali let the power of her inspiration stomp on it, wishing it would also stomp on Jory's implacable face. She pushed herself from her chair and strode onto set.

Cali planted herself in front of Dan. "How much time do we have?"

"About fifteen minutes."

"Could you squeeze out twenty?"

"Maybe, but time ticks."

Cali turned to catch Jory prowling over, poised to pounce on her idea. She summoned her most authoritative voice, the one that said, *I am the director and I am about to bestow the best idea in the Universe on this very scene.*

She hoped she wouldn't squeak.

"I want to shoot the sheets, so I need one more setup with handheld," she declared.

Jory looked like he wasn't sure which part of her ridiculous sentence he should negate first. "We don't have a handheld camera."

"We need something messy, something energetic, something wild." Cali squared her shoulders and felt sweat squelch in her armpits. "We need to see the sheets flutter and rub and move and undulate. It will be beyond sexy."

He let out a long sigh, and repeated, "We don't have a handheld camera."

"You used the camera we have today as a handheld in *Battalion's Folly.*" Cali knew this for a fact because of the many rabbit holes she'd traveled down studying Jory's style.

"That was different."

"So are you saying we don't have the camera or you don't want to operate it?"

Dan's eyebrows shot to his hairline, and he took the slightest step back.

Jory's jaw tensed. "It would look shaky and unwatchable, like—"

"Like someone waking up from a nightmare. Or like someone who's been caught." Cali's growing excitement leaked out in the form of a tiny bounce.

Jory opened his mouth and then shut it. He took a quick survey of the surrounding crew, who were busy not listening to everything they said. He turned to Dan. "Give us a sec."

"Alright, but again with the tick tock."

Jory nodded tersely and stalked off, assuming Cali would follow like an obedient dog.

Dan shot her a warning glance. Acknowledging him with a dip of her head, she followed Jory into the shadows.

He had stopped two sets over in a pool of darkness, his back ramrod straight. When her eyes adjusted to the lack of light, she saw they were on the CEO office set. A behemoth mahogany desk with a high-backed executive chair dwarfed

Love, Camera, Action

two matching leather club chairs, all placed in front of three huge windows looking out onto "Central Park." A fitting place for Jory to give, what Cali could only assume, a dressing down. She mentally pulled on her big-girl boots.

"Okay. I've seen this a lot." He turned, a bastion of patience. "And I hope you'll excuse my candor, but it's a classic first-time director mistake."

"I've directed two films and three TV series."

He put out a hand to mollify her, as if she hadn't understood him. It made her hackles rise. "You want to try out some fancy shots that aren't close to the look of the show—the look I created—to make your mark and prove you are a director of vision. But the question you need to ask, the question the seasoned director asks is: Is this new shot worth sending us into overtime, costing the production money, pissing off the actors and crew, and forcing the producers to rethink why they hired you, when that shot probably won't make it to the final cut?"

When he put it that way it sounded like she was about to make the biggest mistake of her career. The mistake of a director who placed her ego above the show. Her confidence crumbled. *He's right. You don't know what you're doing. Better to be safe.*

But . . . no.

Lots of directors survived on bland choices, made their careers on them even, but Cali wanted something better, to *be* something better. Her instincts were screaming that this was the shot, despite the risk. Jory's fluttering script sheets filled her mind's eye, and she fixed her courage to the image.

"We can be fine or we can be exceptional. And I know you care about being exceptional."

Jory bristled. "You don't know what I care about."

"It's not that different from that incredible cabin scene you shot in *Dead at Sunset*."

"Yes, but I had a handheld cam—wait." Jory drew back, his eyes narrowing in suspicion. "You saw that?"

"Are you kidding? Of course I saw that. The dinner scene? All shot from below, making every character into a villain until you didn't know who to trust? I mean, come on! I literally shouted out, 'No way' in the movie theater." The empty movie theater, but still.

Jory opened his mouth to respond, but Cali plowed forward, her epiphany driving her toward probable doom. "You could use the same technique here from the kitchen fight, getting vignettes, snapshots of moments, moving on instinct—the shakier the better. But instead of knives and drawers and cabinets framing the shot, you use the bed sheets. It will give the scene an authenticity you don't get in the rest of this show."

Jory stiffened. "That's a strange tactic. Complimenting and insulting in one breath."

Cali forced herself to stay quiet. She'd made her case. Any more talk would detract from the power of the inspiration.

They fell into silence while they sized each other up.

She wondered what Jory saw. A frightened girl desperately trying to make her voice heard? The poor, scrappy, passionate upstart who was cute, but easily ignored? Or did he see a woman of ideas, of value? She schvitzed under his burning gaze. He was just so *much*. And they were standing so close. Close enough for her to catch his scent. What was that? Cedar? Some kind of tree, for sure.

His eyes cut to her mouth and then away.

Love, Camera, Action

Heat swept through her body. Jory Blair had looked at her mouth. In *that* way. If she weren't so intent on him, she would've missed it, but there it was.

He met her eyes again, leaning in the tiniest bit, probably trying to intimidate but only underscoring the crackling energy between them. He brought up a finger. "One shot."

"One shot." Cali nodded.

Jory held her gaze a moment longer, then he was gone, booming across the set, "One more, Dan."

Cali huffed out a breath. That was either the smartest thing she'd ever done, or she had just blown whatever sliver of respect she may have had.

Whatever she'd done, the inspiration had better be worth it.

Jory was sweating. Uncomfortably.

He had only been shooting for fifteen minutes, but he'd jumped all over the set—lying on the floor shooting up at Paolo, standing on the bed shooting down at Thalia, squeezing behind the headboard to shoot through the spindles, and jamming his back against the wall to get their feet—all while using the sheets to frame the shot as he balanced a forty-pound not-handheld camera on his shoulder.

Paolo had flipped Thalia over nine times and thrust against her fourteen, while she raised her legs anywhere from a slight knee lift to a full-out ankle clasp around Paolo's butt, ever mindful of where the sheets were on their bodies.

Cali called out each move like an army general, bossy and relentless.

Jory knew his muscles would be screaming at the end of the day, but he also felt the tiniest inkling of something else. Fun?

No. He was *not* having fun. There was nothing fun about bouncing around the set like a twenty-five-year-old on a student film. Sets should be predictable. If he were running things, scenes would be knocked off like clockwork. None of this searching for magic and inspiration and *fun* that inevitably wasted time. He remembered his first gigs, the producers scrounging for investors, the directors grasping for creative solutions because of a lack of money or talent or time. On one horror film, they couldn't afford a jib arm for the slow rise he wanted of the killer's feet walking up the porch stairs. So instead, he'd shimmied under the house through the dirt and the bugs and the things he didn't want to identify to shoot through the gaps in the steps. It was disgusting.

But man, it had been a great shot.

"I think we've got it." Jory wiped the moisture off his brow with a handkerchief from his back pocket.

Ignoring him, Cali said, "Dan, how long have we got?"

"Three minutes."

She pinned Jory with her gaze. "I want you to go under."

"Under what?"

"The sheets."

"What?"

"I'll lift them."

"This is getting a bit much." Jory put the camera down.

Cali regarded the camera as a gauntlet thrown. "Have you ever seen a shot like that?"

"No, because it's a pain."

Cali lifted the sheet that covered Paolo and Thalia, who weren't baiting each other for once because they were too busy trying to catch their breath. "Think of the quality of light as it diffuses through the fabric. Like in a nineteenth-century harem. It'll take two seconds," she promised.

"You get it's only nine thirty in the morning, right? We have another ten hours of this."

"I'm aware of how production works."

Jory raised an eyebrow that said he didn't think she did. Cali stubbornly returned his glower, as though immune to his most formidable of looks, and shook the sheet to make her point.

He had to admit, it would look good.

"Fuck it." He picked the camera back up.

Cali turned to the actors. "Can you guys do one more?"

Shaky, they both nodded. Thalia pulled herself up to straddle Paolo again while makeup swooped in to blot their ever-worsening sweat shine.

Cali flew to the bottom of the bed and lifted up the sheet. Jory gave her one last glare that went unacknowledged, and ducked underneath.

He calibrated the camera and took a deep breath to slow his heartbeat so the camera on his shoulder wouldn't pulse along with it. When he peered through the lens, he almost gasped.

The diaphanous quality of the sheet gave Paolo and Thalia's bodies an unearthly glow. Bronze skin on olive became luminescent as the flowing sheet created an undulating wave like parachute silk. It was sensual and carnal, and he wondered why they hadn't been here all along.

And that annoyed him. It annoyed him that they only had three minutes left. It annoyed him that Cali had come up with it and he hadn't. But mostly it annoyed him that the shot might have been lost because of his stubbornness.

Jory made one last adjustment, then said, "Camera speed."

Through the muffle of material, Cali called, "Action."

Thalia and Paolo began to move.

As their bodies twisted and slid, the sheets became a part of them, billowing and rolling in response. The atmosphere ached with intimacy, ethereal yet earthly, and Jory heard a voice whisper to him from the boundaries of his carefully crafted borders: *That's it.*

Jory felt the gray recede as he moved in sync with the camera. A familiar flow took over as he came alive to intuit every shift in the scene unfolding in front of him, guided by their breaths, their bodies. This was what he was meant for, and the thought galvanized his resolve to switch to the director's seat. He couldn't let others control his environment any longer.

Then, Paolo suddenly veered in a way he hadn't before. He pinned Thalia's arms over her head in an aggressive act of dominance that forced Jory to pull back and into someone standing behind him who fell to the floor with an, "Oof!"

Disregarding whoever it was, Jory reframed in an instant to capture the panic that swept into Thalia's eyes. And the swift knee she slammed into Paolo's balls.

Paolo bellowed in pain as Thalia shot out from under him, hip-checking Jory on the way and knocking him off balance. Jory steadied the camera as much as he could, holding onto the shot for as long as possible, but felt himself going over. Suddenly two hands were at his back keeping him balanced, allowing him to capture Paolo's writhing form for that last crucial moment.

Jory heard Cali call, "Cut!" and when he looked back, he saw it was her, on her knees, bracing him from the fall. It was Cali he'd knocked over, but she didn't look like she cared. Instead, alarm lit her face, her eyes screaming the question, *"Did you get that?"*

Jory gave her a quick nod, and a smile burst out of her. He drank it in, letting her exuberance sluice through him to his bones. Her hands were still on his back, warm and solid, fusing them together as their chests heaved in tandem. He had the strangest urge to bring those hands around his neck so they could wind their way through his hair.

"I'm so sorry!" Thalia's panic pulled them apart. "Oh my God, I'm so sorry! I didn't mean to do that."

Cali rushed to Thalia while Jory awkwardly went down on one knee to check in with Paolo, who was now clutching his balls and rolling from side to side.

Jory winced in sympathy and asked, "You okay there, bud?"

Paolo gave a pathetic thumbs-up while he tried to breathe.

Dan clicked his walkie. "Better send in the medic."

Jory gave Paolo a clumsy pat of assurance and stepped back so on-set Wardrobe could dive in with Paolo's robe, clucking and soothing as though he were going into shock. Jory handed the camera off to his assistant, Alison, and set his covert attention on Cali as she attempted to calm the near hysterical Thalia.

"I don't know what happened. It's just that he—"

"I know." Cali grasped Thalia's upper arms, steadying her. "You weren't expecting it."

"It was a reflex."

"He surprised you."

"It's not his fault." Thalia's breathing quickened.

"It's not yours either," Cali responded.

"It was. I just—I just—"

"It's not your fault." Cali's tone was steel, and Thalia's eyes flashed to hers.

Jory glimpsed something lightning quick pass between the two women. After a long moment, Thalia shakily nodded.

Cali gave her arm a reassuring squeeze. "Why don't you go relax in your trailer? Paolo will be fine. I'll have someone bring you some tea, yeah? Some chamomile?"

Thalia nodded again, and Cali called for the third AD to escort her to her trailer. Something warm spread through Jory's chest. He rarely saw directors take an interest in actors or their well-being. More often than not, actors were treated with the thinnest veneer of respect, under which flowed the opinion they were passably trained monkeys who were more trouble than they were worth. But Cali's eyes, blazing and protective, held nothing but concern. Jory couldn't help but wonder what it would be like to be on the receiving end of that care.

A male voice boomed through the set. "What is going on?"

Jory groaned inwardly. God had arrived.

Howard Fox strode onto the scene. He was the showrunner, top executive producer, engineer of all things creative on the show, and TV royalty, having helmed some of the best-known series in the world. He had graced *The Demon* with his venerable presence and was now clearly in the mood to reign down some holy terror. He was also the key to Jory's next career move.

Cali met the imposing man with a quiet confidence that surprised Jory—most directors would be quaking in their boots. Howard was a big personality, dwarfing those around him with his Old Hollywood presence. He was blustery, blunt, and definitively un-woke, but was often a generous benefactor, the man behind skyrocketing careers. He could also decimate someone for what he saw as incompetence. Howard was not someone with whom to fuck.

He inflated his chest and set his decibel level to stun. "Why has a medic been called down to the set?"

At that moment, the medic, complete with first aid kit, rushed to Paolo's side. Paolo winced at his arrival and tried to close in on himself, clearly embarrassed.

Cali took in the medic's arrival and, voice steady, turned back to Howard. "Hi, Howard. We had an incident during the scene—"

"You're Cali Daniels, I presume." Howard focused a cold stare on Cali. "Melanie's hire."

Jory winced. With two words, Howard effectively removed any responsibility for Cali and placed it firmly on Melanie, who, if Jory were honest, should be the one calling the shots on this show.

"Yes." Cali flashed him a self-deprecating smile. "I would have liked to have met under different circumstances."

"Me too." Howard's smile was just shy of shark. "Why is there a medic on set?"

Now was the time for her to delicately throw Paolo under the bus. It was his fault for changing the choreography without consulting Cali—a rookie move. Howard was the more important person in the grand scheme of things; it was he she needed to impress.

"There was a certain improvisational quality—"

"Improvisation? I thought the scene was rehearsed."

"It was, but I decided the authenticity of the moment—"

"Our actors' safety is of the upmost importance. We would never want to endanger them." Howard's voice was concerned but loud, aimed to humiliate. Jory felt the need to step in to clear up the situation but stopped himself. He wouldn't want someone to interfere on his behalf—why would she? This was her battle, and she would resent him trying to rescue her. Besides, Jory wanted to draw as little of this type of attention as possible.

"Definitely not. Nor would I." Cali's eyes darted around the set, taking in the crew who uncomfortably watched the exchange. Her tone became diplomatic. "We were able to capture a fresh take on the scene that—"

"I was under the impression part of the reason Melanie brought you on was for your particular expertise. And so I'm a bit confused, after discussions around the delicacy of this scene, *why* we would need the onset medic?"

Cali hands clenched. "It was my call to go outside the plan."

"*You* went off the plan? I see." He squinted as though weighing his words. "I understand it's your first day, and I know Melanie has a lot of confidence in your talent. I myself am grateful you were able to help us out on such short notice and am excited to see your work, but I need to ensure everyone is safe. I hope this isn't a harbinger of things to come. We need to keep things professional."

Jory bit back a growl and shoved his hands in his pockets so he wouldn't deck the guy. Howard was an old-school showrunner, who ruled through manipulation and fear. But since most people's reputations were only as good as their last job, to earn a bad review from Howard Fox would be devastating. He could make three phone calls and Jory's career would be over, no matter how in demand he was now. And Jory could forget about the director's chair—it would never happen.

Love, Camera, Action

Now Howard's sights were on Cali. She had to shift blame or she might not be given another chance. Yet Cali stayed quiet, tacitly taking responsibility as Howard turned to address the crew with one of his fake smiles.

"Don't worry, everyone! Paolo seems okay, and we'll be moving on. But please, let's stick to the script, shall we?" Howard shot Jory a glance that clearly said *"Keep her in line,"* before lumbering off the set.

Dan stepped into the void. "Moving on! Scene sixteen. Daytime. Health food store. Rafe finds something mysterious in his smoothie."

Cali drifted away, and Jory felt the strangest pull to follow her to . . . do what? Make her feel better? Tell her Howard had been too harsh? Assure her what they got was great?

That would accomplish nothing except drawing notice from Howard. He wasn't about to sacrifice the good humor of a powerful man for a newbie who showed up on his set that morning, no matter how good her ideas were.

His attention lit on Dan, quietly talking into the phone. Jory always knew when Dan was chatting with his wife— he seemed more boyish somehow. His body relaxed and a slight smile lifted his lips, as though he was flirting, even though they'd been together for twenty-two years. Jory had just sent them an anniversary gift. Now Dan dragged a hand across his face as he paused for long periods while Jory suspected his wife gave him support over what had just gone down on set.

Jory had wanted that. He had wanted someone to call between setups, to download the latest disaster. Or even just to discuss dinner that night. What his parents once had. He wanted to share the beach house, his sanctuary, not hide in it all alone, terrified by numbers on test results. But he couldn't draw someone into an uncertain future, drag them through the pain and loss of an unhappily ever after. He wasn't that cruel.

His gaze drifted to Cali, who was off in a corner, hunched over her script, isolated from everyone. Jory walked over to Dan as he ended his call. "I'm going to drop that dolly shot in the hair salon this afternoon. We don't need it. And ax the jib for the hell scene."

Dan studied his ever-present clipboard, brows raised in curiosity. "Dropping two setups before we get to the scenes. That's not like you. Something going on?"

"I want to make sure we make our day." Jory's eyes strayed back to Cali, who was now in deep conversation with the props master over the size of a candelabra.

Dan cleared his throat, and Jory realized he was staring. "I've never seen you show such interest in the schedule before."

"It's more efficient."

"I think it's very positive."

Jory tried to ferret out Dan's meaning. But he was forever inscrutable. "What's very positive?"

"Your interest in the schedule."

"Yes. The *schedule*."

"Exactly. I think the *schedule* could use some help."

"If the schedule doesn't come up to speed, it's not really my problem," Jory defended.

"No, it's not." Dan flipped a page back in place, closing the clipboard—and the conversation.

"I want to be a team player and make sure things get done right." Jory pushed, feeling like a petulant office manager.

"And that will definitely help the schedule. Thank you."
Dan thrust the clipboard under his arm.

"You're welcome." Jory stormed off to the camera, not really comprehending what had just happened. Dan had a way of say something without saying anything that was infuriating.

Howard had made it clear he needed Jory to take control of the set. So that's would Jory would do. He'd keep Cali from making impetuous decisions while he steered the shoot. Really, he wasn't helping her out. He was helping the production. He was helping himself.

He gathered the familiar gray around him as he stared through the eyepiece in the camera without seeing a thing. Cali Daniels was going to have to figure out how his set worked or she'd be gone by the end of the day.

And he wasn't sure why he felt loss at the thought.

CHAPTER FOUR

Cali fell through the door of her home for the next six weeks: a gleaming, spacious condo in Buckhead. She stumbled into the foyer with her suitcase, which she tripped over. Missed the black hallway table with her keys, and abandoned them where they lay on the polished hardwood floor. Then staggered to the pristine white sectional couch, where she crumpled more than sat. She put her head in her hands and debated whether she should cry.

What a fucking day.

After Howard left, a steel door had slammed down between her and the crew with a definitive clang. There was no room for joviality, let alone creativity—just the clear message: *Don't touch us with your wrong-side-of-the-producer cooties.* Despite the collective cold shoulder, Cali had rescued the time she'd lost on what was now being called "the incident," and ended the day fifteen minutes early. Not that anyone said anything.

Love, Camera, Action

Jory in particular had sunken into a deep—no *deeper*—freeze. He'd only spoken to her when necessary and had put as much space between them as he could. So much so that, at one point, she'd tried leaning toward him to see if he would fall out of his chair. Instead, he'd sprung up in a panther-like way and loosely walked over to the camera to bring a shot in line she hadn't even realized was out.

Irrationally, she felt what had happened to Paolo, and the resulting chaos, was her fault. She could have kept to safe choices instead of endangering the actors or alienating the crew for a moment that might never see the light of day.

She sighed. There was no undoing the past; she could only move forward. She needed to distract herself from her own dumpster fire and focus on someone else's. She picked up her phone and hit the only name on her Favorites list.

Her ever-snarky sister answered. "Took you long enough."

"What's wrong?"

"Whoa! How about hello? Or *'How are you, darling sister'*? You've got your director voice on, and I am not one of your crew."

"Sorry. Hello, *darling sister.*" Cali rolled her eyes, hoping they were loud enough to be heard through the phone. "What's wrong?"

"Nuh-uh, it's still there. Primo bossy. What's wrong with *you*, I might ask?"

Patsy was a genius deflector and incredibly stubborn. She was also incredibly beautiful. Her blond hair, brown eyes, and forest-animal features were diametrically opposed to Cali's Valkyrie vibe, due to the fact they had different fathers. She was one of those people who was full of light when she wasn't face deep in a pool of booze, crying over her latest breakup.

Her actual name was Clio, but when she was eleven, their mother thought she was getting too high and mighty over her smarts and looks, and so started calling her Cleopatra. Clio got fed up, and instead of ignoring the taunts, she leaned into the name, making everyone call her Cleopatra, including her teachers. It was eventually shortened to Pat, and then Patsy, which Mom despised because it reminded her of that *"uppity bitch who sold Nevada tickets at the bingo hall."* Clio, of course, wouldn't give it up, and she'd been Patsy ever since.

That same stubborn tone was in her sister's voice now, and Cali didn't think she had the strength to battle it. "I'm fucking up."

"Really? Or are you just freaking out?"

"Yes."

Cali listened to Patsy take a long drag from her cigarette. Patsy was waiting for Cali to spill. Her patience was legendary and her judgment profound. She'd sit there and smoke in silence for the next two hours if that's what it took. Cali let out a groan of frustration and dropped her head forward into the hand that wasn't holding the phone. "It's hopeless. I've finally lucked my way onto a legitimate show, and I can't deliver. Everyone knows I'm a hack. I can't do this."

It hadn't been easy for Cali to learn how to direct. School hadn't been an option, which meant she'd learned from experience. She'd started from the bottom, gathering knowledge on the ground in the most abused and underpaid positions, and then slowly worked her way up through the various departments while making her own films on

Love, Camera, Action

weekends. Her education was trial by fire, and sometimes people could smell the ash.

"Do you want to bail?" Patsy asked.

"Yes, I want to bail. The showrunner thinks I'm a dud. The DP is one of my idols and also thinks I'm dud. He might be an asshole, but I can't tell yet. And I got the lead actor kicked in the nuts because I couldn't let go of an idea. They know I don't know what I'm doing."

"Sorry, what was that one about the nuts?"

"I don't know what I'm doing!" Cali jumped up from the couch in agitation, knocking over a freestanding lamp with her bag. She dropped the phone to scramble after the lamp before the glass shade could smash on the hardwood floor. She managed to catch one of the legs that made up the tripod stand and righted the lamp, but not before upending her bag and dumping all its contents onto the floor. She sat back down and brought the phone to her ear, catching her sister in mid-rant.

"For fuck's sake, so what if you don't know what you're doing? No one else knows what they're doing either. No one. And the ones who think they know what they're doing are sociopaths who *for sure* don't know what they're doing—they just don't know it."

Cali huffed out a laugh.

"Have you eaten something?" Patsy demanded.

"Um . . ." Cali surveyed the open-concept layout of her blindingly modernist chrome-and-white kitchen that looked like every surface was coated with an industrial cleaner. It was glorious.

"Go eat something. You know how you get. I'll wait."

When Patsy was six and Cali was nine, Patsy had figured out that when Cali couldn't remember the plot to

Patsy's toilet-paper-roll-doll plays, it was a sign that she needed to eat. Patsy would go to the kitchen and bring back whatever she could find—usually candy canes from two Christmases before because that was all she could reach. Or was all they had.

Cali sighed. There would be nothing waiting for her in the fridge, but as she lowered her eyes in defeat, she saw the glint of cellophane peaking from under the couch—a casualty of her bag's battle with the lamp.

She grabbed the granola bar she'd taken from the on-set food table earlier that day and hastily ripped it open. She'd barely eaten because of her nerves, but that hadn't stopped her from obsessively shoving food into her bag. An absurd move since snacks were abundant, but if she didn't always have something to eat at her fingertips her judgment got clouded. Now, after a full day on set with an empty stomach, the granola bar could have been Soylent Green and she would've eaten it. Actually, Soylent Green would've been preferable. Lots of protein in Soylent Green.

Cali took a bite and garbled into the phone, "I'm eating."

"Okay, so go back to the basics. Aphrodite gives Psyche—"

"How are Aphrodite and Psyche the basics?"

"The Greek gods are always the basics, you uncultured boob. When Aphrodite found out Psyche got together with her son Eros, she was *pissed* and decided to give Psyche the bullshit task of separating a mound of mixed-up seeds before dawn, or Psyche would be killed."

"As goddesses do."

"As goddesses do. Psyche's all 'Waaaah, I've lost my hot boyfriend, and I'll never see my family again, and my mother-in-law's a bitch,' when an army of ants comes to her rescue and sorts out the seeds one at a time until they're all in neat little piles, infuriating Aphrodite and getting Psyche one step closer to reuniting with Eros. Which is representative of the soul becoming whole, but that's another thing. So. Be the ants."

"Be the ants."

"Take it one seed at a time."

A burn had started in Cali's throat, an itch climbing up her nose. She fought it because they didn't cry with each other, having made that unspoken pact even before Patsy knew where to get the old candy canes. Pushing the feeling away, Cali skimmed her hand across the rise in the upholstery of the couch, back and forth, creating dark and light patterns. "This place is the polar opposite of our apartment. It's so clean. I'm sitting on a white couch, and there isn't one wine stain on it."

"Clean is for the rich or for people who don't have anything else better to—

"—do with their time. Yes, yes. Some people just like to be clean, you know."

"I rebuke those people." Patsy dragged on her cigarette.

Cali pulled herself back into big sister mode. "So what is wrong? You sent me an ellipsis."

"I sent you no ellipsis. Ellipses are for the weak."

Cali tried a different tack. "How's Colin?"

"He's terrific. Really terrific. Did I tell you he's taking me to his cottage?"

There was something slightly manic edging into her voice despite the air of casualness. Cali's anxiety stirred. Patsy could just be in the honeymoon phase of her new train wreck and wanting to keep the high to herself, or something deeper was at play, like the relationship was about to implode and her along with it. "You did. Is there a thing?"

"I don't think there's a thing. If there was, it's not a thing anymore."

"If there is a thing and you're not telling me because of my thing, then there will be a thing."

"Don't you have a play to read?"

"Screenplay. Teleplay to be exact."

"Huh. Go read your *tele*play."

"You can just call it a script."

But Patsy had already hung up. Cali peered down at the now empty granola bar wrapper. Still hungry, she found an orange had rolled under the glass table. After inhaling a few segments, her blood sugar began to rise, and she was able to mull over the day.

One seed at a time.

A big seed was undoubtedly Jory. Cali had learned from the many sets she'd been on that one's inner voice was paramount, and that inner voice was telling her that, while Jory Blair might be an asshole (scratch that: a *hot* asshole), he also cared about the craft. Someone who created such beautiful images had to care. If she could get him onside, it would be easier to finesse the even bigger seed that was Howard. Howard had worked on some of the greats, so it made sense he would be tough. All he needed was some time, and maybe a good word put in by a certain DP, to see Cali was the right choice.

Despite Jory's coldness toward her, she couldn't help but flush at the thought of him. His body hummed with electricity as he moved around the set. She would blame her fascination on her dry spell between hookups, but there was something else that held her interest. The way he took

Love, Camera, Action

control of his team yet helped with the grunt work that wasn't his responsibility, lifting and moving the heavy cameras that made his shoulders bunch and flex under their weight. In the way he dryly flirted with the matronly catering woman, eliciting giggles and arm smacks. How she'd catch the tail end of him considering her before he looked away. She'd had to switch all of her settings to "Ignore" just so she could get through the day.

Regardless of his appeal, he'd made it clear he did not appreciate her ideas. If she wanted to excel at this gig, she would have to turn him into an ally.

So.

Option one: Sweeten him up. Cajole him into an easy relationship that could lead to collaboration.

She rejected that option immediately. Jory would see the tactic a mile away and would capitalize on it until he had complete control of the set. He needed a firm hand so he knew who was boss. Not in a sexy way, of course. Although maybe she'd entertain that scenario later in her mind.

Option two: Go head-to-head.

Cali didn't think she'd come out on top if she dug in her heels and went against him. The show had already been shooting for four months with Jory as the constant while directors came and went. Jory would have the crew on his side. Once she finished her episode, she and her "vision" would be long gone, leaving Jory and the crew to finish the series under his creative watch. Plus, directors could get blacklisted on a dime if they were deemed difficult to work with, especially women.

Option three: . . .

What was option three?

Option three always held the answer. Hopefully, it would materialize before she was fired.

The orange now nothing but peel, she found one last bit of contraband spilled from her bag: a theme-appropriate poppy-seed muffin. She put it on the practically invisible glass coffee table, placed her script beside it, and began to plan the next day, one seed at a time.

Jory listened to his heavy footsteps thud on the foyer's walnut floor and his keys clatter onto the teak table. He'd been living in this bougie chrome-and-white McCondo for over four months, and he didn't feel like one speck of his skin dust inhabited the place. He was suspicious that some tiny condo elf came out during the day and removed all the molecules that didn't belong there. All of *his* molecules.

Right about now his cousins and aunts would be settling in on the back deck of the beach house, having invaded each room with kids and pets and water toys. They'd all eat too much pie as they toasted his father and Astrid's engagement, one eye on the kids to make sure they didn't drown in the sunset-lit water, the other on their wineglasses to make sure they didn't get too low.

And he was here. Working. Alone.

What a fucking day.

He walked into the kitchen, carrying the box he'd picked up from the concierge, and poured himself a glass of water from the filtered tap. He hadn't eaten since breakfast, needing to prep for the endoscopy he'd finally scheduled and then canceled in the wake of the new director. So that

Love, Camera, Action

meant . . . a croissant. And coffee. He tested his breath to judge whether it was on the meltable scale or not. It seemed fine, which was a minor miracle. He should have some protein and cruciferous vegetables to maintain the strict diet he'd put in place to optimize his digestion, but was too tired to do anything about it. Easier to try again tomorrow.

He moved to the living room and sank onto the white couch that seemed to come with all rented condos. *"Millennial-rubbish design,"* his grandmother called it. He gingerly placed the box on the glass coffee table and pulled back the cardboard flaps. Reaching inside, he lifted out a black leather case slightly bigger than his hand. He ran his fingers over its surface, softly wiping away the embedded dust that had burrowed its way into the textured rise. He felt along the underside and found the button, turned it over to delicately pop open the catch, then lifted the case top. With reverence, he pulled out a 1970s Canon 310XL.

The camera was small, light, and simple—designed for home movies. It sounded cliché, but these cameras were built to last, mainly because of the materials available at the time: metal components instead of plastic, leather casing instead of synthetics.

He'd spotted this one in a pawnshop while on location scout a few days before, and he'd had one of the production assistants deliver it. Jory examined every detail of the camera, checking for dings or grime, scratches on the lens, or misaligned threads. As he did, he mused about the new director.

He'd watched Cali closely all day while considering what tactic he should take to keep her in line. She seemed to be everywhere at once—checking in with Lighting, Makeup, Wardrobe. Jory's usual MO was to assume everyone knew what they were doing and only made comments when something went off the rails. Cali instead took time to notice what was going right and marked it, which meant the crew was gaining respect for her despite the rocky morning.

On the surface it seemed as though she came up with her ideas in the moment—a state of being that made Jory's nerves sizzle. His craft was built on precision and focus. He had no time for notions of spontaneity, because that usually meant the director wasn't prepared. But Cali seemed to gather her spontaneity *from* preparation. As though she'd gathered all the possibilities and then waited for the right one to reveal itself. The thought made him nauseous.

Howard's tacit order should have made Jory happy. Well, at least comfortable. He didn't think his job made him *happy* anymore. But there was something about controlling this new director that rubbed him the wrong way, and his inner gray deepened as the silence of the night came on—an old friend and relentless enemy.

Jory checked his phone notifications and tapped his voicemail. When he heard who it was, his body relaxed.

"Hi, Jor." His father's voice had a smile in it, like Astrid had just told him a joke. "Hope the shoot is going well. I'm up to my ears in wedding plans, since Astrid keeps asking me what I think. I never knew I had so many opinions on seat covers. I don't even know why we need seat covers. But still, I had opinions. Maybe I should get into the wedding business. It's a real racket."

His father uncharacteristically paused, and Jory guessed what was coming next.

"Just wondering if you'd gone in for that checkup yet to get the all clear? Don't want to pry, but I won't say I'm not a little anxious about it. Anyway. Hope the shoot's going well. Oh. I think I said that. Okay. Talk soon."

Love, Camera, Action

Guilt and worry flooded his body. When Jory's mother had been diagnosed with stomach cancer, the tests showed that she also had Lynch syndrome, a condition that raised the risks of certain types of cancers. There was a fifty-percent chance Lynch syndrome would show up in her children, and the year before, Jory's father had insisted Jory get tested. It came back positive. And it also revealed a suspicious growth.

The growth was benign, but the doctors wanted to test him again in a year to make sure it stayed that way. Jory knew he needed to get the test, just to put his father's well-founded fears at ease, instead of continually postponing the appointment for the flimsiest of reasons, shoving it to the back burner every chance he got. His dad didn't want to lose his son the same way he had his wife. But the thought of doctors and hospitals and clinics turned Jory's stomach, and so he'd delayed. Jory should stop being a chicken and call the clinic again. Call them now, in fact, and leave a message on their machine.

He started to do just that when the phone rang, making him start. The name that lit up his screen made him groan. As it rang, Jory debated whether to pick it up, hoping it would go to voicemail early so he could hide. He pressed "Accept."

"Howard."

"Blair!" Jory could feel the bombast blow through the digital waves. "What the fuck was that all about today? I gave Melanie some slack to find a director on her own, and this is who she gets?"

He should agree. Keeping Howard onside would further his ambitions as a director. But to deny the flair Cali had brought to her scenes felt like a betrayal of the work. Not of her, of course. "I don't know—I think she has potential."

"Do you? You're more generous than I am. Hopefully, she can make it through the two-parter. I'll have to keep a tighter rein on Melanie to make sure she doesn't make any more blunders."

Jory rubbed his face. Melanie didn't make blunders. Besides being incredible at her job, she couldn't afford to, and Howard was why. Howard's old-school vibe bled into his worldview, and that came along with comments no longer deemed appropriate. Like "Thalia doesn't look fuckable." Or "Paolo needs to step up like a man." Melanie always scrambled to clean up the mess, not because she wanted to endorse his behavior, but because she knew the network would pull out if Howard was gone. Experience still trumped being woke.

"You're the man with the street cred." It was a benign enough comment. Jory took a drink to settle his clenching stomach.

"That I am. That I am. Listen, I just got off the phone with Jeff Cummings, singing your praises."

Jory almost choked on his water. Jeff Cummings was the new darling in prestige TV, helming three hit series in the past five years. His shows were progressive in style and content, and he had a reputation for being a creative powerhouse. Jory would kill to work with him. "That's great, Howard, thanks. I love what Jeff is doing."

"Turns out he's got a little show that's starting up with a small budget, and he's looking for a director who could also double up on camera. I told him you might be his man."

Jory couldn't believe it. When he'd put out the word he wanted to move into directing, he'd imagined he'd do one or two episodes on some backwater show. He couldn't have asked for a better launch with Jeff Cummings, or a more

Love, Camera, Action

frightening one. Business lore was if you screwed up once, his doors would close for good. Jory didn't mind the pressure; he thrived on it. To direct *and* shoot meant the creative control would be entirely in his hands. He was almost giddy at the thought. "I'll give him a call."

"Not so fast there, Jory. It's not a done deal. These things have to be managed with a delicate hand."

"Sure, sure." Jory's excitement escaped with his exhale. He should have remembered there was always a catch with Howard.

"I'll keep working on Jeff so you're free to focus on *The Demon*. I need someone to be my eyes and ears down on the floor. Saves me a lot of hassle knowing I have someone there I can trust."

It sounded like Howard wanted Jory to be his spy on set and was dangling Jeff Cummings to solidify it. The trick would be to keep Howard happy while avoiding being his errand boy. Jory rubbed at a sudden cramp in his neck. "You know me, Howard. I want what's best for the show."

"Great, great. Glad we're on the same page. Gotta give Melanie hell for another thing she's screwed up."

Before Jory could say another word, Howard hung up. Jory heard a crack and felt something snap.

He looked down and saw the camera groaning under the pressure of his clenching hand. Anxiety flooded him as he quickly gentled his grip, delicately turning the camera to see if he'd done any damage. Luckily he'd just pushed a clasp off its hinge. He breathed out his relief. He forced his attention back to the camera, letting its fragility take over his musings and banish the worries he would have to confront in the morning. As he realigned the threads on the clasp, a rush of memories hit.

Opening up his first camcorder on the floor under the Christmas tree, his mom's eyes brimming with excitement. Jumping in and around the guests at his parent's vow renewal ceremony on the beach. The light from a window, softly cutting across his mother's hospital bed. The crack in a door framing his father at his desk, the desolation on his countenance softening when he realized he wasn't alone.

Jory tipped the camera over, and his finger grazed the tiny window that revealed a yellow square behind it. This was what he wanted. The camera itself was a find, but what was *in* the camera was the real gold. A film cartridge, loaded perhaps dozens of years before, with images recorded and forgotten, sold along with the camera until it found its way into Jory's hands.

The day sloughed off him as his skin prickled with possibility. This little gem used eight-millimeter film cartridges that only lasted about three minutes. Three minutes of whatever bit of life this stranger needed to capture—a kiss over a wedding cake, the table at Passover, a winter afternoon as a toddler learned how to skate. Three minutes out of billions, immortalized as golden moments dancing across the frames.

He suddenly wondered how Cali would react to whatever might be on this film. If that childlike glow would alight like it did when she was watching a good scene unfold before her. If her focus would be as intense, as engaged, as curious as what he saw in these forgotten images.

The roll wasn't finished and needed to be shot out so he could get it developed. He slid his fingers through the camera's handgrip as he stood and walked to his chrome and white bathroom, ignoring the soft sound of despair that

Love, Camera, Action

floated through his consciousness, finding it replaced with Cali's infectious energy. He couldn't help but smile at that returned wink of hers, the sass of it, of her. Flipping on the light and staring into the mirror, Jory aimed the lens at himself and rolled the camera, using up the last of the film inside.

CHAPTER FIVE

Cali walked onto set, buzzing with ideas on how to make the day's scenes sizzle while bringing the crew back onside and Jory to heel. She was going to kick some ass and take some names. She was going turn this ship around. She was going to knock this out of the park. She was going to insert whatever comeback cliché and get a result of optimal awesomeness.

What greeted her instead was the sight of Howard standing on the kitchen set, swiping his arms through the air and proclaiming, "I see a wash of blue for this scene—metallic, cold," while Jory nodded at the floor and Dan furiously took notes.

Her feet stuttered to a stop, but her torso kept going. She straightened herself at the last minute, saving herself from tumbling over, but not from the betrayal flooding through her. Was this a thing Howard just . . . did? Usurp his directors' vision in favor of his own? Or had he lost complete faith in her already? She'd of course witnessed this boys'

Love, Camera, Action

club maneuver before, but catching Jory as a part of it cut deep. Which was ridiculous—she barely knew him.

Her old friend, doubt, leached through her skin. Maybe they hadn't consulted with her because they knew that she knew that they knew that she didn't know what she was doing.

No one else knows what they're doing either. Patsy's voice cut through her pity party. *Plus, they're being sexist dickwads.*

Right. They were being sexist dickwads. The dickiest of sexist wads. Cali mentally bucked herself up. She had tons of experience, even if it wasn't on big network TV shows, and the type of work she'd done meant she was perfectly suited for this job. Cali nodded to herself and put in motion her usual tactic in this situation—barging in and taking over. "Good morning, gentlemen. I heard the word 'blue.'"

Jory's head snapped up, and he blanched. At least he had the courtesy to be embarrassed.

She raised an eyebrow at him that could only be interpreted as, *Oh yes, I caught you in your sausage fest.*

Meanwhile, Howard nominally acknowledged her as if she'd been there all along. "Blue matches the tone of Rafe's discombobulation when he sees the demon reflected in the toaster."

Cali inwardly winced. At that point in the script, Paolo's character Rafe glimpses the fires of hell grasping for his soul. The last time Cali checked her demon reference book, the fires of hell tended toward red. Or at least orange. Maybe yellow. She could argue the point, but Howard's vibe told her she'd get nowhere. She'd have to implement another go-to tactic that would bewilder the leader of the club while flushing out the true opinions of the others: embrace the idiocy.

67

Cali forced an air of contemplation. "Blue is an interesting choice. It upends our culture's notion of how hell is represented in the usual Dantean approach to fire, brimstone, and rings of despair. Instead, you're offering a thesis about hell burning so hot it's actually cold. Very fresh."

Howard turned to her fully for the first time, looking ever so slightly pleased at her acumen. He nodded his approval.

Dan kept his face buried in his clipboard while Jory squinted up at the lights and fidgeted. Not a huge fidget. More of a fidge. But just enough of a fidge to tip a person off who might have been watching him obsessively the day before in order to know that Jory didn't fidget or fidge.

Cali knew what that fidge meant. He hated the idea. Hate, hate, *hated* it. He hated that he had to entertain it, let alone execute it. Which made him a lying liar. A liar by omission, but still.

Cali tried not to sound too self-satisfied when she addressed him. "Jory, how do you feel about the cold fires of hell as represented by the color blue?"

He leveled his eyes to hers, and Cali felt winded from their impact. There was an emptiness in them that spoke of hell's own torment, the icy glare reflecting journeys from the depths and back, and Cali wondered if Howard's inspiration for blue came from the intensity of what gazed at her now. "Cold can burn," he agreed.

Geez Louise. His voice, on the other hand, was anything but cold—it was a deep rumble that evoked throbbing embers promising an inferno once kindled. Cali took a metaphoric gulp and scrambled to cover her visceral response of melty knees and flushing warmth. She had to take control of this interaction with Howard, or she'd be bulldozed in every future decision. She set her tone to "Full Patronize."

Love, Camera, Action

"Cold *can* burn. It really can. I'm sure that's what Howard was thinking. But as I remember, our lighting set up is for red. How long will a changeover take?" she asked.

Jory's face was neutral, but a tic in his jaw belied his obvious annoyance.

Dan answered for him. "Forty-five minutes."

"We can do that for Howard, can't we? A wise man once told me that ninety percent of the job was to make everyone happy." Cali gave Jory her biggest smile.

Jory's tick developed into a full-out clench, even as something sparked in his eyes, making the jaw tic equivalent to *"Touché."*

Just then Alison, the pretty, sweet, and curvy camera assistant, cautiously approached their circle to offer a clipboard for Jory's signature. Without moving his eyes from Cali's, he signed, and Alison scuttled away with her head down.

Unaware of the challenge roaring between them, Howard marked Alison's departure. "Glad you agree, Cali. Let's do it," he said, and left the same way Alison did.

Cali stared Jory down even as she became aware of the set bustling around them. The props assistant flew by with dishes and cutlery to set up Rafe/Paolo's breakfast nook, and a set dresser fussed with the curtains surrounding the window that let in the "sun." A coffee urn percolated at the food table, and she could smell those awesome breakfast egg-and-bacon cup things Cali wanted the recipe for but would never make. Her stomach growled, inconveniently taking her badassery down a notch.

Dan nervously tapped his clipboard. "I'm just going to go over the . . . um—oh hey, Cesare!" And he was gone.

Left alone with Jory, Cali let her smile drop, her anger threatening to leak while she forced a frigid professionalism.

"Do you have any suggestions on how to achieve Howard's creative insight?"

Jory looked off to where Howard had disappeared, and ground out, "That discussion shouldn't have happened without you."

Cali did an inward double take. She'd never heard a man acknowledge her getting edged out before. One time a producer had actually blamed her for missing out on a decision because she'd been late, even though she had been forty-five minutes early. "It's not as though it's never happened."

"Well, it shouldn't happen on my set."

"*Our* set." Cali couldn't let that one go by.

Jory swung his annoyed gaze her way. "Now that you're here on *our* set, maybe you have some ideas on how to realize Howard's creative vision, with which you completely agree."

Cali crossed her arms. "Since Howard is intent on flipping the collective understanding of hell, maybe we should also add some wind-whistling sounds and make Paolo shiver like he needs a sweater."

Jory mimicked her crossed arms and had the audacity to appear pleased as she scowled. "Maybe we should get a snow machine. Then Santa can put in an appearance in a blue suit."

"Christmas is the opposite of hell."

"For some."

Cali couldn't argue with that. "Well, everyone loves blue Christmas lights."

"Everyone does not love blue Christmas lights." Jory snarled. "Blue Christmas lights are an abomination."

"Wow. Finally some strong feelings about something," Cali mocked.

Love, Camera, Action

Jory's forehead wrinkled. "I have strong feelings."

"Uh-huh." Cali wondered what his strong feelings might be like if they were aimed at her, and held back a shiver.

She banished the thought with a deep breath. Everyone needed to calm down. She pulled her eyes from his and considered the kitchen set. "Maybe we could move the camera back so Paolo looks smaller in the frame. It will give him an air of isolation and powerlessness."

"Do you mean *I* could move the camera back?"

Jory's usual stony expression was edging toward magma. She guessed her calming vibe wasn't getting picked up. "Well, *I* wouldn't be doing it. But I like to collaborate with the other creative heads."

Jory flinched, but he didn't back down. "Send me your ideas in the form of a shot list, and I'll consider collaborating with them."

Gawd, he was condescending. "Fine. I'll have a new shot list ready for the blue hellfire scene in fifteen." She turned away from Jory's barely concealed sigh and threw an accusatory glance over her shoulder. "And I'll make sure to come in earlier tomorrow, in case there are any more creative discussions with Howard."

To her delight, a storm cloud crossed his face. Smirking, she turned her head back around . . . and walked smack into a wall.

Which wouldn't be so terrible if the thing was an actual wall. Since it was particleboard, it wobbled precariously along the length of the room, causing kitchen utensils to fall off the barely anchored shelves. Whisks and egg slicers clanged and crashed around her, amplifying her embarrassment while Cali grabbed the doorjamb to stop the whole thing from toppling over. When she heard the heavy scrape of something bigger sliding down the flat, she scrunched her shoulders to brace for the impact.

It didn't come. With a thump, strong arms slammed beside her, caging her against the wall. When she opened her eyes, Jory was there, holding an oversized ceramic angel saltshaker an inch above her head.

Jory's body relaxed with the kind of relief that only followed panic. They stood nose to nose, breathing hard as the moment stretched on. The heat from his body enveloped her, and she suddenly felt the urge to relax into him, happy to stay there for the rest of the day. He didn't move an inch, but took deep breaths as if to steady himself. Cali searched through her rational mind for something cool to say but could only eke out, "Thanks."

Jory slowly returned the angel to its place and stepped back. Cali scrambled to exit but ended up walking into the wall again.

"It's still there," he said with thinly veiled mockery.

Mortification was the only word for what her body was awash with. She straightened and changed her trajectory slightly to the left so she could move through the door.

Dan's shout ricocheted around the set, "Good morning, everyone! We're starting with scene fifty-four B, Rafe sees doom in his toaster."

Carrying two brown recyclable take-out containers, the first soggy and bulging, and the second neat and light, Cali swam through the humid, one-hundred-degree Atlanta heat. After four brutal hours of trying to make up for the forty-five-minute delay because of Howard's "fresh" idea, she needed an escape.

Cali stopped for a moment outside Thalia's trailer to gather herself. She was still shaky from the morning and couldn't afford to be off her game around her star, so she closed her eyes and breathed in, thinking, *One seed at a time.* She then attempted a knock that sounded both friendly and commanding. A small voice inside rang with welcome, and Cali threw open the door to meet the blast of air-conditioning. *Phew.*

"Oh, hey! I was expecting a production assistant. I'm not in trouble, am I?" A smiling Thalia emerged through the bedroom doorway, smoothing lotion over her forearms and wearing a silk bathrobe and a healthy glow. "Resplendent" was the only word Cali could come up with for what Thalia embodied. A goddess in a benevolent mood.

"Just in trouble for doing a great job." Cali winced. "That was awful. Sometimes I try to be clever, and I just come off sounding like an awkward keener on the yearbook committee. I brought lunch."

Cali plunked the take-out containers on the small dining table while Thalia carefully pinned back her blown, curled, sprayed, lustrous black hair. "Oh good. I can relax now. I'm a nerd too."

Cali put a hand up to the air-conditioning vent. "May I?"

"Use my air? I bestow upon you my very important AC." Thalia waved her arm like a grand dame.

Cali suspected Thalia had a playful side she didn't show often. Many actresses maintained a strict air of professionalism so they would be taken seriously, especially those of color. Any hint of goofiness might place them in an unfavorable light. Thalia had opened a door, but if Cali wanted

Thalia to really relax, she would have to walk through it first. So she stuck her chest right into the vent, pulling her shirt away from her sweaty skin and groaned as the air found its way down to her belly.

Thalia smirked, her shoulders loosening a fraction. "I know, it's murder here. I mean, I'm from San Diego—I get heat. But there's something about this town that's unbearable."

"I thought it was just because I'm Canadian, but this is brutal." Cali turned around, lifted her shirt from the bottom and bent over slightly. "How could you have ever been a nerd?"

"I was in the debate club."

"The debate club could be cool."

"Not if you're the only one in it and spent your lunch hours trying to recruit stoners in the stairwells," Thalia drawled.

Cali snickered. "You were *that* girl? Yikes."

"You done hogging all the air?" Thalia slid into a seat behind the tiny table.

Reluctantly, Cali stepped away from the air conditioner and took the opposite seat, the table an inch away from her ribs. They opened their respective containers. While Thalia's was an elegant salad of greens and broiled chicken, Cali's was a sloppy mess of meatballs, coleslaw, sweet potatoes, and corn on the cob. "I eat a lot."

Thalia shot her an irritated look. "Don't brag."

Cali indicated their containers. "While your tray could only be described as refined, mine has all the attributes of slop. I can't pass anything on the catering table without taking it, even though I know I can't eat it all. But in the end, I do. Eat it all, I mean."

"Why do you think I don't go to the lunchroom? I sit here and imagine there's only broiled chicken and greens."

Love, Camera, Action

Thalia jabbed her fork at Cali. "Don't shatter my carefully constructed fiction about this."

They focused on their lunch for a moment, settling into a surprisingly companionable silence. Cali didn't have much contact with women in the business, since it was still very much a man's game. So when she found women she liked, she tried to hang on to them, soaking in their energy. But this visit wasn't about her; it was about Thalia and the elephant in the room. Cali had to tread carefully.

While Thalia took mindful, methodical bites of her salad, Cali studied her forkful of slop and pasted on an easy expression. "I thought I'd check in. See how you're feeling about yesterday."

Thalia pushed her greens around the container. "How's Paolo?"

Cali waved her concern away. "He's fine. More embarrassed than anything. He spent the rest of the day burying what happened with jokes."

Thalia nodded, a troubled look clouding her face. Cali knew that look. *Shame.* Shame for something she probably shouldn't feel shame about.

Cali was careful to keep her tone light but firm. "Paolo shouldn't have gone off script like that. Because he's so new, he probably didn't realize how easy it is to stray into dangerous territory during a sex scene. It was my fault for not being clearer with him."

"It wasn't you. I just got . . ." Thalia put her fork down and jammed her hands under her legs. "Overwhelmed," she finished.

"Of course. Who wouldn't?"

Thalia shot Cali a searching gaze, assessing Cali for her sincerity. Cali knew what it was like to be cornered into a bad situation. When she was a PA, the production manager would schedule Cali to be alone with him in the office during night shoots. He'd tell her how beautiful she was and offer to drive her home, even though she had her own production vehicle. Which he knew about because it was her job to drive around and get things. He'd signed off on it, for fuck's sake. Cali couldn't afford to lose the job, so she'd kept her distance by constantly asking about his wife and kids. "We've all been in situations we felt we had no control over."

Thalia went back to stabbing her lettuce. "I did a sex scene once where the other actor took the director's suggestion of improvisation pretty far. The director kept pushing the boundaries, and I went along with it, even though I didn't think . . . it worked for the character."

Thalia went quiet, lost in the painful memory. A lot of men took advantage of actresses under the auspices the job demanded they be free with their bodies. Once Cali saw an eighteen-year-old girl bullied into taking her clothes off for a scene that was only going to be shot from the shoulders up. Cali later heard the girl had stopped acting altogether. "That shouldn't have happened, Thalia. I'm sorry."

Thalia's eyes misted as her voice hardened. "I'm not afraid to do anything. I'm a professional, and I believe in getting the moment right. I just don't want to be surprised."

"Of course." Cali returned to a casual tone, sensing it was safer for Thalia. "I think, for the next one, I'll insist on an intimacy coach, and we'll strip the crew down even more, to just Jory, Paolo, and me."

Tension crept into Thalia's shoulders, her knuckles turning white around her utensils.

Love, Camera, Action

Maybe Cali had gotten it wrong. "Unless you have a different idea?"

Thalia studied her chicken. "It might be better if *more* people were around. The last time there were barely any, and it was . . . isolating."

"No problem. Whatever you need." Cali wanted to incinerate that director.

Thalia dabbed her mouth with her napkin and rose from the table, signifying the discussion was over. "I still have that tea you sent over yesterday. Want some?"

Cali blew out some air to release the tension of the moment, but also from her lunch bloat. "No thanks. Chamomile makes me sleepy."

Thalia eyed Cali's not so subtle belly rub. "I have salabat. It's a kind of ginger tea that's good for your stomach." Thalia indicated Cali's demolished lunch tray. "You had a lot of coleslaw."

Cali was too distended to be embarrassed. "Yes. That. Please."

Thalia carefully placed the tea bag in a clear glass mug, then poured the water in while slipping into a too-casual stance. "How is it going for *you*?"

"Yeah, great. The team is great. I love the episode. The show is great. It's all really great." Cup of tea placed in front of her, Cali made a show of breathing in its sweet, citrus, and honey notes. "This smells great."

Thalia slid back into place and blew on her own cup while studying Cali over the rim. "That's a lot of 'greats.'"

Cali hid behind her cup, examining the golden-brown liquid.

Thalia ventured, "I find it can be exhausting being around men all the time, like a part of you can never relax."

"Yes. The pressure to be a part of their club while never really being invited. The bro code and all that," Cali replied.

"How's it going with Jory?"

"Good. Yep, good." Cali bobbed her head and took a sip too soon, burning her tongue.

"He's an excellent DP," Thalia granted.

"Yes. Amazing. Really great."

"He's also a condescending know-it-all."

Cali sputtered, dribbling tea from her mouth. She quickly grabbed a napkin to wipe her chin. "No. No. He's fine."

Thalia was smiling and Cali knew she'd been made. "My mom would say you have to let men think they're the ones teaching you."

"I hate that."

"I also hate that." Thalia put her tea down. "My grandmother took a different approach. She said you need to know your enemy."

Cali's eyes flashed up in surprise. "*The Art of War?*"

"A copy was on her coffee table."

Cali nodded, wondering what kind of house her grandmother had run.

Thalia continued, "Sun Tzu says, 'Victorious warriors win first and then go to war, while defeated warriors go to war first and then seek to win.'"

Cali frowned. "The set isn't a war."

"No, of course not." Thalia went silent for a moment, then picked her tea back up. "But make no mistake, they see you as an enemy combatant."

"They do?"

"They do."

Cali flashed back to the morning and how the tone of the conversation had changed when she arrived. How the men had no trouble making decisions without her being there and had almost seemed put out when they needed to adjust for her. True, Jory had apologized, but that didn't erase the doubt she'd felt. Or the anger.

Thalia took a careful sip. "Just know you have allies." Thalia pointed two fingers toward her eyes and then swept them out, a benevolent goddess no more.

Jory escaped down the dark hallway toward the edit bays. He'd pulled himself out of another conversation with Howard in the lunchroom, where the illustrious exec had praised Jory over the blue hell scenes—as though he'd had anything to do with it. Howard should have thanked Cali for making his stupid idea even passably work. *Blue.* Like it was some kind of brilliant idea. Like it even made sense.

Fucking blue.

Howard kept going on and on while Jory frantically searched for a way to extricate himself from a prime opportunity to do some political maneuvering. He used to love listening to stories from decision-makers like Howard, men who had shaped film and TV. And Howard had worked with the best: Coppola, Scorsese, Tarantino. But Jory couldn't muster up the energy to care. He'd grown tired of wading through the bad behavior and bullying to get to the insights about the art of storytelling. Jory wanted to hear from voices that didn't get the same airtime. Stories someone like Cali might tell.

Now he was hiding in a hallway, no lunch eaten, worrying Cali would find out they'd been talking without her again.

Not that he should care what a newbie director thought. He shouldn't. He had more important things to do, like . . . delivering the forgotten film cartridge in his hand. Yeah. That.

The unmistakable sounds of someone having sex wafted out of an edit bay, stopping Jory short. They weren't porn-y sounds—a studied gasp or an inauthentic "Oh baby, your cock is so big." It was a sharp intake of breath, made by someone caught up in the heat of the moment. A dick-thickening sound played over and over and over. Loud.

A similar sound had escaped Cali the day before when Alison demonstrated the new night vision camera they'd brought in for the demon-ops scene. He'd watched her handle the camera with a languorous yet reverent hand that to Jory bordered on lascivious. Her stance turned commanding as she gave instructions to Alison on what she wanted done with the camera, and Jory mused on what it would take for her to make that sound again and then have her turn that commanding gaze on him.

Jory shook himself. The sex noises were not helping.

Just then, the inspiration of his musings rounded the corner and screeched to a halt at the sight of him. Jory flushed with embarrassment, like a teenager caught with his dad's skin mags. Cali's eyes turned curious at the sex sounds bouncing between them.

Jory stepped forward with the urge to clarify, but found his jeans suspiciously tight. Instead, he twisted his hips to a forty-five-degree angle he imagined made him look like a deranged line dancer. He shrugged toward the sounds, all casual-like. "Yesterday's scene."

"Ah." Cali relaxed but turned her regard on him, probably noting his obvious blush. He was thirty-five years old, for crap's sake. He didn't blush.

Love, Camera, Action

The soundtrack to this mortifying scene progressed from sounds to words. *"Oh that's it . . . that's it . . ."* He nonchalantly dropped his hand holding the film cartridge in front of his pants.

Stifling a grin, Cali motioned to the hallway. "Is Melanie's office down here?"

"Uh, no." He cleared his suddenly parched throat. "It's around the corner, down past the coffee makers, and then a left."

"You like that?"

"Yeah . . ."

Cali scanned the hallway Jory had indicated and then peered down the opposite side, her brow furrowed. She lifted her hand to twist a lock of hair around her finger. "Past the coffee makers? Isn't that where Wardrobe is?"

"Don't stop . . ."

"Yes, yep. Wardrobe is down there, but if you take a left, then you'll hit Melanie's office." Jory willed the throbbing in his blood to slow down.

"Oh baby, please don't stop . . ."

Cali tapped her lips with a finger, confused.

What didn't she get? It was pretty clear. Unless she was fucking with him. Was she fucking with him? Because it would be great if this little exchange could end *yesterday*.

She tipped her head to the side. "Sorry, I have a terrible sense of direction. Give it to me again? I take a left at the coffee makers and go past Wardrobe . . ."

"No, no, no. You don't go past Wardrobe. You take a left *before* Wardrobe." He was sweating now. Blushing and sweating.

"My left or your left?" Her lip curled the slightest bit.

81

Yep, she was fucking with him. The brat was enjoying his discomfort. He didn't know whether to laugh or curse. "Your left."

"My left—got it."

Desperate for escape the second time that day, Jory walked backward, awkwardly pointing behind him at the edit bay. "I'm going to go check on that scene."

Her smile turned evil as she dropped the charade. "You do that."

Jory fumbled for the door handle and burst into the room. "Do you have to play that so goddamned loud?"

The editor jumped from his chair at the intrusion, quickly stopping the footage in mid-image with a yelp. The shot on the screen was of Paolo and Thalia's entangled legs, their skin glowing with an ethereal sensuality under the diaphanous sheet. It was electrifying, just as Jory had known it would be.

Michael, the editor who'd been working the footage at such an unnatural volume, put a hand on his heart. "Man, don't freak me out like that. You know how into it I get."

It wasn't Michael's fault Jory'd been caught in a night-mare of awkward sexual tension with the woman he was firmly banishing from his mind and definitely having no inappropriate thoughts about. "Sorry. It was just . . . loud. And I . . . uh . . . yeah."

Michael let out a breath and threw his arms over his head in a big stretch. At over six foot two, he was taller and broader than Jory, and exuded an undeniable Idris Elba sexuality not even Jory could deny. As Michael lowered his arms to scratch his belly, Jory had the fleeting thought he'd definitely tap that if he weren't straight. Hell, if he was honest, he'd tap Michael regardless.

Love, Camera, Action

Michael's voice returned to its normal sleepy drawl. "That's some good stuff you got yesterday."

Jory pulled himself together. "Yeah, you like it?"

"Jesus, yeah. I'm not even supposed to be working on this scene, but I did a quick scan of the rushes and after going through all that blancmange stuff you guys did at the beginning—" Michael froze over the blunder. "Don't get me wrong, I'm not throwing shade. That stuff was fine, but when I came across this, I was very much—yeah." Michael nodded in agreement with the footage. "I mean, *yeah*. And have you heard the audio?"

Jory rubbed the back of his neck. "Just all the way down the hall."

"Oh yeah, sorry about that. I had to jack it up to hear the nuances, and then got lost to it." Michael didn't seem the least sorry. "And there's more of those little gasps and sighs. From Paolo even."

"You get to the end?"

Michael nodded. "Hilarious. I mean, *ouch*. But hilarious."

"Yeah."

"Anyway, that shit is hot. The shots, not Paolo getting dinged."

Jory figured the sex scene would be good, but he hadn't imagined it could be *this* good. Begrudging respect seeped into him. He wasn't often proven wrong, but when he was, he took notice and made sure kudos found a way to the source. The sexy, smart source. "It was Cali, the new director's idea. The shots."

"Well, let her know for me." Michael spotted the film cartridge in Jory's hand. "You need another transfer?" Jory passed it to Michael, who turned it over in his hand. "Super eight today. What are you doing with all this footage?"

"Just a personal project."

Michael's body stilled as all his attention shifted to the doorway, where a flurry of woman blew in. Jory glanced over his shoulder and saw Melanie brimming with all the energy of being on top of a million things, plus ten you didn't consider.

She typed away on her phone. "Hey, Jory. Michael, we have notes on episode two from the network. Did you get them?"

"Ah, no. I got caught up in something else." Michael motioned to the screen.

She glanced up from her phone to the monitor with the sex scene footage. "Oh yeah. How does that look?"

"Really good." Michael cleared his throat. "Very good."

Jory pondered the sight of Michael in a rare display of nerves. His physical presence tended to put all the women and most of the men on the production into a state of "aflutter." And here he was acting like the proverbial schoolboy while Melanie didn't seem to notice.

"That's why we got Cali." Melanie turned her intense perusal on Jory. "How do you like her? Is she working out?"

Jory stilled. This was one of those moments. Jory knew his response wouldn't make or break Cali's career, but his yes or no could definitely nudge her future down a particular path. He couldn't deny her absence would make his life a lot easier, not only with his Howard campaign but also with the uncomfortable attraction he was finding difficult to tamp down. He also couldn't deny her work was good, that she was bringing an energy to the material the show sorely needed. That *he* sorely needed.

"I'm not sure yet," he hedged.

Melanie narrowed her eyes. "You're not sure yet."

Love, Camera, Action

"No."

"You're always sure."

Jory shrugged.

Melanie crossed her arms while Michael considered Jory with an air of interest.

Jory scowled.

He had to give them something. His lack of opinion would rouse suspicion one way or the other if he didn't. "Well, she has a complete disregard for schedule when she gets an idea, but those ideas are often good. She talks to the actors too much but gets performances I didn't know they had in them. She's in my business about where the camera is, but sometimes the shot looks better as a result. She's constantly eating and is always, *always* bouncing her knee."

Melanie turned her laser gaze up twenty degrees. "So, she's good?"

"Hey! Is that the footage from yesterday?"

The trio broke apart as Paolo sauntered in. Actors weren't generally allowed in the edit bays. Seeing themselves onscreen either put them in a panic about how "bad" they were or gave them an unfounded sense of power that they were in a position to give advice. Paolo was in the latter category. He raised a fist bump to Michael, which went ignored.

"Can I say something about the newbie director?" Michael pointed to the monitor where Thalia's profile stared up in ecstasy at Paolo. "That scene is fire, and when I get my teeth into it it's going to be transcendent. If that's what she came up with on her first day, I can't wait to see what comes next."

Paolo half sneered. "Yeah, but she got it in a totally unprofessional way. I mean, you can't endanger one of your best assets, am I right?" Paolo took a step back, indicating himself.

After the briefest pause, during which Jory imagined Melanie had to take a fortifying breath, she plastered concern on her face. "Absolutely. We take the safety of our artists very seriously." She gently took Paolo's arm to steer him out of the room. "Paolo, can you walk with me? I have a question about your contract."

Paolo swaggered beside her. "Mel, I have people for that . . ."

Left alone, Jory risked a glance at Michael and immediately regretted it. The guy was all smirk. "She bounces her knee, huh?"

"Shut up, man."

Jory stalked out of the room. He'd better find a way to control Cali. The woman was dangerous to his sanity.

CHAPTER SIX

"It's big, isn't it? Bigger than you'd think. Heavy and thick," Cali said.

Paolo took in the long wooden pepper grinder in his hand, considered its size, its weight, its girth. Cali's lips quirked up in a little smile, and she snuck a glimpse at Jory, who, to her delight, was ever so slightly shaking his head, as though she were acting like a badly behaved teenager. Which she was.

She had survived—so far. This was her second week on *The Demon*, and this morning they were shooting the real-life meeting between Paolo and Thalia's characters, Rafe and Anna. Having so far only connected in the dream world, Anna's corporeal form was ramping up her possession of Rafe by way of an in-person meeting at the chichi restaurant where Rafe worked his day job. Paolo looked devastatingly ethereal in crisp server blacks while he waited on his literal dream woman, Thalia/Anna, and her blond

"Best Friend" as she was named in the script. The restaurant was all chrome and glass minimalism, accentuating Thalia's dangerous dark beauty and knockout curves caressed by a fuchsia cashmere sweater. Extras sat at the other tables, bored but quiet while the crew made final adjustments.

Cali, meanwhile, was deep into her option-three battle plan, which was, in essence, to chill everyone the fuck out. Stage one of the third option involved smoothing out her rocky start with a series of methodically placed bricks of efficiency. Every night, no matter how little sleep she got, she came up with a watertight plan that made the crew breathe easy and appeased Jory's regimented nature. If there were issues, she was quick to find solutions. Shot taking too long? Cut time from the following scene. Problems with clunky dialogue? Have a quick consultation with the writer, to come up with better lines. Framing not quite right? Show deference to Jory without giving up too much control, resulting in a begrudging grunt of respect.

It helped that Howard was back in LA, dealing with some issue in the writer's room. The entire cast and crew had collectively dropped their shoulders, able to do their work without worrying how it would be judged and torn apart.

Then she'd begun stage two: Jory needed to play.

Cali's smile grew as she remembered the exchange she'd had last week with Jory outside the edit bays. Watching his icy facade melt away under boyish embarrassment as the sex sounds wove around them? Hilarious. And she couldn't pass up the opportunity to ruthlessly tease him. He'd been a *mess*. He'd actually begun to stammer, and when the realization of what she was doing dawned across his face, his mortification was priceless.

Love, Camera, Action

He was all brisk efficiency and cool consideration, but there was no joy in anything he did. And maybe if he had more fun, he'd let go of the reins so she could do her job without interference. She had to show him that, despite the arduous schedule and warring egos, shooting a TV series—and about a demon no less—could be a hilarious riot. When you thought about it, what they did every day was kind of ridiculous. They had long discussions over whether a cape looked evil enough, or if the amount of water the rain machine sprayed on Rafe's window was foreboding or maudlin, or what size the hellfire portal should be in the ice-cream parlor. Somewhere along the line Jory had lost his sense of play. Assuming he'd had it in the first place.

She started her campaign with the crew. She'd rejected Thalia's view that all the men were enemy combatants. Antagonism would only raise tensions, and it wasn't really her style. Instead, she gave out prizes for the most creative T-shirt. She had the crew whoop when the actors got a shot in the first take. She started a betting pool on when they would finish each day. The strategy was working on the crew, and on Jory as well.

He still moved around like a professional robot, but wry smiles or huffs of surprise occasionally eked out, and she was able to sneak in her ideas more freely. She watched closely for those tiny chinks in his armor, collecting them like shiny pieces of glass.

And he watched her. She didn't know if it was to make sure she was following the rules or because she was an incomprehensible entity he couldn't figure out, but she knew he was watching, even if he didn't. Which made her the teensiest bit reckless. How far could she push him while still staying in the realm of professional behavior? In the restaurant scene, this particular brand of play she was experimenting with was on the cheeky side. And his little scandalized headshake was a good indication she was on the right path.

Cali focused on Paolo, his pepper grinder in hand. "Have you ever been a waiter, Paolo?"

Paolo let out a "pfft," as though he would never stoop to such levels. At the table, blond, blue-eyed, and buxom Best Friend giggled, clearly smitten. He rewarded her with a dazzling smile.

"Okay, well . . . it's a busy job that requires you to appear in control. Servers are always on the edge of chaos, even as they try to keep everything smooth and easy, to make sure their customers feel attended to. At the same time, those customers want something that's a waste of the server's precious time—more water, a cleaner fork, to know how much paprika is in the special. These lovely women here"—Cali gestured to Thalia and Best Friend—"want freshly ground pepper. Do you think they need pepper? No. Have they tasted their food to see if they need pepper? No. They just want some pepper ground onto their food because they think it looks fancy. So the best way to look fancy is efficiency of movement."

She grabbed the pepper grinder from Paolo and brandished it like a pro. Mainly because she had been a pro. When she couldn't find a gig on a set, she'd served at restaurants that ran the gamut from high-class to grungy, in order to pay for her expensive filmmaking habit.

Cali caressed the pepper grinder ever so subtly, showing it off to Thalia and Best Friend. "First you offer it as though it were a gift. The gift of your pepper grinder."

Love, Camera, Action

Cali stole another glance at Jory, who was rubbing the back of his neck. She wrapped her fingers around the wood with the slightest suggestion. "A firm grip on the base with one hand and a quick twist at the head with the other, and the pepper comes shooting out."

Jory coughed.

Zing. Another chink in the armor. "Efficient, controlled, effective. And if you do it like that, it will be even more awkward when you grind your pepper into the mimosa of the woman who has been invading your dreams."

Cali slapped the grinder back into Paolo's hands, and Thalia shot Cali a smirk.

"What?" Paolo asked Thalia.

Thalia shook her head à la *"If you don't get it, I'm not going to tell you."*

Paolo shrugged her off. Cali was beginning to wonder if his defensiveness was a cover for being deeply shy. If she could take a guess, Paolo had big respect for Thalia and was slain every time she mocked him.

Best Friend pursed her perfectly full, red lips. "I like pepper."

"Oh, I like pepper too," Cali said. "That's just what the server is thinking."

"Really?" Best Friend's eyebrows shot up as though she was surprised servers had thoughts at all.

"Yes." Cali turned back to Paolo. "Keep your eyes on Thalia's—remember, this is the first time you've seen her in real life—and angle the grinder down so it crosses your chest. Holding it like that, um . . . highlights your biceps."

Pleased with the setup, Cali walked off to Video Village. She sat in her chair while she waited for the scene to start.

Empty spaces of time could wind her up more than anything, allowing her internal chatter to seep through the silent cracks. On the surface, she knew most people saw her as a calm but energetic person who was always in control. Internally she was thrashing around in a fast river of anxiety, desperately fighting to keep from being swept away. She'd learned being calm meant her mother might not descend into despair and/or fury quite as fast if, say, the dinner spilled on the floor, or the package didn't arrive, or the date was canceled. And that outward calm helped her on set. But Cali's boundless internal energy would always spill out, no matter how much she tried to squelch it. She did her best to monitor her breathing while her leg began its inevitable bounce.

Jory drifted from set to his chair beside her. Talk about efficiency of movement. No action was wasted, every motion purposeful: his strong fingers adjusting the focus of the camera; his shoulders straining through his T-shirt as he aimed a light; his smile like an aphrodisiac to the office staff, whom he left tittering in his wake. He was all languid confidence and easy sexuality. So chill, she sometimes wondered if he was even breathing, not *trying* to breathe like she was.

She pulled her attention back to the monitor, put on her Jory blinders as the set readied, and called, "Action."

Paolo sailed into the scene like he'd been serving all his life. She'd had a hunch he would respond well to physical direction, and it was paying off. Any coaching that involved him having to use his head didn't make a stick of difference to his performance, but give him something to *do*, and he was all ease and fluidity, as though he were born to act.

Love, Camera, Action

He masterfully wielded the pepper grinder to land at just the angle Cali had shown him, with a subtle cheekiness that caused Joanne, who was onset Makeup, to let out a little guffaw. *Huh.* Paolo could be funny. Who knew? Even Thalia registered surprise before she segued into an expression of wry amusement more in keeping with her character.

What the actors didn't realize was that Cali had angled the grinder that way to place a visual barrier between Paolo and Thalia in obvious symbolic innuendo—a wall to be climbed, a boundary to be crossed, while signaling the mounting sexual tension between the characters. Cali loved those simple embellishments that added psychological weight to a scene, even if those cues were only subconscious. Plus, the pose really did show off Paolo's biceps.

Jory sat forward, squinting at the screen. Cali stopped her breath entirely. This was it. Jory was about to rave over her quiet ingenuity. He raised his long finger to the monitor in slow motion, and she followed that finger along his muscled forearm, across his sculpted shoulder, and up to his eyes—those intensely focused eyes that now pinned her to her director's chair. "Your little phallic symbol is making the bad guy look like a bobblehead."

Cali's gaze shot to the monitor where "the bad guy" stood in the doorway, watching the scene. Tragically, only his head was visible. Cali's pepper grinder–cum–phallic symbol blocked the rest of his body, making him look like, yes, a live bobblehead.

Cali's shoulders slumped. "Damn it."

"Paolo has to move the pepper grinder." Jory sat back.

"I'm trying to use that pepper grinder as a—"

"I know what you're trying to do with the pepper grinder." He answered her in a tone she could only describe as chastising. "Your thinly veiled attempt at sex symbolism needs to go."

Cali's mind raced for an alternative. "What if we changed the angle of the camera?"

"You'd rather change the camera's angle than the pepper grinder's?"

"When you put it like that, it sounds frivolous," Cali whined. Ugh, she hated whining. She straightened in her chair and cleared her throat.

"This is not the symbol you want to die on. Pick another one."

He leafed through his script, already moving on. No discussion. No collaboration. Decision made, edict delivered. Cali realized, as much as Jory had begun to loosen up over the past week, he had also delivered equal doses of condescension that fed the doubt percolating under the skin, turning her mood as black as unexposed film in the light. "You won't discuss the possibilities?"

"I've already run through the possibilities, and it won't work."

Cali got off her chair and walked closer to the camera, taking in its sight lines. "What if you moved the camera to the left?"

He burrowed into his chair, appearing more and more like a jaded king issuing orders from his throne. "Then we lose the light from the overhead counter, thrusting—" Jory raised an eyebrow in obvious sarcastic homage to her innuendoes, "Paolo into darkness."

"What about to the right?"

"Then I lose Thalia."

Love, Camera, Action

"What about from below?"

Jory squeezed his eyes shut. "The only option is to raise the camera higher, but then we'll have to change where the actors sit *and* their lights, which will take another half an hour."

He really had thought through all the possibilities. She should have known. While obsessing over his manly form, she'd clocked his nearly constant, infinitesimal changes to each frame, his busy mind calculating every element coming into play for the shot. He also never factored her ideas into those calculations.

"I would like to bring some psychological depth to the scene." Cali lowered her voice, aware of the crew around them, yet unable to control her petulance oozing out. "Or didn't you study film theory at AFI?"

Jory scoffed. "You want to talk film theory?"

"It's a simple concept."

"Yep. Phallic symbols are pretty simple. Where did you go to school?"

Cali blushed. And of course, he noticed. He slid out of his chair, keeping his volume low while his body vibrated with intensity. "Ah! The school of experience. Not much film theory taught there, from my understanding. If by chance you *had* read any theory lately, you'd know no one cares about that stuff anymore. Symbolism is dead."

Cali knew the crew was listening, that they couldn't keep the intensity of the argument from them, but her temper was edging out her good sense, fueled by his patronizing tone. "*I* learned on the ground that people want meaning."

"No, they don't. They don't give a crap about what they put in their eye holes."

Cali stepped closer in an attempt to keep quiet, and a current shot down her spine at his nearness. His body tensed and a flush ignited over his skin. "I think they watch because something calls to them, to whatever they yearn for inside, some kind of connection."

"It's a pepper grinder!" he exclaimed.

"It's a phallic symbol!" she answered.

On set, Paolo piped up, "Is this grinder supposed to be my cock or something?"

Thalia blasted out a surprised laugh. "*Ding, ding, ding!* You got it!"

Paolo gave her a smug look. "This is nothing compared to what *I* got, baby."

"If you're bigger than that pepper grinder, I don't want you anywhere near me."

Any hope of keeping the argument between them vanished, and even though Cali knew she shouldn't involve the cast and crew, Jory's inflexibility infuriated her. She marched over to set and motioned between Thalia and Paolo. "This needs spark. Some unknowable something that moves between them that the audience can pick up—a signal that these two are already half in love."

Jory crossed his arms. Cali could feel the whole crew still as they watched their creative heads square off. "The audience will see him look at her and her look at him, and fill in the blanks themselves. It's called 'projection.' Nothing needs to spark."

"We"—Cali motioned to everyone, her arm gestures getting bigger as her frustration mounted—"need to differentiate one look from another, to signal they recognize each other as 'The One' rather than just another person they're passing in anonymity."

Love, Camera, Action

"'The One'"—Jory made sarcastic air quotes—"can't be represented by a phallic symbol. And people don't fall in love with a look. Love is deeper than that. It's not gazing across a table; it's years of commitment."

"You don't believe in love at first sight?"

He snorted. "Do you?"

"I don't believe in 'The One' at all." She mimicked his air quotes. "It's the audience who believe in 'The One,' and watching the initial connection gives them a thrill. But no, love at first sight isn't a thing. If love is a thing at all."

"It is too a thing." Suddenly Joanne from Makeup stepped from the shadows onto the set, pushing her fire-engine-red hair off her brow, demanding to be heard. "I knew the second I laid eyes on my Joey. Bam! I almost fainted." She let out a big laugh, lost in the memory. "Joey didn't know right off, but that's men for you."

"Whoa, whoa, whoa." From the other side, Dan waved his arms. "When I saw Kelly, my heart stopped. Literally. I went to the doctor to make sure I hadn't messed up my ticker."

Cali's excitement rose. Her personal opinion that romantic love was hogwash, a concept designed to make prey of vulnerable women, was unpopular. She'd watched how it had destroyed her mother and sister time and time again. And how it rocked Cali's world by default: she'd been out of school for weeks because her mother couldn't get out of bed after her breakup with Patsy's father, and she'd had to hide grocery money so her mother wouldn't give it to Rick. But the crew was making her point, so who cared? "And what was it like?" she asked.

"It was like . . . um. It's hard to explain." Dan squinted at Joanne for help.

"Yeah, it's like . . . well . . ." Joanne screwed her face up, stumped.

"It's like your whole world was washed in gray and then suddenly explodes into color." Paolo's voice had entered the fray, steeped in painful, bittersweet understanding.

Jory blanched.

Paolo went on, "It's as though you weren't breathing before, and now that you are, every breath scrapes across the pain of loneliness you feel without them. But you relish that pain since it means you exist only because they do."

The room fell silent. Paolo started, as though surfacing from a trance, and blushed just as Dan stepped in to save him. "Yeah, it's like that."

Joanne smiled gently at Paolo. "It's exactly like that."

The unexpected tenderness from them both allowed a sad smile to surface. And then Paolo wiped it away as he tipped his head down.

Thalia snarled. "That's just a myth the patriarchy cooked up to ensnare young girls into thinking they're unworthy unless they find love. It's a complete fabrication."

Cali privately agreed with Thalia but kept quiet so her point carried.

"It is not a myth." All eyes swung to Jory. "But it's also not something you can capture with a glance or a sigh or a phallic symbol or whatever the fuck. Because it is something deeper. It is something better, something more solid and ephemeral than anything else in the world. Love *is* the world, and it envelops everyone in this beautiful blanket that not even death can deny. We should be striving for *that*, but instead we have to bow to whatever cliché people will swallow." Jory let out a growl of frustration. "And none of this matters when a fucking pepper grinder is blocking the entrance of the next actor. We've wasted enough time. Dan, set the scene up again. Paolo, move the grinder."

Jory stormed away and the set fell into silence.

Cali wasn't sure if she should be embarrassed for herself that Jory had usurped her authority in front of the crew or embarrassed for him because he'd thrown a hissy fit.

She held her hand up to Dan to signal she needed five, and followed in Jory's wake.

She found him a few sets over, bathed in darkness and quiet, standing among wood-paneled walls and lush armchairs. It was the Demon Overlord set, imposing and luxurious. It spoke of privilege, history, danger.

She approached gingerly so as not to startle him. "You're right about the pepper grinder. I shouldn't have dug in on it. We'll take it out."

Jory scrubbed his face, as though trying to scrape a memory away, and nodded without meeting her gaze. She sensed him retreating from her with every movement, and even though she was still riddled with doubt over her abilities, and anger at his stubbornness, she felt desperate to pull him back, to stay here with her. "We could do something different. Something you want to try?"

"I want something greater," he implored. "Something that isn't run of the mill."

Cali felt compelled to get to the source of the pain she saw in him and stepped closer. "We could figure it out together. Something better than a stupid pepper grinder."

"It wasn't stupid." He searched her face as though looking for the answer to an impossible question. He stilled and Cali got the strangest feeling he was about to kiss her.

He stepped back. "It's fine. I'm being a brat. Let's just get through the scene."

Cali stiffened. She didn't know when his good opinion had become so important to her, but she couldn't be dismissed again. "I don't want to just get through the scene. You may not think what we're trying to say has value, but no one ever cried their eyes out over a perfectly lit and framed shot." Jory went slack-jawed. She pushed. "It's the imperfection, the messiness of emotion that brings people to their knees."

"Are you saying that what I do isn't important?" His shock disappeared, replaced by fiery anger.

"No. I'm saying what *I* do is important. My job is to bring everything together, to marry the perfectly constructed shot and the heart of the scene. Form and spirit combined."

Ice smoothed out his features, forged by a fury Cali didn't comprehend. "And I'm telling you: No. One. Cares."

He walked off, leaving Cali alone.

"I care," she whispered.

The room sucked up the sound as if she hadn't even spoken.

CHAPTER SEVEN

Jory stood in Spiral Burgers, trying to keep apart from Atlanta's hipster and financial elite as they filed in for anchovy-beet–virgin blood burgers and rum-vodka-absinthe lighter-fluid cocktails. He hadn't had lunch again, to prep again for his test, and then he'd had to cancel again because the shoot went over time. Since Spiral was steps away from his condo, he'd forced himself to wade into the infamous burger joint to get some calories in the form of takeout.

After his conflict with Cali, the whole day had fallen apart. With no pepper grinder in hand, Paolo's performance had become leagues worse than even Jory could have imagined. Paolo knew he was flaming out, which he first tried to cover with bravado and jokes, then with sulky bitterness as he blamed Cali for changing things at the last minute. Who knew a pepper grinder would make such a difference to the hack?

Cali had.

Meanwhile Cali had become quiet and withdrawn. She'd stopped engaging the crew and the actors, only giving the most cursory direction while pouring over her notes, anxiety thinning her lips as she second-guessed, then triple guessed, her choices.

Jory knew he was the reason for the fallout. He'd been out of control all day, a logical progression from the week he'd had. He'd been sleeping for shit. He knew the results from the endoscopy could potentially put his mind at ease, as well as his father's, but Jory kept thinking back to that time before they'd known about his mother's cancer. How simple life had seemed, how ordinary. Then the frenzied rush to live life to the max after her diagnosis, the trips they'd taken, his parents' vow renewal ceremony, the school he'd skipped just to be with her. Then the constant sickness, the treatments, the relentless hope, the desperation, and finally the lonely emptiness that never seemed to end. He didn't want to think about the possibility, even a remote one, of going down that path and taking his loved ones with him.

Maybe that's why he couldn't stop thinking about Cali. She'd filled the vacuum of his thoughts with an unintentional campaign to capture his every waking moment. He tried to keep things professional, but then she'd walk by, and he'd watch her long legs cross the set; or she'd tweak a light, and he'd be delighted by the effect; or she'd make one of the burly grips laugh, and he'd wonder what it'd take to make her laugh like that.

On the other side of the mind-fucking spectrum, there was the nightly call from Howard, "checking in," which really meant he wanted to gossip, to wheedle information from his operative on the inside, who was forced to try to

Love, Camera, Action

find damning evidence that just wasn't there. Jory deflected most of Howard's questions with variations on "everything's going better than well," or by telling convoluted stories that never went anywhere, leaving Howard slightly confused.

If anything, Jory was the problem on set, losing his cool over Cali's callous view on love. It's not like he wanted love himself—dragging someone into his morass of possible medical issues was the last thing he wanted to do—but to deny the depth of the real love he'd witnessed between his parents felt like some kind of betrayal. Especially because that love hadn't been reserved just for them, but had enveloped everyone who came into their sphere. When his mother died, his father had been devastated. But instead of closing off, he'd opened up, merging his despair with Jory's so they could face their future together in the shared knowledge they had each other.

To hear Cali say love didn't exist had shaken him. For someone so passionate, so full of creativity and life, to not believe in love felt deeply wrong. Like discovering beautiful colors skimming across water were made by an oil spill. The beauty above covering something ugly underneath.

His skittering mind slowly returned to the present as he vaguely took in the terrifyingly efficient brunette at the cash register when she shouted out, "'70s Elvis?"

"That's me," someone called out.

"And—" The brunette peered over her shoulder as a teenager dressed in white prep cook linens handed her two bags: one bulging and sweating grease, the other neat and orderly. The woman turned back to wave Jory forward. "The cheeseburger."

He reached for his bag and brushed shoulders with the owner of the '70s Elvis. Immediately he pulled back to apologize and froze when he saw that it was Cali Daniels.

Her eyes widened with horror as she took a step back. She forced out a tremulous fake smile. "Oh, hey."

She looked tired and drawn. Her hair fell across her forehead, and he noticed the careless waves had tangled in places because of the hectic day. He had the sudden urge to run his hands through her hair to set it to rights.

Cali shoved her own hands in her pockets. "I just got some takeout to take home. To eat."

"Hence the name *takeout*."

Cali sighed and her "friendly" look melted into one of exhaustion. "Yeah."

Jory immediately regretted his poor attempt at a joke. Was he this much of a dick to everyone? Or was he just noticing it in her presence, each thoughtless wound he inflicted written across her expressive face. He was so tired of himself.

He searched for some small talk to ease the tension. "The production assistant told me this is the best burger joint in Atlanta."

Cali nodded.

He nodded back.

They awkwardly nodded.

Another customer bustled into the restaurant, pushing his way past Cali to the cash register, forcing her to move closer to Jory. The efficient brunette put their bags down to talk to the new customer while Cali searched for an escape. Nerves assailed him. "I don't usually eat burgers, but I didn't have any lunch, and I couldn't bring myself to translate the bespoke menus at the other restaurants in this hood."

Cali's features flooded with concern, all trace of their awkward exchange gone. "You didn't eat lunch?"

"No." He frowned as he tried to understand her sudden change. Was she worried about him? An incomprehensible, soft glow bloomed in his chest.

"Why didn't you eat lunch?"

"Uh . . ." He shifted his feet, not wanting to admit the real reason. "I usually run at lunch. Or do Pilates."

A stupefied look replaced the one of concern. "You run at lunch. Or do Pilates." Her gaze traveled his body as though assessing the truth of his words, and he felt his internal temperature rise.

"I can't bring weights to work, and Pilates is a good way to train without them. Because you use your body weight."

"I know how Pilates works." Cali's mouth quirked into an almost smile.

He shifted again. Why did he feel so uncomfortable? He was a grown man. He didn't have to justify himself.

"So, you didn't eat all day?" Cali asked.

"I had a muffin." At least he thought he'd had a muffin.

"That's not eating."

Jory shrugged. "I just . . . forgot."

Cali turned her attention to the brunette, whose focus was back on them, her amenable customer service facade wearing thin. "How can men simply forget to eat? I would never forget to eat."

The brunette shook her head. "I would never forget to eat."

Cali shook her head along with her, compatriots in the struggle to understand the ridiculousness that was The Male.

The brunette held up the bags and shook them. "Luckily you have food right here."

Cali nabbed the two bags and handed his over. "You're also staying at The Towers, right? Come on. I'll walk you."

"Because I might faint from starvation on the dangerous streets of Buckhead?" Jory quipped.

"I'm sorry." Cali stopped suddenly and brought a hand to her ear. "Was that a joke?"

"I hope so." Jory wasn't sure. He couldn't remember the last time he'd had to actively charm someone. Charm used to come easily to him, especially with women. He'd had a lot of relationships in the past, some short, some long, but all fun and interesting and experimental, and never straying into anything too serious. His life as a DP meant long hours and sometimes months away on location shoots. Most women who wanted something deeper figured out he wasn't physically available and left him, with no hard feelings, for more stable pastures. He'd had vague thoughts of settling down before his health scare but those quickly vanished when the test results came in.

For some reason, he wanted to impress Cali with his adroit sophistication and cosmopolitan outlook, but at the moment he couldn't string a coherent thought together.

Cali raised her eyebrows at the brunette in a telepathic message. *Look at him making a joke . . .*

"You'd be surprised how dangerous this neighborhood is." The brunette turned to Jory. "The real estate agents can be vicious."

Cali called over her shoulder on her way out, "I'll make sure he doesn't take anyone's card." She pushed open the door, pausing for him to follow.

Love, Camera, Action

Jory forced a saunter, trying to regain his equilibrium. He stopped when he reached her, holding the door so she could precede him, his grandmother's etiquette lessons taking over. They walked toward their condos in slightly less awkward silence as he frantically searched through those etiquette lessons for polite conversation starters.

Cali beat him to it. "The condos are nice."

He was flummoxed again. He despised the production condos; their lack of personality drained his own. He couldn't help but compare his family's beach house to the condo. The warm wood floors instead of concrete. The large windows looking over the ocean instead of the city. He'd spent weeks there last year during his scare, swimming in the water alone, breathing in salt air and soaking in the chirps of the sand pipers.

He wondered now what it would be like to share that sacred space with someone who'd never been there. Someone who might appreciate its small miracles. His eyes flitted to Cali and he struggled to remember what they were talking about. "Sure."

"You don't think so?" Her voice quavered, the new kid trying to figure out what's cool.

Oh right, the condos. "They're fine. The usual."

"Sure." Cali grew quiet.

He cursed himself. This might be her first time doing a shoot out of town. He supposed the pampering that was de rigueur for a director could be exciting for a newbie. At least he guessed it could be exciting. He should be able to find something neutral to talk about for God's sake that wasn't about the stupid condo or work. She seemed obsessed about food. Maybe that. "What's on a '70s Elvis burger?"

"Pardon?" Cali started, as though shocked he would ask her a direct question.

"The '70s Elvis burger. What's on it?" He motioned toward her greasy bag.

"Oh. It has deep fried bacon, plantains, and peanut butter."

Jory blinked. "That's disgusting."

"I'm hoping it's on the delicious side of disgusting." Cali's face filled with excitement. "I like all of those things. Why wouldn't they go together?"

"Because it's not natural," he blurted out, appalled.

"Possibly, but I like variety. Change keeps things fresh. Can't let yourself get stuck with one burger. Plus I need the extra energy. I move around a lot."

"Yes. You do."

Cali stole a glance at him, and he could see she was trying to figure out if he was giving her a compliment or not. All Jory knew was when she moved he watched her do it—and watched nothing else.

He put up his hand, counting off his fingers. "You move from Video Village to the set upward of twenty times a scene to give direction when most directors would either yell over the flats or go through Dan. There's the going up and down of ladders to investigate lights or explore odd angles where you hope to put the camera, which is why I ask Cesare to hide them."

"I was wondering where the ladders had gone."

"The ADs are constantly searching for you either in wardrobe or the trailers or in set dec because walking 10,000 steps a day seems to be an interior goal."

"I've always wanted to clock that."

Love, Camera, Action

"I'll get you the app. And then there's the obvious knee bouncing." Jory went quiet, realizing he'd revealed just how much he did watch her. To her, and to himself.

After a moment, as if sensing his embarrassment, she took pity on him. "What did you get to eat?"

Jory eyed his bag, disappointed in himself. It wasn't a red meat day, and he was irritated he'd gone off his schedule. "Cheeseburger."

"Yeah, but with what?"

"Just a cheeseburger."

"Just a cheeseburger?" Her eyebrows furrowed in confusion.

"Just a cheeseburger."

"You just got a cheeseburger at Spiral?"

"Yes."

"No habanero relish or fried pickles or onion rings?"

"No."

"No candied pineapple or creamed avocado or chocolate chips?"

"What? God, no. That's a thing?" Jory screwed up his face, wondering who had come up with that offense to basic cuisine.

"Huh." Cali regarded him like he was a bug under glass. A rare, ridiculous bug.

Jory narrowed his eyes. "You're awfully judgmental about my burger."

"While you were so open minded about mine. But it's fine, I get it. You like things simple." A knowing smile curved her lips.

"Yes."

"Clear-cut."

"Yes."

"Straightforward."

"I assume there's tomatoes and lettuce and some kind of secret sauce."

"Secret sauce? No!" Cali gasped in faux shock.

Jory stopped walking. "What. Is wrong. With my burger?"

Cali giggled. She actually giggled.

He should hate that, but he didn't.

"It just seems to me that if you're at one of Atlanta's most popular burger joints that's famous for its wacky toppings, you might indulge in one topping of wackiness. That's all."

Jory tilted his head back as though beseeching the heavens for guidance. "You think I'm boring."

"No, no!" Cali backtracked. "I think you have clear ideas of what is the most effective way to be in the world. For example, you might be one of those guys who has a calendar of what you're going to eat that day. Tuesday, grilled salmon and kale. Wednesday, chicken breast and kale. Thursday, kale with a side of kale . . ."

"I'm feeling a definite making-fun-of-me vibe." Jory started walking again, hoping the movement would cover his blush over being found out.

"Not at all. It's very responsible."

They arrived at the condo and stepped through the sliding doors in sync.

Jory put on a kindergarten teacher tone he hoped would annoy her. "Wacky toppings distract from quality. When it's simple you can taste the burger, see if the meat is juicy and thick, if it's cooked just right, if it's fresh or organic. You can tell if it's the real thing. Not some processed crap that is disguised by the taste of a fried pickle."

Love, Camera, Action

"Yeah, but fried pickles are sooooo good."

Cali pushed the elevator button and he watched her as she considered his point of view. He was suddenly curious about what she would come up with. "I think I like what it means to take the proven basics and pair them with the unexpected. Turn something simple into another thing you'd never imagined if you hadn't taken the risk. Even if you end up with something inedible in the search. Hey!" A wide smile bloomed. "We've got a little metaphor going on with our burgers."

"No. We don't." Jory feigned a scowl.

She returned his scowl with a mock one of her own, shaking her head with him in agreement. Jory remembered a time when he was experimental. His youth had been full of films he'd made just for the hell of it, because they'd touched some chord of inspiration in him. Films that would never lead him to the greater goal of being an A-list DP or a director for Jeff Cummings. Films scoffed at by men who could make those things happen for Jory's career if he only did a little dirty work. He vaguely recalled that spark Cali so easily exuded with every breath.

He followed her into the elevator, keenly feeling the close quarters of the space. She turned her attention to the floor indicator as the elevator rose and he found himself contemplating her mouth. He got the sudden urge to see if that spark would travel from her lips into his if he kissed her. He made a little growl in his throat and stubbornly turned his eyes to the floor indicator too.

Cali sighed. "My burger is probably going to make me sick."

"Don't back down now. You're in, you might as well enjoy it."

Cali's burger bag rustled by his ear. She spoke in an enticingly low voice, "You want to try a bite?"

Fuck yes, he wanted a bite. And if he didn't get out of this elevator in the next two seconds he was going to push her against the wall and take it. Rules about biting colleagues be damned.

"I'm not eating your gross burger."

"You might like it," she sang.

The elevator door opened and Jory stepped across the threshold with a rush of relief. But he couldn't help turning back as the door slid between them. "It's Tuesday. I don't eat peanut butter on Tuesdays."

Cali gasped. "I knew it! I knew you had an eating calendar!"

The doors shut closed with a *whoosh*.

Jory walked down the hall, irritated by the smile on his face.

CHAPTER EIGHT

Cali walked onto set buoyed by her impromptu burger chat with Jory the night before. It seemed as though there was a human in there. A human who made jokes and could be teased and could tease back. A super-hot, deeply talented, sexy human. Surprise, surprise.

When she first saw him that morning, he dipped his head in a nod accompanied by a shy smile. It was as though a breeze blew through her, soft and warm. A harbinger of better things to come. Throughout the morning, she found herself staring at him while he worked, how his long, strong fingers delicately handled a lens, the easy stance of his legs as he inspected the lighting grid, the patience in his tone as he worked with Alison, his camera assistant. He always found time to explain an angle, to discuss a shot, never too busy to take a moment. Cali also noted the ease with which he talked to Melanie, strong in his opinions but deferential to hers. He was confident in his roll, happy to teach or collaborate.

Now, he stood alone, considering the scene—a shadowy bar lit to feel sexy and dangerous. The action had Paolo/Rafe chatting up a woman when he gets a phone call from his senior operative. It's the first hint that Paolo/Rafe isn't just a server being tormented by the demon Thalia/Anna. Jory was considering where to put his camera next, serenity coursing through him like a powerful current, a force field erected around him to repel any unwanted distractions. The crew kept their distance, which gave her an unadulterated view of his thighs straining against his jeans, his T-shirt hugging his toned shoulders, his forearms flexing as he raised them behind his head to stretch.

He nodded slightly to himself, a decision made, and his body uncoiled into movement. He dropped one hand from his head while dragging the other through his hair as he walked away. Cali felt her internal muscles clench and she arched her back to relieve the tension, unable to stop herself from moaning, "Oh my God."

"I know, it's ridiculous."

Cali jumped. Joanne stood beside her, rummaging through her giant makeup bag. Cali sat up straighter in her chair, fixing her perfectly fine T-shirt that suddenly rubbed rough against sensitive skin. "Sorry?"

"I mean, he's not my type. But empirically, yeah, he's ridiculous." Joanne cracked her gum and sauntered toward set.

Cali bit down on her tongue. *Get it together, Daniels. You can't have the crew clocking your lust for the DP.*

Speaking of the crew, there was an odd vibe to them today. A change in energy. Thinking back on yesterday's conflict, she wondered what had pushed Jory into such a volatile space. He seemed so contrite at the burger joint and

Love, Camera, Action

now his stance was easy, relaxed. But the crew appeared unsure of whom to listen to—her or Jory—for the answers to their questions, settling on neither. She would have to remedy that.

Cali pulled out her phone, staring at the innocuous outgoing text she'd sent her sister last night: *You good?* It hadn't been returned. Patsy went radio silent for two reasons—a translation wormhole or a bender caused by a breakup. When Cali had left, Patsy had just been hired by the university to translate a history of Cyprus from an ancient Greek text, so maybe she was deep in it, oblivious to the world.

Or she'd gotten drunk, passed out in front of their building, and had been eaten by raccoons. Toronto raccoons were no joke.

When Cali looked up from her phone, Jory was frowning at her, concern on his face. The moment she caught him, he jerked quickly away and went back to the camera he'd just left to check the focus. Again.

Cali shook her head to get back in the game. What was happening? Ah yes, Paolo's disastrous acting.

It was a simple scene. Paolo flirts with a woman, gets a phone call from a mysterious male voice who informs him his orders have changed due to the termination of Agent Twenty-Nine, his best friend. Paolo had to start with charm, go covert, and end in shock within a few moments.

He was *awful.*

Charm was good. Covert was fine, if only because blank looks came naturally to him. But the moment he had to show emotion over the death of his friend and colleague, he'd start laughing. Or forget his line. Or awkwardly shift out of frame. By the eighth take he was blathering, "No, it's cool, it's cool. I can do this. Seriously. Sorry, everybody. I can do this. Seriously."

Cali was running out of ideas.

Her heart went out to Paolo. He reminded her of what she was like at the beginning of her career—terrified, bumbling, hoping no one would notice her lack of experience. Her first directing gig had been on a no-budget horror film with tons of gratuitous BDSM scenes. On the first setup, she blithely told the grizzled DP which lens to use. The guy had been in the business *forever* and that shitty movie was his last gig. He'd pulled her aside out of earshot of the crew to tell her the lens she chose *might* make the actors on the spanking bench look like they were in a fish bowl. Before Cali could bluster out a reply, he gently and kindly guided her through the various options, effectively teaching her under the guise of collaboration.

She blushed at her audacity in those early days and relived the rush of gratitude that she'd met such a generous mentor out of the gate. She still sent clips of her work to him, for advice and praise, even though he lived happily on a beach in Costa Rica.

But who was there for Paolo?

She searched around the set for inspiration on how to help him. What if she got him to do some acrobatics with his drink? Or a sleight-of-hand trick with the coaster to impress the girl . . . The whispers of an idea tickled her ear.

"We gotta move on," Jory rumbled.

Not an idea tickling her ear—Jory. She fought a shiver. "I want one more take."

"I have enough footage to work around him."

"I think he can do it."

Love, Camera, Action

"I don't know why." Jory sank into his chair with a harrumph. He kept his volume low as the crew did their final checks. "He doesn't have the chops. Let's move on."

She could feel Paolo's fear and embarrassment through the lens and knew he was on the brink of shutting down. "He can do it. I just haven't given him the right cue."

On the monitors, Paolo wiped his sweaty forehead with the back of his hand. Joanne batted his hand away, trying to powder his failure glow while he dodged her with a scowl. Joanne put her hands on her hips and gave him a mom stare that could melt glass. He petulantly sat still.

Jory grunted in annoyance. "We could be here all day, and you wouldn't get anything different."

Maybe Jory was right. It wasn't important to help Paolo out. He was just the studio hire after all. She shouldn't feel any responsibility for him.

Still, why couldn't Jory open himself up to the possibility that something new and unexpected *might* happen?

"We should give him a chance."

"We've given him eight," he huffed out.

Crew began to congregate around the monitor; her conversation with Jory was drawing attention. Cali got up out of her chair and tipped her head for Jory to follow. She stopped just off to the side, at the window looking into the bar. The frame was covered with a thick masking that allowed the lamps to shine through to emulate streetlight, and also gave them a modicum of privacy while they could still watch what was happening on set.

Cali turned to Jory. "From the first take, you've been making adjustments to the angle because you're positive he's going to fail. He picks up on that."

Jory snorted. "I don't think he would pick up on a nuclear explosion."

"Don't these work-around shots mess up your *tone*?" She snapped her mouth shut. She shouldn't have said that. Her jibe was highly inappropriate and out of character. "Sorry. That was . . . sorry. I just want him to succeed."

"That's sweet." Cali's hackles rose at his condescension. "Those shots are what got us through his bad acting before you showed up. There's no diamond in the rough here."

Cali watched Paolo muttering to himself on set, probably trying to psych himself up for the next take. "Anyone would be scared knowing their failure was flushing thousands of dollars down the toilet every minute they didn't deliver. Some actors need support."

"You know what kind of schedule we're on here. Actors who work in TV should be able to perform on a dime," he chided.

Jory knew Paolo was flailing but his indifference, his *disdain* for Paolo's weakness cut Cali to the core. Maybe Jory didn't know what it felt like to be the one everyone knew was screwing up, what it felt like to have no one there to help. She was suddenly desperate for him to listen to her, not only for Paolo's sake, but to find some understanding of vulnerability within Jory. "I might have an idea that will help."

"Another idea." Jory sighed and crossed his arms. "Save your ideas for actors who can use them. We have to move on."

She'd never get through to him. He would always be a hard ass, never letting in a new idea or inspiration. Sticking to the rules instead of having a heart. The face of her grizzled, teddy bear of a DP flooded her mind—a man who never gave up helping, right up until his last gig with a young, untried director.

Love, Camera, Action

Cali dug in. "I want one more take."

"You're wasting your time!" Jory threw up his arms. "It's not you, it's him. He's the problem."

"It *is* me. I'm the director." She couldn't stop her pitch from rising, a sense of powerlessness taking over her common sense. "I have to figure out how to direct him. It's not the fact that *he can't take direction!*" She barked out the final words, trying to get through.

Suddenly a hush fell over the crew. Cali and Jory snapped their heads up to see why.

There was Paolo, standing on the other side of the window, a few feet away, his face stricken. What Cali had assumed was a wall of masking was in fact a flimsy piece of ND cellophane placed a few feet in front of the flats, allowing anyone to step between them and hear their argument. Cali frantically cast back in her mind to what she'd said, for what he might have heard . . . and . . . fuck.

Cali pulled out a shaky smile, hoping she was wrong. "Paolo, I'm glad you stepped back here. I want to do another take."

"No, that's cool. I get it." His jaw turned to granite, his fists clenched.

"Get what?" Cali's stomach flipped. She knew that look. She'd seen it a million times when Thalia shut him down. A look that was equal parts shame, self-derision and anger. *Fuck.*

"I'm done." Paolo dismissed her and focused on Jory. "You got them, right? You got your cover shots?"

Jory nodded warily.

"Great. I'm out." Paolo turned to leave, his body strung tight.

"Paolo, wait." Cali put a hand out to stop him. "I think we can get it."

He wheeled on her, skin red with fury, teeth clenched. "I'm. Out."

Cali watched helplessly as Paolo stalked off the set, unbuttoning his jacket and throwing it at the wardrobe assistant on his way. The crew went back to their duties, giving Jory and Cali a wide berth. This was catastrophic. Cali had failed him. Even if Cali could convince Paolo she believed in him, it was clear he didn't believe in himself.

"Can't take the heat." Jory shook his head.

She whirled on him, incredulous. "That's what you want to say right now?"

"That guy's an asshole."

Oh, hell no. This could not stand. Any disbelief in her own abilities were extinguished in the protectiveness she felt for that misguided man. She pointed her finger at Jory's chest and hissed under her voice. "You're the asshole in this situation."

"Me?!"

"You can't do that to an actor. He's pretending to be a tough guy because he's actually a sensitive novice who's being asked to bare his soul in front of your camera with dozens of people standing around judging him. He was stuck, and you just tripled his insecurity because you were impatient. And now he mistrusts the only person willing to help him."

Jory squared his shoulders to her. "I know when someone can't get there."

"And you just made sure he won't. This "—she gestured between the two of them—"is not your thing. Human emotion—frailty, vulnerability, inspiration—is not your thing. Stick to capturing what everyone else can do, but you can only film. Stay out of my sandbox."

Love, Camera, Action

Cali moved to stomp away but thought better of it. She raised her voice, for whoever listened, keeping her tone professional but making her intention clear. "Jory, I understand you've been worried about making our day and I've come up with a solution for you. We don't need that crane shot this afternoon. I'm cutting it."

Jory's mouth fell open. "That's the keystone shot of the episode. I've been planning that for days."

"It's too complicated. Find another shot to die on." She walked off, mentally dropping the mic. She'd probably just killed any chance she had of making this two-parter work and would wake up tomorrow in deep regret and worry over her future, but it felt amazing to see the look on Jory's suckhole face.

As she stormed away, Cali swore she heard glee in Dan's voice when he practically sang, "Moving on!"

CHAPTER NINE

Boring, banal, blancmange. Jory was blocked. He knew it and everyone else knew it too.

It had been a week since Cali had drawn her metaphoric line in her sandbox and there was a distinct chill in the air. He was trying his best to be the originator of that cold front, but if he was honest, he was the one freezing to death. It wasn't anything overt, but there were whispers. Maybe not whispers so much as currents. Frigid, whispered currents that flowed around him, nudging him to the conclusion that he might have been, in fact, the asshole in the situation.

He wasn't a bad guy, he told himself. He was a good guy. He'd endangered his career ambitions by steering Howard in such confusing circles that the check-ins had stopped, meaning Cali was, for the time being anyway, safe. Jory had kept a lid on his attraction to her, definitely not noticing she moved with a new relaxation he hadn't seen before, a kind of loose languidness that made her hips sway. And he definitely wasn't grumpier because of it.

He watched her ruthlessly chip away at scenes until the crew had no choice but to go along with her directives, like a school of fish swept in the surf and surge of a swirling ocean. An ocean the color of Cali's green and brown eyes that were big and bright enough to be an ocean themselves— changeable and turbulent as the storms he'd watched through the windows of the beach house. He had always wanted to go out into those storms, but never moved from behind the glass.

He felt like he was behind glass now as he watched her hands comb through her shiny auburn hair, lifting the heavy mane off her neck and holding it there in a rare moment of stillness while she considered the scene. Then she released her hair in a *whoosh* as she walked toward what-ever idea she would summon into reality.

But the rest of the crew was . . . off. There was a whiff of hostility bubbling from an underground cavern Jory only now suspected existed. On the surface, their days were orderly and efficient. But the women in Wardrobe were avoiding him. It was nothing so obvious he could mark— they generally ignored his directives, but now they were *pointedly* ignoring his directives.

Across the set, Thalia talked to Joanne in that quietly intense way women did when there was something not to their liking. He'd seen his aunts in that cross-armed, obtuse-angled stance casually plotting the demise of those around them, usually the men, and a shiver ran through him. They lifted their heads in tandem to stare at him and pursed their lips in dissatisfaction.

He turned away and bumped into the man responsible for the sharpness of any image Jory shot, his focus puller, Guillermo. His whole camera team had been sticking uncomfortably close to Jory. Secret service close. Like they were protecting him with their very lives. Only his camera assistant, Alison, stood apart, efficient and capable as ever, but standoffish and cool.

Then there was Paolo. He'd attached himself to Jory, all bouncy and full of energy, wanting to have conversations about parkour—which Jory thought was a beautiful, balletic response to humanity's deepening relationship to urban environments—or, God forbid, MMA—which Jory thought was ridiculous because there was a reason you stuck to one martial art and it was called discipline.

Paolo's attention made Jory feel something uncomfortably akin to regret. Regret for not setting him straight about the misunderstanding, instead delaying because he didn't want to appear unprofessional to Howard. Possibly even regret for hurting Paolo's feelings, and not recognizing there was, possibly, maybe, a vulnerable person in there. But every time Jory made the move to explain what had happened, Paolo would cut him off with an inane attempt to be buddy–buddy, which dug under Jory's skin until he turned away in a huff. The exchanges went something like this:

JORY
Paolo, can I talk to you?

PAOLO
Question: Why are you using a fifty-millimeter lens on this scene?

Love, Camera, Action

Paolo bounces.

>   JORY
> *Because it's slightly comic.*

>   PAOLO
> *Oh, Why is that funny?*

Paolo skips.

>   JORY
>   *(Sighing)*
> *A fifty-millimeter lens is as close*
> *to what the human eye sees which*
> *allows you to take in everything*
> *that's happening while still feeling*
> *in on the joke.*

>   PAOLO
> *Oh yeah. Right. Right. Hey can I put*
> *the lens on?*

>   JORY
>   *(Grinds his jaw)*
> *No.*

>   PAOLO
> *What's it called, swinging the lens?*

>   JORY
> *No.*

>   PAOLO
> *Aw, come on. I'll be really careful.*

Noël Stark

> JORY
> *Step away from the camera Paolo.*

> PAOLO
> *(BACKING AWAY)*
> *That's cool. That's cool. I'm here if*
> *you need me, 'kay?*

And . . . scene.

Jory had to figure out what was going on. This was his set, his to protect, to lead. So he went to the source of all knowledge—Dan.

Jory sidled up to him, enacting a casual stance, speaking in a hushed tone. "Do you feel something weird with the crew? I mean, there's a vibe."

"Oh, I feel it." Dan didn't glance up from his paperwork.

"You feel it?" Jory's poker face fled.

"I feel it."

"It's like everyone's in some kind of Illuminati secret society." Jory analyzed the busy crew as they worked. "And they've made me the Grand Pooh-bah without telling me what the secret is."

"Mm-hmm."

"What do you think's going on?"

"Oh, I know what's going on. I'm just surprised you don't."

Jory did a double take. "Why would I know what's going on?"

"Come on, Jory." Dan huffed out an exasperated sigh. "You're usually more perceptive than this."

"I'm just doing my job." Jory tried to sound nonchalant but came off pouty instead.

Love, Camera, Action

"Mm-hmm."

"Stop *mm-hmm*-ing me. You're not my grandmother."

Dan gave him a decidedly grandmotherly look.

"Okay, don't tell me," Jory pouted. Dan moved to walk away, but Jory grabbed his arm and hauled him back. "You're really not going to tell me?"

Dan sighed, again. The man was a geyser of disappointment. "Lines are being drawn."

"What kind of lines?"

"Battle lines."

"Battle lines."

Dan nodded.

"And . . . ?" Jory circled his hand to nudge him along.

"The crew are swearing fealty."

"Swearing fealty to who?"

"You or Cali."

"What?!" Heads turned at his sudden exclamation.

Dan stayed silent.

Jory lowered his voice. "The only thing they should swear fealty to is the script." His voice climbed back up. "Plus, I'm not doing anything! I'm fine!"

Dan pinned Jory with a glare. "You haven't been talking to Howard about scenes behind Cali's back?"

Jory's stomach turned over. "Well, that wasn't—"

"You haven't been digging in on your own ideas simply because they're contrary to hers?"

"Now, some of her ideas—"

"You haven't let Paolo believe Cali called him a bad actor when it was, in fact, you?" Dan asked.

Jory stopped at that one. "I was about to clear that up." Jory rubbed the back of his neck while Dan's face cooled. "I have made some mistakes and perhaps crossed some lines."

127

Jory shoved his hands in his pockets. "But I've been with this crew for four months. She's been here three weeks and look at the commotion she's made. If there's any fealty swearing, it should be to me!"

Dan closed his binder with a snap and jammed it under his arm. "And there's the rub. I'm not going to explain the intricacies of your relationship with Calliope. For whatever reason, and I can probably guess, the Jory I know has been usurped by a Neanderthal. Scene's up."

Off he went, leaving Jory alone.

"Intricacies" of his and Cali's relationship? There were no intricacies, Jory scoffed to himself.

Unless . . .

Maybe Dan suspected Jory'd been lusting after her since day one. Maybe he sensed the struggle Jory confronted everyday as he wondered how their relationship might take shape if they hadn't met in this place, at this time. How he'd turned over in his mind what it would be like to watch a movie with her and argue over the choices made. Or to feel the texture of her lips against his own. How he struggled to protect her from Howard's notice while trying to land his dream job. Maybe Dan understood that Jory kept away as much for her sake as the sake of the set.

Dan was uncommonly intuitive, but he couldn't be *that* good.

Jory searched Cali out and found her sitting in her chair, considering the shot on the monitor, confident and thoughtful, all fired up with ideas and complications.

It wasn't his fault he lost all rationality when he was around her. It *was* his fault he'd let his personal feelings develop into a rift. He couldn't let his crew work in unsavory conditions, especially when he might have had a *small* part in creating them. As much as he hated the idea, he would have to build a bridge between he and Cali so they could work together in harmony, while not losing his mind.

With a frustrated breath, he caught her eye, lifted his arm, and beckoned.

Cali blinked. Was Jory *beckoning* her?

Surely not. He'd barely looked at her the past week. Which was just fine by Cali because his lack of input had made her job, and her life, that much easier. She should have read Jory the riot act the very first day. No one was going to give her control, and now that she had taken it, her confidence had fallen into place with a satisfying *snick*. She felt fantastic. It was true that much of the joviality among the crew had disappeared. A frosty, if not frigid, atmosphere had descended, and some of that glacial regard found its way to her, mostly from the camera team. But she was Canadian—she thrived in the cold.

Jory, meanwhile, had become a vibrating storm of grump. She couldn't help but marvel over the sheer determination it must take to keep his Byronic aura burning. The man could *brood*. The riotous cloud that churned across his gorgeous visage would make Heathcliff, Rochester, and Angel from Buffy bow to his glower.

And now he beckoned.

Well, beckon all you want, buddy. I'm not giving you an inch. A princely come-hither wave will not compel me to concede.

When she didn't move, he gestured more emphatically, as if she didn't get it. She noted a pang of sympathy—he looked so frustrated. She'd have felt bad for him if he weren't such a jerk. But she stayed where she was, straightening her spine as she raised a brow.

Jory narrowed his eyes and then rolled them. He stalked over to her. Inside her mind, she shouted a "whoop, whoop" but was all bland curiosity once he arrived. "What's up?"

"We have a problem."

"Oh?"

"Could we . . . ?" Jory gestured to an unoccupied corner of Video Village.

Cali took a moment to consider, pushing the silence to just shy of uncomfortable, then rose from her chair like a queen.

Once they landed, Jory took a moment, choosing his words carefully. "Have you noticed anything off about the crew?"

Cali gave him a noncommittal shrug.

Jory's scowl somehow deepened. He surveyed the crew, who were setting up the scene just out of earshot, as though suspecting a mutiny in the making. "They believe you and I are at odds, and they're picking sides."

A warm feeling coursed through her. The crew *was* mutinous. Mutinous for *her*. "There are crew members who have picked my side?" She put a hand up to her heart. "That's so sweet."

"It's not sweet!" Jory exclaimed.

"I would have thought they'd all choose you, and I'd be ignored at best. This is great!" Cali let out a giant grin.

"It's not great!" Jory sputtered.

Love, Camera, Action

Cali couldn't remember when she'd been chosen over anyone else. In the past she'd taken director gigs no one else wanted to get her foot in the door. She'd begged producers to give her a chance who'd never heard her name. Even on *The Demon*, she was filling in for someone who'd been fired. Finally, here was proof. Proof that her style was working. Proof she was a director of worth and ideas. So much so that members of the crew were standing with her against Jory. Jory!

"Are you upset they didn't side with you?" She put away her grin. Barely.

Jory waved her off. "No, of course not."

"I mean you've been here the whole time." Cali laced her response with faux pity. "It must be upsetting that some of them would jump ship. They must really be pissed at you."

"They aren't pissed." Jory checked his rising volume. "You're missing the point here."

"Probably."

"The crew is like a machine. If one piece is out of joint, the whole system shuts down, and the work suffers."

"It's interesting you should describe the crew as a machine—a cold unfeeling entity without consciousness." Cali went full tilt Earth Mother. "I would suggest a crew is more like a family, an ensemble of unique voices, moving harmoniously toward a common goal." Cali relished the snort that burst out of him. "As for the idea of an unhappy crew making bad TV, I've been on sets that were miserable, and the final result was magic."

Jory pinned her with his gaze. "Are you saying a toxic environment makes better TV?"

Cali faltered. She would never want anyone to work in a toxic environment. Sets were tough enough as it was, with the long days and exhausting pace. Add negative emotions on top of that and each moment became a living hell. "No, of course not."

Guilt washed over her. Had she been so happy to have finally found her stride that she ignored the emotional well-being of the crew? She had intuited something was wrong but had taken one week—one week!—where she could bask in the thought she actually knew what she was doing. Now she felt as though she had selfishly abandoned responsibility for those who followed her.

Sniffing out a weakness, Jory's tone became patronizing. "We haven't had this issue before, so . . ."

"Ah, so it's the way *I* work." Cali's defenses slammed back up.

"You do have a different approach."

"Than most directors you mean."

"In my experience, yes."

"Most directors that are *men*." It was a risk to openly talk about the inherent sexism of the industry, but she was tired of keeping quiet about all the microaggressions that came at her and the other women on set. "It obviously couldn't be the way *you* like to control everything."

Instead of reeling from the accusation, Jory squared off. "Don't make this about sexism. You're a creative bully."

"I am *not* a creative bully!"

"You get an idea and you steamroll everyone until you get what you want."

"I trust in the inspiration of the moment."

"And sometimes people use inspiration as an excuse to bully."

Love, Camera, Action

Jory's superior tone burned away Cali's guilt. "Inspiration can be scary for *some,* especially when they're too set in their ways to try anything new."

"Whoa!" Jory's exclamation was loud enough to turn heads.

"Hi, guys, can I have a mo?"

Cali and Jory wheeled to confront the interloper. Melanie speared them with a cold smile. Brooking no argument, she turned and walked deeper into the studio, her heel clicks commanding their compliance. Cali and Jory fell in step behind her, passing the doctor-office set, around the ice-cream parlor, and through the convenience store, where Melanie stopped.

She fixed them with a hard glare. "I've been hearing reports that our set isn't the peaceful family it usually is."

"Our *family*"—Cali leaned into the word to telegraph the win to Jory—"has been working their professional best, and I think you're going to be really pleased with the results."

Jory scoffed.

Melanie raised an eyebrow. "Jory?"

Jory leveled his shark stare on Melanie. "Everything's good."

Melanie wasn't fooled. "From what I understand, everything is not good, and apparently it's you two who are the cause of the fracture within the crew. I think it would be best if you could settle this between yourselves instead of hissing at each other in corners and stressing everyone out."

"Everything's good, Melanie," Jory repeated.

"Yep, everything's good," Cali agreed.

"Listen, I get it. You're both wonderful artists at the top of your game. But," she said, looking pointedly at Cali, "whether or not you have a great idea that will put the schedule in jeopardy"—she swung her eyes to Jory—"or you cause tension because you think you're always right, if either of you cost this production one penny over budget or I get one more complaint from a crew member, I will go to Howard. And trust me, you do not want me to go to Howard."

Cali and Jory shuffled in place, two children caught in bad behavior.

Melanie put a hand to her chest, beseeching. "I like to be happy. How can I be happy when my crew is not happy?"

Melanie wedged herself between them, looping her arms through theirs, and gently shepherding them deeper into the studio. "You know, I come from a family of five kids. My parents didn't have the time or the emotional capacity to deal with all of our conflicts. So in either a genius parenting move or a thoroughly Darwinian one, they would lock us in a room together until we worked it out."

Melanie stopped in front of what appeared to be an office door. "Now, I'm not your parent, and I would never lock you in a room together because that would flagrantly disregard our HR policies. But we don't have all afternoon to get over this. So, I'm giving you fifteen minutes to voluntarily sequester yourselves so you can come up with a solution together like adults and we can continue on as a joyous, harmonious, *functional* family."

Melanie opened the door and stood aside, her message clear.

Channeling her most adult walk, Cali strode through the opening and Jory followed.

Melanie slammed the door shut behind them.

CHAPTER TEN

It took a minute for Jory's eyes to adjust to the darkness. The door Melanie had guilted them through did not lead into an office, but to the back of the sets—a long, narrow passageway with flats on one side and the north wall of the studio on the other. It was dark and dusty and just wide enough to allow a few inches on either side of their shoulders. A blue light from high above spilled into the space, making the passage glow with an eerie quality heightened by the distant promise of a glowing red "Exit" sign.

They were quiet, as though the new space had robbed them of language, the change in scene banishing the arguments they'd erected between them until all that was left was the energy that hummed under their skin in each other's presence.

When Jory finally raised his attention from the floor to Cali, his breath hitched. Her gaze flitted about like a butterfly unable to land, her lush lips parted and trembling. As though she might bolt toward that "Exit" sign to get away.

An insane urge to wrap her in a protective hug washed through him. He didn't know how he could go from fighting with her one minute and wanting to kiss her the next. Maybe desire was linked in that way. He'd never found passion for a person, like the passion he'd once found in his work. Now he couldn't shoot his way out of a paper bag, and was being forced into tiny, dirty spaces to work things out with a woman who could barely look at him. He shouldn't have let things get this bad.

It wasn't all his fault, he reasoned. The constant speculation and uncertainty about what she was thinking was exhausting. This would never happen with a guy. There was a shorthand that flowed between men—a well-placed grunt or hand gesture was all that was needed to convey what was required, a system developed over eons of male privilege.

Understanding seeped into him along with a good dose of shame. He was pissy because he had to learn something new—*someone* new. He was the problem, not her. His knowledge of how to communicate was limited to one language, and despite Cali's efforts to reach him, he hadn't listened. Instead, he'd shut her down.

It was her first kick at a major television show. A show that would be daunting for seasoned directors. And here she was, probably worried she was going to get blacklisted as trouble—or, worse, as incompetent—just as her career should be about to skyrocket. Yet she still bravely took control, using her voice in a world that wasn't accustomed to hearing it. This world was set up for people like him, and he had always taken that for granted.

He had to take responsibility for opening that world, open himself. To stop the bickering and help Cali instead of grinding down her spirit to keep the set under his control.

He felt ashamed of his complicity and knew things needed to change.

He needed to change.

Cali's gaze landed on the ceiling as though the answer to their conundrum might be high above them. Her hair sparkled like a chiseled sapphire under the strange light, all deep blues and blacks shimmering in the darkness. He at once wished he had a camera to capture it and was glad one wasn't near, so he could keep the image to himself.

Before he could think twice, he said, "I've been an idiot."

Cali's head snapped from the ceiling, and her eyes shot round with surprise.

"But I'll do better." He stared at those eyes that were black in the light—well, one of them anyway. The other was covered by a wavy swath of hair like Veronica Lake in negative. Cali had a beautiful face—one you wouldn't notice right away. Her aesthetic wasn't the flashy kind of beauty he always saw through the lens, but an other-time kind of elegance. One that was classically Grecian in its softness, with no hard planes or fairy features like those that dominated the TV world. Her eyes were the standout, full of intelligence and fire.

A forbidden urge swept up, and although he knew he shouldn't, knew he was crossing a line that couldn't be uncrossed, he reached up his hand and drew her curtain of hair aside, revealing both eyes to his gaze.

Cali let out a held breath, the air between them thick and heavy and impossible. He stood stock-still, shocked over what he'd done, over what might happen next.

Cali stepped forward slowly, as though she were approaching a scared rabbit. He was frozen, unable to comprehend what she was doing but desperately hoping she wouldn't stop. When she was only a sigh away, she leaned in until her lips found his.

It was a soft, introductory graze. Not even a kiss, really. An impression that was gone in an instant when she pulled away. She searched his face, gauging his response. He, meanwhile, had petrified, but he guessed his look said something different, because she moved in closer and kissed him again. She tested the waters, taking little, unhurried nips, raising a hand to his neck, where her touch anchored both of them. Jory's muscles relaxed into liquid, his mouth softening. Almost without thought, he began returning her attentions, sucking her bottom lip into his mouth. A groan rose from the depths of his chest, his limbs filling with heat as he snaked one arm around her waist to pull her against his body while slanting his mouth across hers in what could only be called a claiming.

She sucked in a gasp and then drove him against the studio wall as she devoured his mouth, turning his claim into a surrender.

He couldn't remember ever letting a woman lead a kiss before, as he had always been the one to take control. With Cali he felt like a teenager getting tutored by the hot, untouchable senior, who, for some unknown reason, had decided to school him in the world of female electricity.

Their slick tongues explored, flirting with the danger of electrocution, the charge twisting down his neck, through his core, to spark in his boots.

Jory plunged his hands into her blue-black hair and was rewarded with a shaky sigh when Cali managed to take a breath. A sigh full of relief and frustration that fueled him to take more, to go deeper. He swung her around to get more

Love, Camera, Action

traction, pinning her against the wall in the same position he had been in moments before.

She used the wall as leverage, angling her hips against his, and slid her hands down his sides. On a groan, she grabbed his belt loops and pulled him snug against her, grinding into the erection he was suddenly painfully aware of. He put a hand against the wall so she wouldn't rock him back into the flats and, if he was being honest, to steady himself from crashing to the ground in some kind of nineteenth-century faint. What the hell was she doing to him? It was like she was unleashing all her energy, and he had no choice but to absorb the fury of it. But he was happy to. Oh, how he was happy to. The kiss turned ferocious as he met her, bite for bite, grind for grind, growl for growl, each battling the other for control.

"Scene's up!" Dan's voice ripped them apart as surely as if he'd thrown a bucket of water over the top of the flats.

Jory stared at Cali as he tried to catch his breath, watching her naked hunger turn to horror.

Dan rang out once more, "Finals!"

Jory leaped away from her, knocking into the flats, making them wave and wobble with the impact. Cali shot out a hand to steady them, her face filled with alarm. Once they stilled, he motioned to her plaid shirt, which was askew and unbuttoned, presumably because of him. She shakily straightened herself while Jory took another step away, this time to the side, to give her a wide berth to the door.

As her hand went for the doorknob, he stopped her with a light touch on her shoulder. She jumped and snapped her eyes up to his.

Jory put two hands up in an I'm-not-going-to-maul-you gesture and mouthed, "Your back."

She peered over her shoulder, trying to see what was on it, but instead turned in a circle, chasing her tail. He made a motion asking permission to touch her. She nodded, turning her back to him. With the deft touch of someone diffusing a bomb, he lightly wiped the dust that covered her flannel shirt, from being slammed against the brick wall.

He finished and stepped away as she turned. She gave him the finger swivel for him to present his back to her, and she removed the dust from him with brutal slaps.

When he turned, she was taking a moment to steady herself. He wanted to say he was sorry. He wanted to tell her it was a mistake. He wanted to kiss her again and say to hell with the shoot. Then, she opened the door with a confidence he doubted he could replicate and strode out into the light. He caught up with her, and walking side-by-side, they purposefully strode to set, careful not to look at each other or anyone else.

Dan approached them with studious professionalism. "You guys good to go?"

"Yep. Yep." Cali put on a too-big smile.

Jory turned to her and graveled out, "I'll just check the . . . uh . . ."

Cali vigorously nodded. "Yep, for sure. I'll see you over . . ." She motioned to nowhere.

"Yep, great. Good."

"Great."

They turned their backs to each other, Jory floundering for a direction, settling on the camera. The camera seemed good. That's where he usually went . . . right?

On his way, Jory adjusted his jeans as surreptitiously as he could, wincing under the restricting denim. When he

Love, Camera, Action

arrived, he pretended to assess what his team had prepped while his mind raced over that what-the-fuckery.

He had never, *ever* gotten physical with another person on a production. It was his unspoken rule, his steadfast law—the don't-shit-where-you-eat policy. And now he'd gone and not only kissed a woman who clearly didn't like him, but had done so in an atmosphere where any kind of sexual missteps were highly scrutinized. Not to mention he wanted zero romantic complications when he might have to fight for his actual life if the test he still had not gotten came back positive. What was he thinking?

He hadn't been thinking. At all. When Cali had made the move, he had been all instinct, which had definitively said, *"Yes. We are doing this now."* He'd had no thought of repercussions—only of Cali and her mouth and her hair and her grinding hips. Of how he'd wanted to pull her jeans down and kneel at her feet. To sink into her wet heat and follow her directions to the letter until she came apart around him. He could easily have set up a nest in that dusty corridor, never to emerge.

He shook his head at himself. He'd placed his career in jeopardy by stealing an illicit kiss behind the flats, of all fucking places. Maybe he deserved to lose his career. Maybe he'd been a predator. Maybe he was a Bad Man.

He caught sight of Cali talking to Cesare, the key grip, motioning to the lighting grid with big hand gestures while blathering out a goofy laugh. She was as shaken as he was. He wondered if she was overcome by the power of what had transpired between them or because they'd crossed a dangerous line.

Cesare leaned away from her frenetic gesturing and shot a glance at Jory as if to say, *What's up with her?* When Cesare saw Jory's face, his eyes went into a scrunch, clearly thinking, *What's up with* you? He returned his attention to Cali, nodded in agreement as he stepped away, then got the hell out of there.

Cali let out a tremulous breath and then, as if a secret laser connected them, swung her gaze right at Jory. They froze together in a state of shared disbelief.

Suddenly Dan stepped in front of him, snapping his fingers. "Hey, space case. You up or what?"

Jory batted away Dan's offending finger snaps. "I'm up. I'm up."

Dan tipped a glance at Jory's tightened jeans and turned away with a smirk.

Jory swore under his breath and beelined to the monitors. His head wasn't even close to being in the game. He should be focusing on the scene instead of stifling the weirdest urge to giggle. *What the fuck did I just do?* He sat with a thump in his chair, relieved Cali had chosen to stand in front of the monitors while also missing her presence beside him. Her arms were crossed, and she was obviously trying to concentrate on the image before her.

Jory knew better. She was too still to be concentrating.

He straightened and threw back his shoulders in a desperate attempt to force his attention on his job. The scene had Paolo walking into a café to leave a message for his superior, in the guise of a coffee order. Paolo was late to set, so they had arranged everything without him. It was a simple scene, but as Jory's eyes strayed to Cali's now slightly swaying hips, he knew she was getting an idea. Those hips were giving *him* ideas.

Jory squirmed in his chair. He stood up and approached her at the monitor. "What are you thinking?"

Love, Camera, Action

Cali started. When their eyes met, the frisson between them sparked back to life. Cali gave him a small, almost awe-filled smile and then shook her head. "Um. Nothing. I don't want to go off schedule."

"What are you thinking?" Jory put his hands on his hips, and gave her his best stern look.

She studied him—searching. He watched her expression go from passive deference to steely resolve in a nanosecond.

God he loved that.

She pointed at the monitor. "This isn't very covert from a camera perspective."

Jory considered the frame. It *was* pretty paint-by-numbers.

Cali continued. "In the next couple of scenes we find out Paolo's being followed. Would it be so weird if we started feeling that here?"

"We place a camera in the far corner." Jory pointed at the café door. "As if someone were watching. A voyeur."

"Very Hitchcock." Cali traced a path on the monitor. "And if you follow him at the same time with the Steadicam, that cuts the scene down to two shots, bringing us in under time." Cali's face broke into a giant grin.

Jory responded with a goofy grin of his own as he shouted, "Camera's on the move!"

Reluctantly breaking their gaze, Jory strode away in full general mode. "Guillermo, you get camera two set up in the corner of the café. Alison, I need you to set up the Steadicam as quick as you can. I'm operating."

Jory buckled into the harness Alison held up for him while Cali gave orders to Dan. Listening to her confident leadership made his heart beat faster under the straps. When he looked up, he was surprised to see Alison peering at him from under her bangs with a smile. She approved. His twenty-year-old cam assist approved of her boss's new collaboration, and that gave him a dose of humility. He was supposed to be setting an example, not tearing down people's ideas. He stuttered out a word of thanks as she tugged hard on the straps, giving him a pat of support. Jory looked up to see the crew scrambling with excitement to meet the new direction. A direction set out by Cali and Jory together.

"Scene's up!" Dan shouted. "Have we got Paolo?"

Everyone searched around for the errant actor.

The distant sound of Melanie's heels clicked toward them. When she arrived next to Cali, her body was rigid. This wasn't good.

Jory walked over with his gear strapped to him. "What's up?

"Paolo won't come."

Cali winced. "Why?"

"He doesn't want to work with Cali." Melanie huffed in frustration. "He saw the two of you fighting and now thinks she's trying to sabotage the show. He'll only work with Jory."

Jory's mouth went slack. "What? But I'm not the director."

Melanie's skewered him with her gaze. "Well, until we get this sorted out, for Paolo you are."

Jory's body flooded with dread as his eyes shot to Cali's. Her face was a mask of anger directly aimed at him.

CHAPTER ELEVEN

Cali sat alone in Melanie's office, lost in a cloud of doom. This was bad. Very bad. Paolo wouldn't work with her, half the crew thought she was a hack, and this little visit to Melanie's office was probably the first brick to be laid for Cali's eventual firing. She investigated the space in an attempt to distract herself so she could get her racing pulse under control.

Most production offices were hastily made, temporary affairs with white walls and overhead fluorescents that brought out the black scuff marks made from years of cheap furniture being moved in and out as one production replaced another. Melanie had somehow made her office into an ecosystem all its own. The stark space was lit by softly glowing mid-century modern lamps, their metallic finishes quietly gleaming underneath transparent bulbs that showed off their filaments. Each light was perfectly placed to add a chic warmth, a stylish coziness. Exotic plants were sprinkled throughout, flourishing beside *objets d'art* and books on film.

Melanie's desk was clear of items except for a green desk light reminiscent of a film noir detective's, and a penholder decorated with fuzzy pink octopi.

Fuzzy pink octopi? Does Melanie have a kid?

Cali searched the office for clues and found a small picture frame just behind Melanie's desk, slightly obscured by one of her plants. Cali leaned closer—it was of a little boy maybe six or seven. A nephew? A son? He had the same dark hair and blue eyes as Melanie, but he was lanky, indicating he was going to be tall. He was a cutie. A cutie Melanie had never mentioned. That wasn't surprising. Cali knew quite a few women who kept the fact that they were mothers quiet, afraid of being discriminated against because "their focus would be split." She had friends who didn't get hired because they had children.

Sitting back into her chair, Cali felt the events of the past two hours crash in.

Paolo wasn't wrong to take his stand. She *had* been fighting with Jory, and it was fracturing the crew. Completely unprofessional. That said, Jory was no better for not clearing things up with Paolo and taking some of the responsibility. She should be furious with him. But then he'd gone and confessed to being an *idiot* and vowed to do *better* and brushed her *hair* aside, and all her other thoughts were drowned out by memories of the kiss.

Oh, that kiss.

Her fingers floated up to lips that still tingled. Her nerves had been replaced by a craving that coursed through her when she'd taken what she wanted. Which was his mouth, again and again.

It had been an awful idea. She'd never imagined they'd actually do anything physical. She'd been happy seething and lusting from afar. And the thought that the kiss could

Love, Camera, Action

turn into *something* was a horrifying one. If she and Jory were ever found out, she would never be taken seriously as a director again, not to mention Cali had zero emotional space for someone else in her life. An all-consuming career, chaotic sister, and depressive mother were enough.

After witnessing her mother fall apart after Cali's father left, and then after Patsy's father left, and then—*shudder*—after Rick left, Cali had more than enough evidence to close the relationship coffin. But then watching Patsy go through the same cycle on a biannual basis was the final nail.

The kiss had been incredible, no doubt, and she would be revisiting it tonight, alone in her bed. But it was better to keep the indiscretion to themselves. Go back to smoldering across the set, having the occasional sexy bicker, and then part ways at the end of the shoot. Never to see each other again. Perfect. Great.

Great.

Melanie bustled in, her high-octane energy in overdrive as she slid around her desk, opened her laptop, and started typing as she sat down. Melanie's ability to multitask was a thing of beauty. Cali would have told her as much if she hadn't been in such deep shit.

Melanie burrowed into her Herman Miller chair and punched the last key with a whack. "Howard would like to talk to you about the situation."

"Howard? Is he going to call me, or should I call him?"

"He prefers video chat. Hi, Howard, I've got Cali here."

Melanie swung the laptop around, and Cali was face-to-face with Howard sitting behind a desk in a sunny office with palm trees swaying outside a giant window. He had a stress ball in his hand and wore a sour expression. "What's going on with Paolo?"

Cali shot a glance at Melanie, who was typing furiously into her phone. Hadn't he been briefed? Cali returned to Howard. "Uh, well, I can only assume he is under the misapprehension—"

"I get this call from the star of the show in a lady panic because he isn't comfortable with the director on set."

Cali balked inwardly. Thalia was the true star of the show, given that it was about a female demon, as played by Thalia. It was the title for God's sake. "So far my relationship with Paolo has been fruitful, but there was a misunderstand—"

"I can't afford having a pissed-off star who isn't comfortable delivering what I need."

Her body coiled tight, fury mixing with disgrace. She hadn't been able to clear things up with Paolo, and his emotional state was, in some part, her responsibility. She'd failed in that. But why did it have to all be on her when the blame was shared? She wasn't sure where to direct her anger: at Jory for not coming clean or at Howard for not giving her a moment to explain.

Howard leaned back in his chair and squeezed his ball. "Listen, Cali, you come highly recommended and have been delivering some fantastic scenes that the network has really loved. Don't think I'm not grateful for the work you're doing and, frankly, for helping us out of the PR bind from the last dipshit director."

Cali tried to focus on the compliment and not Howard inadvertently grouping her in with the dipshit. "Thanks, Howard."

"But not having an actor on board with your directing style causes a lot of problems down the line, not only for us but for you as well."

Love, Camera, Action

Ah, there was the threat. If she didn't turn this around, not only would she be fired, but she'd also be shut out of future jobs. Her big break was breaking apart, along with a life free of scrambling for gigs. A life of doing the job she was born for. Cali gritted her teeth and attempted to rally. "Don't worry, Howard. I have faith I'll be able to bring him onside. He's got talent, and up until now our work together has been bringing out his best. This is a minor setback that we'll get cleared up in no time."

Howard sat in silence for a moment, the red ball squelching in and out of his closed fingers. "I know you don't come to us with as much experience as our other directors."

Melanie stilled over her phone.

Cali suddenly wondered how far Melanie had gone out on a limb for her. Was Melanie's position in jeopardy too?

"But I believe in fostering talent, and I think you show a lot of promise. Fix the issue and we'll keep moving forward." Howard tapped his keyboard and the screen went black.

She was still in the game. Precariously, but still. Cali had worked long enough in the business to know she couldn't take anyone's words at face value. Howard might believe in fostering talent, in fostering her, or he could be lying to her face so she wouldn't sue them for letting her go without just cause. For now, she had a chance, which she needed to take advantage of despite wanting to crawl away into a safe nine-to-five hidey-hole.

Melanie turned the laptop back around and gently closed it. Her phone buzzed, but instead of answering it, she turned it off and over. "I need you to know, I've been watching you work, and I'm impressed."

Cali searched her face. Melanie's usual frenetic energy was completely absent. All her focus was on Cali. It gave her a much-needed sense of safety, of being seen—a feeling she was unaccustomed to.

Melanie continued, the surety in her voice acting like a balm over the ambiguity Howard had stirred within her. "Despite the problem with Paolo, it's obvious you have deep respect for the actors and the crew. The footage you're getting is elevating the style and tone of the show, and when you're working together, even Jory has been delivering images better than his usual—and his usual is phenomenal. Thalia raves about you, and Paolo's performances have transcended what I thought possible for him." Melanie sat back in her chair. "So, what happened?"

Here it was. The moment to clear her name. Where Cali could air what had truly happened with Paolo. She was filled with the desperate urge to shout, *It wasn't me! It was Jory! He's a big jerk who can kiss like a god!*

Instead, she paused. If she told Melanie what had happened, Cali would be throwing shade on Jory, which felt wrong after his vulnerable admission behind the flats. Even though insulting Paolo was his fault, placing blame on Jory would lead to deeper fissures in the crew, not to mention reflect badly on her for blaming someone else. Inexplicably she sensed a certain loyalty growing toward Jory, perhaps because of his whispered vow: *". . . I'll do better."*

There was also the fact her confession would cause Paolo to suffer a second betrayal. From the way he worshipped Jory, that would be far worse than him thinking she didn't believe in him—a relative stranger who would be gone in a few weeks. At the end of the day, she was still the director,

Love, Camera, Action

and her responsibility was to protect the delicate balance on set. Sometimes that meant taking the hit for things she may not have done herself but had overseen.

She wanted to confide in Melanie, to talk the problem through, to get some help. Instead, she swallowed her vulnerability, feeling as alone as ever. "Paolo overheard me say something out of context. Now he thinks I don't believe in him as an actor." It wasn't a lie—just not the complete truth.

Melanie speared her with a look. "Something *you* said?"

Had Melanie heard something? Had someone filled her in on what had happened? It didn't matter; she wouldn't throw Jory under the bus. "Yes."

Melanie's scrutiny remained steady. Then she relaxed, bringing up a hand to massage her temple. "Paolo . . ." Melanie shook her head, as if trying to sort through her thoughts. "Paolo presents as a tough, together guy, but he's really a marshmallow. And like a marshmallow, if he's too close to the heat, he melts into a gooey mess."

"He has a lot of insecurities."

"And they can be difficult to navigate."

Cali nodded. It felt good to have someone acknowledge what she had already intuited. To have a comrade.

Then Melanie shuttered her gaze and became the hard-assed producer once more. "But I do not hold the final power here. See what you can do with Paolo, try to bring him back onside. And you need to be squeaky clean from here on out." Melanie stood up from her desk, signaling the meeting was over.

Cali stood with her. "I'll do my best."

Melanie said wryly, "You'll have to do better than that."

CHAPTER TWELVE

"Paolo, you're looking over your shoulder again."

"Yeah, I'm letting the guy watching me know that I know he's there."

Jory peered up from the small monitor attached to his Steadicam at the walking mannequin he was trying to direct. This thespian. This *actor*. "But you don't know he's there."

"I *feel* him."

"No, you don't feel him. You don't know he's there. You just get a coffee."

"Riiiigggght. I *just* get a coffee." Paolo touched his nose and nodded. Then he bounced away to his first position to begin the scene again.

Jory exhaled. He'd been trying to film Paolo getting a coffee for thirty minutes. Once Cali had been pulled off the set, leaving Jory alone to shoot the scene, Paolo had jabbered nonstop about his intention and emotional landscape.

Love, Camera, Action

To shut him up, Jory had made a terrible mistake. He'd explained what he was trying to do.

Now Paolo was "helping" the scene by acknowledging the unknown voyeur who stalked him. He'd searched the coffee shop in suspicion in one take, glanced over his shoulder on the next, and hadn't come in at all on another, instead just peering through the café window.

Jory couldn't help but ask himself: What would Cali do?

She wouldn't have told Paolo in the first place: that was what.

As the set quietened for yet another take, Jory sighed out, "Action."

Paolo glided in, all ease and confidence as Jory followed with the Steadicam.

Despite Paolo tanking the shot, the scene had taken on a depth that wasn't in the script. The added tension of someone watching Paolo/Rafe without him knowing would deepen the dread in the later scenes. Cali should be here to enjoy the fruits of their inspiration, instead of getting reprimanded—or whatever the hell was happening, in Melanie's office. Guilt and fury bubbled up in Jory at the unfairness of it all. The unfairness he was partly responsible for.

Paolo ordered his coffee and smiled at the barista, taking his cup in a perfectly normal and natural way. Jory's excitement rose. *He's doing it. He's doing it!*

Then Paolo turned and looked directly in the lens with a dead stare before he walked off camera.

Jory had to stop himself for groaning, "Cut" to the ceiling. Hopefully Michael would have enough to piece it all together. He motioned for Alison to help him remove his gear.

Paolo bounded up. "Did you like that look straight down the barrel? It was like I was challenging the audience, telling *them* to stop following me. Totally meta."

"Yep, it was great. Really good. Thanks, Paolo." Jory kept his hands busy so he wouldn't throttle him.

"No problem, man. You are really good to work with." Paolo slapped Jory on the arm so hard he almost fell over. Paolo lowered his voice. "I'm trying to fix it so we can do more." Then he shadowboxed Jory in the ribs and flopped away. The man was the living embodiment of Tigger.

Thank God the day was over and Jory could escape to his condo. Walking through the sets, Jory pulled his phone out of his back pocket, hoping for a message from Cali telling him what was going on, if she was okay, if she needed anything, what she thought about the scene, what she thought about their kiss, what she thought about him. Ugh. He was a mess. When he turned his phone on, a call did come in, just not the one he wanted.

"Howard."

"Blair! For fuck's sakes, what is going on down there? What's the deal with Paolo? I know he's as dumb as a rock, but he tested through the roof with eighteen- to twenty-nine-year-old women, and we *need* that market. How'd the scene go?"

"It went fine." Other than being a dumpster fire.

Howard whistled through the phone. "Good. I'm glad I've got you there. Listen!" Jory had taken a breath to say something, anything, but Howard steamrolled through. "I talked to Jeff about his show, and he's really pumped to have you on board. But he's nervous about pitching you to the network when you don't have any directing experience."

Jory deflated. He knew becoming a director wouldn't be easy. No one ever took a chance on an actual newbie,

Love, Camera, Action

although he'd hoped his hours and hours as a DP would be enough to bypass that step.

"We both know any monkey can direct," Howard continued. "We just need to get you some experience on paper. I've got a couple of ideas where I can slot you in on *The Demon*."

Jory's pulse picked up. He'd never imagined his first directing credit could come from *The Demon*. Working on material he already knew with a crew who trusted him would be best-case scenario. Maybe he could even ask Cali for some tips if he made it clear he wasn't encroaching on her territory. And if she was still speaking to him after their kiss. "That would be amazing. But I thought the roster was full?"

"You leave that to me. You just keep Paolo happy." Howard hung up. Like he always did.

Jory scrubbed a hand across his face and pulled open the door that led onto the crew parking lot.

Keep Paolo happy. Paolo would definitely not be happy if Jory came clean about what he'd said about his acting. That it was him, and not Cali, who believed he didn't have any talent. The smart move would be to keep quiet. But he wouldn't. Even if he hadn't shared that electric kiss with her, not 'fessing up wasn't right. He'd have to set Paolo straight regardless of what it meant to Jory's career. He had vowed to do better, after all.

Still, *The Demon* would be a perfect stepping stone. Could he find a way to boost Cali to Paolo and keep on both of their good sides? He doubted it. Maybe a workshop with all three of them—except Paolo would never go for that. Plus, Cali might be reporting Jory to HR this very second.

Before this, he had been above reproach with the opposite sex on set, especially in the aftermath of the #metoo movement. He was all for light being shed on the unconscionable behavior of the toxic men in the industry who'd been called out, and then thrown out. Now he could be painted with the same brush as those reprehensible creeps, and he didn't want everything he'd worked so hard for to disappear because of one ill-advised moment.

He had to shut down whatever this was between Cali and him. He would walk away. Pretend like nothing had happened, extinguish any possibility of what they might be together, what the show might be with them on the same side, and avoid her at all costs.

Yet, as he drove, Jory didn't go over what he would say to Cali to distance himself, but through their kiss—the heat, the surprise, the guilt, the horror. And then, the synergy *after*. How they had locked into each other creatively with a Borg mind that moved as one. He sensed an inspiration he hadn't felt since . . .

Since when? He remembered having fun on an underwater shoot in the Seychelles for that art house film about a Westerner learning how to spearfish. The light through the water was interesting and the gear they'd used was neat, but was that inspiration? Today he had been giddy over a simple Steadicam shot.

Still, the kiss was definitely not good. Well, it was good. It was really good. It hadn't been *wise*.

He locked his car and walked up the parking garage stairs, barely registering where he was. It all seemed an impossible tangle. Make Paolo happy while supporting Cali as he'd vowed. Manage Howard and his new career while distancing himself from a woman he felt a connection with that he hadn't felt in years, if ever. Go back to where Cali and he had started, silently seething beside each other

Love, Camera, Action

instead of sharing open-mouthed kisses that had a lush and decadent flavor he couldn't pinpoint.

He snapped his fingers. *Chocolate plums.* That's what it was. She tasted faintly of chocolate plums. Was there such a thing? Cali would know. She ate everything on the planet because *she* knew how to grab life, how to hold it in her hands and share its wonder.

Chocolate plums were what he was thinking about when he walked through the doors of his building, the subject of his quandary materializing before him.

Cali stood motionless in front of the elevators, staring into the middle distance, the elevator button un-pushed. With her arms loose at her sides, and her shoulders thrust back, she appeared almost regal, an exhausted queen who'd lost an important battle and now solemnly regarded the carnage laid out before her.

Jory felt like a duplicitous vassal, hanging in the moment before admitting to a betrayal he hadn't constructed, but had obliquely let fester. Stuck between his own ambitions and the monarch he served.

Or maybe he was just stuck between the condo's retracted doors that patiently waited for him to make a decision—in or out. Avoid Cali and retreat into taciturnity so he could squash any tenuous trust they had fostered? Or answer the call of her obvious misery? The prudent option was to retreat, but he couldn't leave her alone, not when she probably felt her world crumbling around her.

He stepped into the lobby, and the doors closed behind him with a quiet whoosh. His body flooded with adrenaline as he approached her with care. "I find the elevator works better when you push this button."

Cali flinched at the sound of his voice, snapping out of her reverie. When she realized who it was, her lips thinned, and she swallowed as her focus flicked from him to the elevator, then to the floor. So not exactly happy to see him, but not shooting daggers either.

She raised her hand to point at the button and widened her eyes in mock innocence. "This round thing here? This . . . how do you say? Butt-*on?*"

Happy for the brief reprieve from reality, he kept his expression neutral. "Yes. It is what signals the moving box that will deliver you to the stationary box you sleep in."

"And this butt-*on* invites the box?" Cali sank into her role, an alien in a strange world.

"Yes, the box slides down a long shaft . . . that stands . . . in the middle . . . of a bigger shaft . . ." His sentence petered out as the joke traversed into a territory he didn't foresee, and he inwardly cursed the blush that definitely lit up his features.

"Slides down the long shaft, eh?" She prolonged the sentence, which only deepened his discomfort.

Jory grasped for a misdirection. "I think that's the first time I've heard you say 'eh.' I was doubting your Canadianness."

"Ah, yes. Americans always believe the Canadian 'eh' a mythical creature, but as you have just witnessed, it is very real."

The amiable moment lengthened past jokey to stray into slightly awkward. Realizing they were still standing in front of the elevators with the *butt-on* as yet un-pushed, they both lunged forward to punch it, bringing their bodies uncomfortably close. They immediately pulled back.

"Sorry. Go ahead," Cali stammered.

Love, Camera, Action

"No, it's cool." Jory jammed his hands in his pockets. "You go. You were here first."

"But you explained its use so well."

Ah, there was her smile, just a bit brighter, her eyes a bit warmer, bringing out the browns that reminded him of a glass of bourbon in front of a fire on the beach. His chest tightened in a not entirely unpleasant way as her gaze dropped to his mouth. He licked his lips.

The motion snapped her eyes up to his, which widened in tandem. He quickly went for the elevator button again, just as she did, causing their hands to brush.

They jumped back.

Cali blew out a laugh. "Wow."

"I'm out." Jory threw his hands up.

"You don't want to go for three?"

"If you don't push the button, I'm taking the stairs."

She slowly lifted a pointed finger between them and announced, "I'm going in."

Jory swept a chivalrous arm for her to proceed and stepped back.

Cali pushed the button as the mischief seeped out of her. "Thanks for directing Paolo on that final scene."

Guilt lit up his body. "It wasn't a great situation."

"It's fine. He feels comfortable with you."

The elevator arrived and emptied of people. While they waited for them to clear, Jory offered an olive branch he hoped would be enough. "I meant to explain to Paolo what happened, but I got . . . distracted by the conflicts on set." A feeble excuse.

Cali fastened him with her gaze. "The conflicts with me."

Jory felt as if his almost apology was being turned over in Cali's hands as she weighed its worth. "Um, well, yes."

"Did you get distracted enough to do nothing about Paolo so you could passively get back at me?"

"What? No. No." But that's exactly what he'd done. Paolo had given him a number of chances to come clean, and Jory just . . . hadn't. He'd been angry at Cali, and if he was honest, had felt a self-righteous satisfaction that the misunderstanding remained. Now Cali was taking his measure, and Jory wasn't comfortable with her conclusions. He wasn't comfortable with his own.

The open elevator doors decided they'd waited long enough for them to board and closed to pick up someone who could make a decision.

"Shit," Cali whispered under her breath as she hit the elevator button too late. She stabbed the button again and again, as if that might bring the elevator back faster.

Giving up, she fished around in her bag to pull out an apple, which she bit into with an angry crack. Jory watched her chew, staring at her lush mouth surrounding the fruit as she went in for another bite. Jory was catapulted back to their kiss—the way she took control like she couldn't get enough of him, his eagerness to grab that control back, making it a game they played. Jory suddenly wished he could be that apple.

Her mouth slowed, and he lifted his gaze to catch worry flooding her features. "Oh, I'm sorry. Do you want one?" She jostled around in her bag, and another emerged.

How many apples was she carrying?

"Or maybe you want a granola bar?" she continued, peering into the bag's depths. "I might also have a yogurt."

He plucked the untouched apple out of her palm to get her to stop, just as the elevator dinged its arrival.

Jory stepped aside so she could precede him, and simultaneously dreading and craving the tight space, he followed.

Inside, the lighting was softer than he'd remembered. He was assailed by flashes of their kiss again—the panting breaths, the urgent touches, the desperate clinging. Inconvenient blood rushed south in giddy response. Cali cleared her throat, bringing his attention back to her as she ran her hand gracefully over the elevator panel like a *Price Is Right* model. "Again with the buttons. Floor?"

"Oh, right. Uh, eleven."

Cali pushed eleven and then floated her hand up to her own number, fifteen. She settled a shoulder against the wall to watch him.

There was something so comfortable about her. In the way she scrutinized him, in curiosity rather than reverence, that allowed him to shed the façade of presupposed genius, the unreachable DP. It made him want to give up his ethics and lose himself in the magic that sparked between them.

No. Stop that. He had to create distance. Not just to avoid the fallout at work but because he had no business exploring "spark" with anyone until he was healthy enough to do so. Better yet, he should seize this moment to clear up what had happened so they could return to being colleagues.

"I'm sorry that happened today. Behind the flats." Although he wasn't sorry at all. He was sorry it hadn't taken place in front of a moonlit fountain or over a soda float or on top of the Eiffel Tower. But that wasn't the point.

Cali's body tensed and she stood away from the wall. "Yes, me too. Me too. Completely unprofessional."

Jory nodded and then Cali nodded, and they were both nodding.

Noël Stark

"Completely unprofessional," she repeated.

Jory stopped nodding. Did she mean she was unprofessional or he was unprofessional? "I mean, yes, it was unethical on both our parts, despite you making the first move, but I completely take responsibility for my part in the transgression."

Cali stopped nodding.

Jory nervously continued, "I just wanted to be clear, because the present climate is weighed heavily, and *understandably*, against men being inappropriate on set. But I want to make sure you knew I wasn't trying to manipulate you with a gross misuse of power and intimidation."

"I didn't think you were trying to manipulate me with a gross misuse of power and intimidation."

"Great. Great."

As the elevator slowed, Jory felt lighter. Maybe they could move past this. Maybe there would be no recriminations. Maybe everything would return to its proper place, where they would work side-by-side a million miles apart, never to explore what could have been. Perfect. He stepped out of the elevator, when Cali's voice stopped him short.

"But you did touch my hair."

"Sorry?" Jory turned, confused.

Cali stepped up to the elevator threshold. "You said I made the first move, but you pushed my hair back and tucked it behind my ear. That's a move. That's more than a lean."

The elevator door began to close, and Jory swept his hand out to trip the sensors. The door wisely retreated. "Your hair was in front of your eyes."

"And you moved it. It's my hair to move."

Jory settled into his calm and rational demeanor, to diffuse the situation. And to bug her. "It is definitely

162

Love, Camera, Action

and absolutely your hair to move, and I take responsibility for moving your hair. But after I, obviously, misstepped in moving your hair, you moved your *body* and kissed me, which is, obviously, more egregious than moving hair."

Cali narrowed her eyes. "I suppose it depends on your intention."

"*My* intention?"

"Of whether or not you were moving my hair so you could kiss me."

Jory's calm and rational demeanor morphed into his terse and annoyed one. "It doesn't matter what my intention was. It was preempted by you actually kissing me."

"And you kissed me back." Cali flushed with what he could only assume was anger. "Neutralizing my initial kiss."

Jory pointed a finger at Cali, banishing the door back again. "You had your hands in my hair."

Cali matched his finger point. "You had *your* hands in *my* hair! And then you pushed me against the wall."

"After you pushed me against the wall!"

"Well, that doesn't mean you can then push me against a wall."

Jory stumbled for a response. "You, you—you moved your hands from my hair to the belt loops on my jeans, grinding your hips into my hips."

Cali sputtered, "I did not—"

"Oh, you did!" Jory leaned in. "You really did. You probably don't think you did because you were so into me."

"*I* was into *you*?"

"You were *so* into me."

"You were so into *me!*"

163

He *was* so into her. He made a last desperate attempt to retreat, from her, from them, and stepped back, hands raised. "Don't kiss me again."

"Oh don't worry. I won't." Cali smirked. "I'm a one-and-done type."

Jory stopped short. "What does that mean, 'one and done?'"

"I don't do repeats."

"You don't do repeats."

"I. Don't. Do. Repeats." She enunciated each word, exaggerating so he would get it.

But Jory didn't get it. "Sorry—you don't want to explore this between us, this *unbelievable energy* between us because you 'don't do repeats?'"

Cali tipped her chin up in defiance. "I don't have the time or the emotional space for romantic entanglements, no matter how good the kiss."

At that, the elevator door beeped its displeasure and slowly began to close. Jory put his hand out to push it back again, but the door had had enough.

Cali slid along with the exasperated door as it closed. "So you don't have to worry about the kiss because we had our one, and now we're done."

The elevator shut on Cali's smug face.

One and done? That was the stupidest thing he'd ever heard. After the connection they'd had, she was going to just walk away? He should agree with her and walk away himself. It's what he had been hoping for, after all, but now that just seemed preposterous. He went to rub the incredulity from his face but found the apple clutched in his hand. He looked at it as though it were poisoned.

No fucking way. No fucking way.

Love, Camera, Action

She wanted one and done? Fine. That one kiss was done. There were lots of other ones to be done, and he would be happy to cross each off on a thorough checklist. And once those were done, so were they.

A warning whispered in the background, a montage of hurt and loss, of empty rooms and a steady flow of quiet tears. That he was flirting with a pain that had nothing to do with his job or the show, and everything to do with his real fears, his true worry.

But God, he needed a reprieve.

He wasn't lying to himself; he wasn't. He knew it was stupid. Knew it was a risk. But at the moment he didn't give a crap about his rules or his career, about Howard or Paolo, about directing or *The Demon*. Or his stupid test. It could all wait. Here was a challenge he could rise to, in more ways than one, and as a plan began to coalesce in his mind, for once the ever-present gray was nowhere to be found.

Jory grinned. Oh, Cali was going down. And so was he.

He bit into the apple, the loud crunch underlining the sentiment.

CHAPTER THIRTEEN

Today was pasta day. A chef was creating made-to-order dishes at a choose-your-own bar with six different types of noodles, four different meats, and fifteen different vegetables. Cali had practically asked for all of them, and now she sat hunched over her food mound, listening to Dan go through the afternoon's shots while idly wondering if she had chosen a rosé sauce because it was two sauces in one.

She listlessly pushed her fork through her half-eaten pasta because, honestly, how could anyone eat this much food? But also because everything was going great. Like, really well. The crew was calm and relaxed; there was no contact from Howard or Paolo; and she and Jory had found an effective equilibrium. There were no jabs, no snark, no conflict. Only a steady, collaborative stride that kept the day on time and the scenes running smoothly. Cali had even thrown in a few signature shots to push the boundaries of the show, and Jory had been on board with every suggestion.

Love, Camera, Action

It was wrong, wrong, wrong.

She had congratulated herself on her maturity for putting a halt to what had been physically brewing with Jory. Well, using the phrase *one and done* wasn't the height of adulting, but the energy behind it was. They couldn't continue down the path they'd started on for all the reasons he'd laid out. They had reputations to protect and needed to focus on the show. Besides, romance for her in general was a hard no.

Cali had never been in a long-term relationship—lots of temporary and dazzling affairs—but nothing permanent. Men were ultimately a drain on one's resources. She supposed some had good intentions, but she just hadn't seen any evidence of it. She wasn't going to allow her ambitions get dragged down by emotional baggage.

A tray clattered next to Dan's, making her jump. On it was an elegant linguine with tomatoes and fresh basil in a simple olive oil sauce. Even knowing such a grown-up pasta would only belong to one person, Cali was still surprised when Jory pulled out a chair to join them. Not only was he eating, he was eating with *her*. Well, her and Dan.

Dan threw him a glance. "Nice of you to join us."

"I thought I'd check in to see if there were any plans outside the usual for this afternoon." His almost friendly tone was unsettling.

While Dan rattled through the scenes, Cali covertly studied Jory. His attention never wavered from their AD, even while he expertly wound pasta around his fork and lifted it confidently to his mouth with strong, masculine fingers. Fingers that raised a napkin to dab a full mouth she now knew the texture of. A mouth that didn't need dabbing because food would never dare go anywhere but between those beautiful lips. Jory had probably taken Tuscan pasta deportment lessons while sitting at a café in a white linen shirt by the Mediterranean Sea.

The table had gone quiet. Cali pulled her attention from Jory to see Dan waiting patiently for the answer to whatever question had been asked.

She blinked Tuscany away. "Sorry, what?"

"Is that all or do you have anything else?" inquired Dan.

Jory turned to her with a wide, guileless gaze that could only be interpreted as, *"I am your vessel, completely open for any and all of your new and interesting ideas."* Cooperative, servile, conciliatory.

You sneaky, little . . .

Jory *had* been doing everything she'd asked that morning. Like, everything. Never a question or a concern or a quibble. He also hadn't offered an addition or suggestion or enhancement. He'd given her exactly what she wanted and nothing more.

Why was he being so helpful? So gracious? So *easy*?

"Do you have anything you would like to add, Jory?" she politely inquired.

"No, I defer to you. Your plans for the day can't be improved on."

Dan choked on his salad and rushed to sip his coffee to bury his reaction.

That had to be sarcasm. How could her plans not be improved on? Maybe he was still worried about her calling him out to HR, and so he was fucking with her by *not* fucking with her. Oh, it was on. He would be the one who was getting fucked with. And nothing fucked with Jory like fucking with his vision.

Love, Camera, Action

Cali sat back in a deceptively calm pose, picking up her fork and pushing the tines lightly into her fingertips, summoning her best Bond villain. "Actually, there is something. I want to bring CCTV cameras into the ice-cream-parlor scene."

A black hole of silence threatened to swallow the table.

Jory cleared his throat. "CCTV cameras? Interesting." He leaned in on his elbows. "I'm listening."

Cali fought to keep it chill. "The security style of CCTV cameras will hint that Thalia's being surveilled and recorded—a Big Brother–type feel. And the gray hues of the footage will juxtapose nicely with the happy pastel colors of the parlor." Cali watched Jory's face flatten to neutral. She hated that look. "It's a departure from the tone you've established, but I think it could give a more original vibe. Don't you?"

Jory dabbed his lips again—still, no dabbing required— as though mulling over the idea. Cali knew he was stalling to cover his barely checked horror. CCTV cameras were grainy and stilted and only captured every other second because they couldn't hold that much memory. Basically, they looked like shit and would destroy the scene.

"How many cameras were you thinking?" Jory's voice held a faint wisp of hope in it. Maybe he thought that if she asked for one or two he could sabotage them.

Cali shrugged blandly at Dan, who now watched them with great interest. "I don't know—what do you think, Dan? Fifteen or so?"

Dan's eyes sparked with mischief, which he quickly shuttered. "We can do that. I think we have three and can probably borrow the others from the *Seedlings in Seattle* production next door."

Cali nodded sagely and turned her best faux innocent smile on Jory. "I'll show you where to put them."

Jory's countenance settled into a granite she desperately wanted to crack. She psychically telepathed to him to tell her off, to say the idea was asinine, to advise where *she* could put the CCTV cameras.

"Great idea. Let's do it." He rapped the table with his knuckles and smiled. He *smiled*. Cali recoiled. What in the god of fuck was going on?

Dan, astute as ever, rose to get out of Dodge. "Let me see if I can source those cameras."

Jory stood with his plate and raised an eyebrow. "Shall we?"

Cali stood too, loathe to leave her apple pie but unable to back down from the challenge. "Let's."

Side-by-side they deposited their dirty dishes into the plastic catering bins and walked out of the lunchroom into the darkness of the studio. It was quiet in the cavernous space. With everyone at lunch there weren't any *tinks* or *tonks* of the crew setting up for the next scene. No *clinks* or *clanks* of props being carried to their tables, no *shuffles* or *swishes* of cables pulled along the floor. The studio was dead quiet except for the steady plod of Cali and Jory's footsteps as they continued their TV version of Chicken.

Cali fumed. She was so tired of having to decipher every emotion from people in her life. Her mother was always a morass of feeling, and if Cali couldn't solve what was wrong on any given day, her mother would chastise her. *"Cali, you're insensitive. Cali, you don't care. Cali, you're cold."* Which of course had made Cali even more hyperaware of her mother's moods, always struggling to head off whatever disaster was coming down the pass.

Love, Camera, Action

She had the same problem with Patsy, but in reverse. Patsy carefully hid what she felt behind clever jokes and sardonic quips, but if Cali couldn't ferret out the downslide, she'd be pulling Patsy out of a ditch that, in a drunken haze, her sister would happily make her permanent home.

Cali didn't have space for yet another temperamental person, especially not a man who barely expressed one feeling and then poured all of them into a kiss.

Emotional whiplash. That's what Jory was. The male equivalent of an undeployed air bag in a violent but non-life-threatening accident. This was why she didn't want a man in her life, outside of the occasional hookup. She was done with guessing.

She stopped deep in the deserted set. "What are you doing?"

Jory turned in apparent confusion. "I'm getting ready for the next scene."

"You're acquiescing," she hissed.

"Not at all. I think CCTV cameras are a great idea. Very original." Jory's features could not be blanker.

"They are not a great idea. They are a ridiculous idea. You know that and I know that, yet you're going along with it. In fact, you haven't disagreed with me all morning."

"I didn't have to."

She wanted to strangle that neutral tone out of his neutral body with her biased hands. "That isn't possible. I've said things I *knew* were wrong."

"No, everything was great." He put a hand to his heart, slain by her self-maligning.

Irrationally, Cali started to panic, feeling as though she were on the brink of losing something. Something vital. She motioned sharply between them. "*This* is not great. You giving in to all my ideas is not great. For anyone. Least of all you and me. Let me be clear: I do not want you to do everything I say. I want your opinions, I want your input, and I want your voice." Cali's own voice cracked. The last thing she wanted was an automaton who did her bidding. She wouldn't deny she had fantasized about him executing her every whim, bending to her every command, but now, with that actuality made real, she was left with a hopelessness she couldn't explain. Out of all the things that had gone wrong on set, this felt the worst.

"My voice isn't what's important right now."

Cali seethed. "How could your voice not be important? You are brilliant and innovative, and you are quashing your creativity so I can get my way probably because you're worried about that kiss!"

Their eyes widened in tandem at the truth of that, but before either could speak, the sound of footsteps approaching ricocheted through the no longer empty studio. Jory opened a random door beside them and whisked Cali inside a deeper darkness.

As her pupils adjusted, she found herself on the tiny set of a dance-club bathroom. The stainless-steel sinks set in black countertops triggered the memory of a night at a rave where, much to Cali's shock, she'd hooked up with a painfully hot guy in a puny bathroom, much like this one. Her blood had sung with the wickedness of it as he hoisted her up on the counter, pushed her back against the mirror and had his way. But although it had been fun and exciting, she remembered being left wanting after he finished, too inexperienced to know how to ask for more.

Cali shook her head to remind herself she wasn't twenty-one anymore.

Love, Camera, Action

Jory crowded her against the counter, the quiet studio outside giving the room a churchlike quality. The church of sexy bathrooms.

"Why are we hiding in here?" she demanded.

He held up a finger to his lips, standing close and looking off, his ear trained to the footsteps. She still didn't understand why they had to hide, but the heat of him fogged her brain, and she didn't have much interest in moving. She took advantage of his distraction to trace the line of his strong neck until it disappeared under his gray T-shirt. His tee was well made, expensive, and classy, while her own came from a thrift store and had a sparkly unicorn playing electric guitar on it. She marveled at how his hinted at solid pecs and a firm torso without completely revealing them. How the muted color brought out his lupine-blue eyes, now entirely trained on her, as though she were a frame he was trying to bring into focus.

As the footsteps faded in the opposite direction, Cali tried to minimize the force of Jory's nearness by mustering up the frustration she'd been feeling all morning, hoping her whispers sounded formidable and cool as opposed to breathy and turned on.

"Are you doing what I want because you think I'm going to call you out to the union?"

"No, I have great respect for your choices as a director and merely want to fulfill your vision," he rumbled.

"Then why are you doing this?" She sounded hurt. *Damn it.* She straightened her shoulders.

Jory put one hand on the counter bedside her, which sexily popped his opposite hip. His scrutiny intensified, and she wondered if she'd fallen into some kind of trap. The door was easily accessible, she could leave at any moment, yet his hungry stare made her feel like a cornered rabbit.

He tapped his finger on the counter, tipping his head down while moving the tiniest bit closer. He lowered his volume to a murmur, telling her a secret. "I'm concerned the conflict we're having is stirring up inappropriate energy."

Cali matched his volume while trying to reason out what he meant. "And you think that if the conflict between us simmers down, so will we?"

He drifted his eyes up her arm to her collarbone, where they lingered, his gaze caressing her skin. "I think so, and you said you wanted things to be done, so . . ." His attention landed on her lips, and she could feel them trembling. "I'm just trying to respect your wishes."

She shivered. "I don't want you to sacrifice who you are for the sake of the conflict between us."

"That's just it: there shouldn't be any conflict." He moved closer. "I should be following your lead. You are the director, after all. And it's about time I honored that." His eyes finally met hers, and although his words were deferential, his stare was all predator, his voice no more than a growl. "So, as my director, what do you want me to do?"

Oh, so many things. So many, many things. Things that would firmly go against her one-and-done rule. The rule she'd made up to gain some ground in an argument so very far in the past that she had practically been a different person. The now person, the one in this fake bathroom with a veritable god in front of her, was definitely not done.

"What do I want you to do?" Cali repeated.

Jory slowly nodded. "To avoid conflict."

"To avoid conflict."

Love, Camera, Action

"And respect your wishes."

Cali didn't know what her wishes were. She certainly wished he wasn't so far away, even though they were only inches apart. She was good at boundaries, good at putting a halt to things when necessary. In a way, it would be *irresponsible* to go against her instincts by denying herself this possibility to explore their creative relationship further. Plus, he looked so good in that T-shirt, his body crowding hers and ready to spring, like he'd waited all day to get her in a dark corner of a set.

"Do you have an example?" she hedged.

He scanned her body in seeming contemplation, his breath coming faster, his pulse hammering in his neck. She'd gasp at the beauty of him if she weren't so eager for his answer. "Well," he said with a hint of gravel in his voice, "if you directed me to put my hand on you, I'd do it."

Her mouth went dry. "That's a bit vague. Directors need to be specific."

"Good point. Let me show you then." Keeping his eyes locked on hers, he slid his hand along the counter, slow enough that she could flee if she weren't frozen like that rabbit suddenly aware of its fate. His hand whispered by her thigh, teased at her hip, and landed firmly on her ass, pulling her into his body.

They both let out a sigh.

"And," he rumbled on, "if you directed me to squeeze your ass, just a little, like it was my ass to squeeze any time I wanted"—he demonstrated with a firm grope that brought her into even more contact with his hard body–"I would do that. I would do everything I could to fulfill your demands. I'm here to serve you."

Her focus fluttered down to his full mouth, making her momentarily forget her role in the game he was laying out before her. "You have Chris Pine lips. Only better."

Jory's voice came out low as a timber wolf's on the verge of attack. "I've worked with Chris Pine. He's very easy to light."

"I bet."

Jory licked his beautiful lips but remained still. Cali realized he was waiting. Waiting for her direction. Could she do this? It was such a terrible, terrible idea.

"I'm a very demanding director," she warned.

"I hope so." He squeezed her ass again, lifting her up on her toes the tiniest bit.

"Okay, then. Bring those Chris Pine lips over and kiss me."

Jory descended like an alpha claiming his due. Her senses exploded. He sampled her taste, licking into her until she whimpered at the rush. Then he abruptly leaned back to examine the effect.

A little moan eked out of Cali as she stumbled forward to follow his retreating mouth. He caught her elbows in a firm grip, steadying her.

"Did I tell you to stop?" she chastised.

He peered at her with a satisfaction that stole her breath, then snaked a hand behind her back, and crushed her against the marble countertop to take full, hungry possession of her mouth.

She was giddy with the thought she had ignited this passion that lay hidden beneath all that control. It became too much to simply receive and she matched his intensity, meeting each stroke of his tongue, earning a grunt of approval.

Love, Camera, Action

His other hand stole across her belly, slowly gathered the hem of her T-shirt in his fingers until the sparkly unicorn disappeared and the curve of her stomach was exposed. His fingers drifted lazily across her skin, just above her jeans and around her belly button, dipping below her waistline with each pass.

She tried to pull her focus back, searching for a direction to give him, to stay in charge of their increasing entanglement, but it was hard to concentrate when Jory's hand was sliding slowly into her jeans as he scraped his teeth along her jaw, raising goose bumps over her entire body.

He murmured into her ear, "Is this good? I want to make sure I do it right. Do you have another direction for me?" He pulled his hand out of her jeans and went back to her belly.

She whimpered in frustration. Those fingers gave her ideas, but she couldn't translate them into words. She'd lost her train of thought entirely, lost it to his energy surrounding her, manipulating her. There was something *she* was supposed to do. Oh yes, taking full control of this very, very sexy situation.

Jory nipped her ear. "I can kiss your neck or pull lightly on your nipples or rub my hardening cock against you. Please, Director. Tell me what you want."

"Keep doing what you were doing," she sighed out.

He lifted his head away from her but kept his hand circling her belly button. "And what's that?"

He wanted her to say it, reveling in the game, leading it but making it clear she had to ask, to give him permission. She had to stop the passive routine, ask for what she wanted, and leave that twenty-one-year-old girl in the past. "I want you to put your hand down my jeans and draw your finger through my slit where it's all slippery and wet, and gently, oh so gently, make me come."

Jory let out a gust of air. "That's very specific."

"I like my directions followed to the letter."

He returned to her mouth, kissing her with a renewed heat as he continued to move his hand in a not so controlled descent, past her waistband and beneath her panties to cup her with a decisive hold. She jolted at the contact and then melted against him, hungry for more. He pushed the heel of his hand against her mound while he slid the tip of his finger along her seam, back and forth, back and forth. He broke from her mouth. "Circles or pulses?"

"Surprise me."

His teeth found the artery that ran down her neck, and he bit down hard as his finger slid inside her. They both moaned at the contact. He worked deeper into her wet folds, grunting in approval at what he found while his other arm scooped her leg to half boost her onto the counter, splaying her wide.

Cali had to touch him. She fumbled her hand across his cock and grasped its mass, weighing it, learning it. Feeling it strain large and heavy in his khakis, squeezing hard as he slid his finger over her clit. She let out a moan as desire flashed through her.

"Shh," Jory whispered. "Anybody could come by and know you were in here getting your clit stroked."

His finger teased her, clouding Cali's cognition as she fought to speak. "By you."

"They won't know it's me."

"I could let your name slip out on one of my—uh . . ."

Jory sunk one of his fingers inside her pussy then, and her head fell back on a groan. His lazy thrusts made her

Love, Camera, Action

bones liquify and her breath quicken, taunting her to keep quiet as he added another finger. She tried to keep her sounds at bay, but when he turned his fingers inside her to rub along that bundle of nerves, her groan became a whimper.

"Shh," Jory whispered.

His fingers continued their slide as his thumb took up a circle pulse on her clit—he'd opted for both—and Cali was at his mercy. She tried to rebel, to pull it together, but she could barely think, and, at this point she wasn't sure she wanted to.

Jory smirked, intuiting her inner conflict. "Tell you what? If you keep quiet, I'll let you come."

The game flooded back, and with her last shred of dignity, she locked her glassy eyes onto his blown pupils, all the blue consumed. "You'll let me, eh?"

His smirk blossomed into a smile of appreciation. He leaned in and purred, "Please, Director, may I make you come?"

Cali burbled out, "Oh my God, that's so dirty," before his mouth covered hers again.

Cali's hand tightened on Jory's cock with little to no finesse, her coordination rocky given Jory's apparent virtuosity at illicit finger-fucking. She was gratified when Jory huffed at the contact and faltered for a moment. But then he renewed his concentration on her, pulling his thumb away and dragging his fingers out of her core, up to circle her and then slide deep inside her again. He repeated the movement—up, inside, back, again and again in a relentless rhythm.

She was completely in his control, and he knew it. As her body began to contract, he crooned in her ear, "That's it, that's it. Come hard for me. Make me feel it." Cali's back arched and her mouth opened in a wordless scream, his fingers never stopping their delicious onslaught. "Shh, that's it. Yeah, baby, that's it. Shh."

And then white light exploded behind her closed lids as her body seized, pulsing around his fingers for what seemed like hours, her consciousness traipsing between astral planes while Jory growled, "Fuck yeah. *Fuck.*"

As her orgasm retreated, she lifted her eyes to find Jory's dark with a furious heat, a smile of deep satisfaction on his lips while his finger lazily circled her, drawing out every last shudder. All her tension over the last week drained out, and she nearly collapsed against him, an emotion wedging in her throat. He pulled his hand from her jeans, and slid his fingers into his mouth, sucking on them with a satisfied hum.

Still enveloped in her haze, she struggled to pull back from the feelings threatening to spill out of her and put her attention on him. She moved to his cock, with directed intent. "Now you."

He captured her hand before it landed. "Uh-uh. We have to go."

She couldn't grasp what he was saying. "What? Why?"

"The scene's over."

Frustration rose in her despite the fact that her body was jelly. She gestured to his hard-on. "The scene's not over."

Jory surveyed her with a self-satisfied smile. "*Your* scene is definitely over." He motioned to the sounds of the crew filtering back to set. "We don't want anyone to stumble in here and get the right idea." Jory backed away from her and opened the door a crack to check if the coast was clear. He turned back to wink as he slipped out.

Cali let out a frustrated snarl. *That wink!* Shaky, she turned to brace herself on the counter, catching a glimpse of

Love, Camera, Action

her disheveled reflection in the mirror. She felt like that twenty-one-year-old girl again, frustrated in a club bathroom. Although, this time, she was the one who'd had the mind-altering orgasm. She flushed with the intensity of what just happened, the utter lush sordidness of it. Dangerous and glorious.

No. Her frustration coalesced into a razor-sharp focus now that her mind was clear of the nuisance that was her burning desire for Jory. This frustration was over the control that had slipped through her fingers and landed firmly in his as he'd sucked her taste from them.

This could not stand.

Cali straightened to her full height, regarding the woman who peered back at her in the mirror. She was a full-grown woman who knew who she was.

And fully-grown Cali Daniels wasn't finished with Jory Blair.

CHAPTER FOURTEEN

As Jory walked to set, he silently crowed over Cali's blazing orgasm. She ran so hot, sensitive to his every touch, blowing bright and fast, as though he'd only just taken the edge off. He bet he could have coaxed two more out of her without even dropping his pants. And even though he was left hard and wanting, he was oh so satisfied with where he had taken her. Even if she was furious after the result.

He laughed outright, remembering her outrage when he walked away. Letting her think he'd regained the upper hand in the game that was the push and pull between them was intensely gratifying. He would have a spring in his step if his suddenly restrictive khakis would allow it. He'd have to settle for a smirk over his devious plan to knock her off balance, which had started with agreeing to all her ideas about the day's shoot. He knew she would take his acquiescence as a personal slight. She needed the spark of conflict between them as much as he did, the spark that made their blood boil. And if that conflict led to a liaison in the back sets, who was he to deny them?

What he hadn't considered was her concern over losing his voice. How she felt it was a crime he put himself away. Cali was a feisty, talented director who genuinely found value in differing opinions. He felt seen. Which made him . . . fluttery.

No, not fluttery. Triumphant over a battle won.

He should have known his victory wouldn't last long.

As the afternoon went on, he realized he'd made a gross miscalculation. Cali was a hand talker who created the shapes and landscapes of her ideas with her body. Now she used those expressive limbs as weapons of subversion and torment, launching a silent campaign engineered to drive him out of his mind with want. When she illustrated her vision for the lighting grid, she brushed the heel of her hand up his arm. When she gestured toward set, she grazed a finger across his ribs. When she scooched by to give an actor some direction, she managed to—God knew how—drift her knuckles along the ridge of the erection he was growing desperate to hide.

If he hadn't been rendered mindless by the constant contact, he would've been in awe of her dexterity. Never once did her furtive teasing appear suspect to others or call her integrity into question—each touch a whispered promise meant only for him.

Then the *actual* whispers started.

"Can you come in a little tighter, a little harder on the tail end?"

Jory blinked as the soft air from her words brushed past his ear. They were sitting side-by-side at the monitors. When he risked a glance at her, she sat innocently reading her script. He had no idea what she was talking about. His mind was fried with lust, and he filled with dread when she turned her hooded hazel eyes to him in expectation of an answer.

Jory swallowed. "Pardon me?"

Half the crew had gathered around the monitors to check their own work—Makeup, Continuity, the art director. No one seemed to notice the fire-hot woman terrorizing him.

She regarded him with that heavy-lidded gaze and slowed down her speech, as though speaking to someone who couldn't form sentences, which wasn't far off. "Can you come in a little tighter, a little harder, on the tail end?" Jory swallowed again. "Of the scene," she clarified, watching him with lazy curiosity.

"Sure, I can do that." Jory shifted his shoulders in his suddenly abrasive T-shirt.

"Start off slow, of course, and then when the climax comes, really hammer it."

"Got it," Jory squeaked. He actually squeaked.

Cali's mouth kicked up at the ends. "Thanks." She turned back to her script with the easy grace of a satisfied cat.

Jory scrubbed a hand down his face. He had to get out of her space, or he wouldn't survive the day. But when he tried to leave, she grasped his arm. Blowing out a breath, he was about to cry uncle, only to be struck dumb by the concern in her eyes.

"And take this." A protein bar glinted at him from her hand. Jory could feel his face crinkle like the bar's cellophane wrapper.

Love, Camera, Action

"You need to eat," she said, standing up and placing the bar in his hand with a lingering touch. "It's cherry," she breathed, patting his shoulder and sauntering to set. He couldn't help watching her heart-shaped ass swing from side to side as she went. He winced. His cock was going to fall off from a case of blue balls.

Someone cleared their throat beside him. Loudly.

Jory was up and out of his chair like a shot, focusing on the monitor, to cover the fact he'd just been ogling the director's butt. He glanced back to see Michael with his arms across his formidable chest. "You good there, bra?"

Jory waved a nonchalant hand in the hope that it would waft away the suspicion in Michael's eyes. "Yeah, great. Was just checking the shot."

"I saw what you were checking," he accused.

Guilt bubbled up despite the fact he hadn't done anything wrong. Or had he? He was so mixed up in the fervor stew Cali concocted, he couldn't remember. He was a good guy—he was fairly sure about that. He diverted his attention to the set where Alison stood in mirror image of Michael, crossed arms and condemnation clouding her face. Did everyone know what was happening? He was a good guy!

Michael smacked Jory in the chest with a plastic case. Jory looked down and saw the film cartridge he'd dropped off with Michael a few weeks ago. "Sorry to say," Michael growled out, "but this Super 8 is too old-school for us to develop. Has to go to New York or LA. Not that it seems to be on your mind at the moment."

Jory took the case. "Um . . . thanks. Yeah. I mean, *no.* I'm just a bit . . . distracted."

Noël Stark

"You keeping it clean, my friend?" Michael poked two fingers into Jory's deltoid.

"Ow!" Jory would've found Michael's protectiveness of Cali endearing if he wasn't genuinely worried about the guy decking him. "Yes! Yes. Kind of."

The two men glanced over at Cali, who was now on set, animatedly talking to the actors. Michael rumbled, "I like her stuff."

"Me too."

Cali reached into her back pocket and pulled out her phone. Her easy air changed to one of dread as she took in the screen. She answered the call in hushed tones Jory strained to hear. "Hi, Mom. Oh . . . No . . . Don't worry. I paid that one, Mom. You don't have to worry about . . . Yes, I went through your bank . . . Yes, with Theresa . . . She is very nice. Listen . . . Listen . . . Have you talked to Patsy?"

Jory could feel her tension from across the set and had the unprecedented urge to catch her eye to see if she was alright. He crushed the impulse, knowing their game had nothing to do with deeper feelings, which was how it needed to stay. He turned back to Michael, who had a look of dawning understanding on his face. "Oh, shit. Okay."

Jory frowned. "'Oh, shit, okay,' *what?*"

"You like her."

"What? No!" Somehow they'd moved into middle school territory. He cleared his throat. "No."

"You *like* her, like her." Michael's heavy hand landed on his shoulder. "If you want, I could put a good word in for you."

"I can handle myself, thanks."

"You can be kind of an asshole," Michael said skeptically.

Love, Camera, Action

"Shut up, man."

For the first time probably ever, Jory was happy to see Paolo bound up to him. "You're directing me again. I like your style, and I don't want to get mixed up with the haters." Paolo sent a sneer at Cali.

Jory's happiness turned to indignation. He pointed a finger at Paolo. "You and I need to talk."

"Yeah, man. What are you thinking for me?" Paolo rubbed his hands together.

"You're directing now?" Michael's eyebrows bunched together.

Jory put his hands on his hips. "No."

Paolo nodded. "Yeah."

Jory shot Paolo a glare.

"What? You're amazing," Paolo said.

"No. I'm not amazing. We need to talk."

"You're not amazing?" Michael innocently inquired.

"I am not . . . oh, shut *up*." Jory searched out Cali as Paolo explained to Michael just how amazing Jory was.

Cali had moved away from set, her fingers pinching the bridge of her nose, lids squeezed shut. "You haven't heard from her at all? Since when? Oh. I'm sure it's fine . . . Right . . . I gotta go . . . As soon as I'm done here . . . Okay. Bye. Love you. Love you. Bye. Bye."

Cali hung up and stared into the middle distance. Blinking, she slid the phone into her back pocket, shuttered her gaze, and walked onto set with a sense of purpose that seemed to be pulled from the ground.

Paolo wrapped an arm around Jory's shoulders. "This guy's been giving me just what I need."

"I haven't been giving you anything."

Paolo shrugged. "That's exactly what I need."

Suddenly a female voice lilted above the flats, cutting through the chattering crew. "I know Cali's around here. She'll vouch for me. Cali? Cali!"

A petite blond woman barreled around the corner of the set, followed by a harried PA trying to stop her. The woman wedged herself between Michael and Paolo, full of a too-bright energy, tone unreasonably loud. "Hi. Have you seen Cali?"

Cali froze at the sound, the whole set going quiet as she turned to take in the newcomer. "Patsy?"

Cali dragged Patsy outside into the Atlanta heat as she scanned her sister's bedraggled state. Dressed in formless black layers, Patsy lit a cigarette, the sudden flare highlighting the dark circles under her eyes and the wrong kind of shiny hair that needed a wash. Patsy leaned against the outside wall of the studio as though it would keep her up.

"You look like shit." It came out more like a motherly scolding than an actual observation. Cali was furious. She had enough on her plate without having to deal with her sister.

Patsy sighed out the smoke with relief. "If by *shit* you mean stylistically waiflike, then you are correct."

"I'm not in the mood for your charming self-destructive mode."

"But it goes so well with the surroundings."

The skies were darkening for the daily thundershower. Every day in the summer, Atlanta had an afternoon storm that no one seemed to take note of. Violent and majestic, these thunderstorms did little to assuage the constant

Love, Camera, Action

humidity, and everything to build the Southern Gothic vibe of entrapment. Patsy always managed to appear ethereal, even in all black and dangling a cigarette out of her mouth like a trucker. A wispy, Twiggy-like beauty with blond hair and blue eyes, she could definitely pass for a Tennessee Williams heroine teetering on the edge of madness.

She was obviously breaking apart now, her hand shaking as she pulled the cigarette from her mouth. According to Cali's calculations, Patsy and—what was this one's name? Carl? Carter? Colin—Colin should've had another four weeks before the inevitable breakup. This one came early, *for fucks sake,* and given that Patsy was on the studio's doorstep, it was bad.

"What happened?" Cali tried to sound empathetic but obviously failed.

Patsy put a hand to her chest in mock effrontery. "Can't a girl visit her sister? I wanted to see you in action."

Irritation flared in the way only a sister could produce. "You drove fifteen hundred kilometers from Toronto to Atlanta to watch me work?"

Patsy paused. "It is a bit dramatic, isn't it?"

"A bit, yeah."

"I know. I'm sorry. I'm sorry." Patsy breathed out a plume of smoke, and they both watched it curl away, slow and heavy like the air around them.

"What happened?" Cali tried again.

"Colin's a douche."

"I assumed," Cali said bitterly.

"Wow, you're really mad." Patsy had the audacity to look hurt.

Cali put out her hand, fingers splayed, and Patsy gave her the cigarette. Cali took a long deep drag, relishing the burn in her lungs and the damage she was doing to them. Cali had briefly flirted with smoking in her twenties, but it never took, keeping her firmly in the realm of social smoker. And of course she smoked when her sister had one of her meltdowns. "It's been a hard gig."

"Oh really, why?" Patsy snatched at the segue like a life-buoy in the middle of the ocean.

"No." Cali pinned her with a glare. "No evasions. Why are you here?"

Patsy grabbed the smoke back and took a deep drag, her bottom lip trembling. "We had a connection, Colin and me. We met at the rare editions library, where we both wanted the same text of Sapphic poetry." Patsy usually started these diatribes with dialogue steeped in the language of romance novels. Reading them was a secret pastime of hers she hid from the rest of the Classics Department. But there was something different in her tone this time. Something hopeless.

"What does he do?"

Patsy studied her shoes. "He's a new prof in the department. Just arrived."

"Oh God, Patsy, no." Cali hung her head.

"Yeah. Then he took me up to his cottage in Muskoka."

"So, he has money."

"Yeah, but not how you think. It's the family cottage."

"Old money."

Patsy paused for effect. "His *wife's* family cottage."

"Oh, Pats," Cali gasped. "That asshole. That classless asshole."

"It gets worse." Patsy peered up at her, tears brimming. Patsy never cried. "Colin might have been my superior on the translation contract. And I might have quit because

Love, Camera, Action

I couldn't stand being in the same room with him, let alone huddling over ancient texts and debating over the various translations for 'oral pleasure.'"

Patsy's work had been the only thing keeping her fragile sister's world together. Translating was an all-encompassing endeavor that required time and diligence. If that was gone, Patsy would have nothing to distract her from her broken heart. Not to mention, there was the money. Always the money.

Patsy grimaced. "I know, I know. I didn't think it would be a problem but . . . it was." She lit another cigarette with the dregs of the last one.

"Patsy! We need that money for rent! I don't know—" Cali swallowed the sentence. She couldn't add her own concerns about losing this director's gig to Patsy's worries. "You know all my money's tied up with Mom."

"I'll get a job. A regular job."

"You can't get a regular job when you're working on your PhD."

Pasty winced. "Um . . . well . . ."

"What?"

"I dropped out of the program."

"You dropped out of the program? You're about to present!" Years of Patsy's life studying, years of Cali taking terrible jobs so her brilliant sister could realize her dream.

"Colin was also on the board." Patsy glanced away. "It became a whole ethical mess."

Rain started to fall. Thunder rumbled and trees blew. Cali and Patsy were gathered under an awning that was doing nothing to keep them dry, and as the water seeped through her clothes Cali began to realize the hopelessness of her situation. She would have to support them both again. She would have to make *The Demon* work, no matter what.

The door to the studio nudged open, and a PA stuck her head out, her eyes taking in Patsy's seedy vibe and then shifting to Cali. "We're going in five."

Cali blankly nodded, and the door closed, leaving them to the storm.

Cali blew out a weary breath and took Patsy's now soggy cigarette. Cali inhaled and focused on the head rush, putting a hand on the wall to steady herself. This was a lot. "I have one more scene to shoot. You wait in the production offices, then I'll take you home."

Cali took another deep drag, then handed the cigarette back to Patsy, who sucked in the last hit and butted it out. Patsy's shoulders were slumped, her posture defeated. Even at her lowest, Patsy had always exuded an imperial air, as though her presence among mortals was due to a sudden whim to go slumming. Now her inner light was snuffed out, and that absence, above all else, terrified Cali the most.

Patsy rifled through her pockets and pulled out a silver gum packet. She popped out one of the small white rectangles. "Take this. You can't have people thinking you smoke like your fuckup sister."

Cali gave her a tremulous smile. Patsy did her best to watch out for Cali, even if it was just with gum.

Cali opened up the door and went inside, Patsy following. Both were silent as they wound their way through the sets and into the production hallways. She showed Patsy into her barely furnished office. "Stay in here. Stream some shows or something on my laptop, but don't move. I'll send someone in with chips and pop."

"Salt and vinegar please," Patsy whined.

Love, Camera, Action

"They put sugar in the salt and vinegar chips here."

"What?" She gasped in mortification.

"I know. I know. I'll send something good."

As she walked back to set, Cali tried to recall what she had been doing before Patsy's manic entrance. An echo of excitement ran through her as she remembered baiting Jory. How delighted she'd been to witness him flushed and clumsy as she continued his torment. How his shots had somehow kicked up a notch, sparkling in their execution, as if they were allowed to shine through when his mind was occupied with something else.

All that had to stop, of course. Cali would have to do everything by the book to make sure she kept this job so she could turn it into steady work. Which probably meant giving up any artistic notions as well. Just tow the party line as Jory had told her in the first place.

An hour and a half later, Cali was shivering through the last shot of the day—the "martini"—so called because the next shot would come out of a glass. She could use some of that liquid warmth right now, seeing as her clothes were still wet from standing outside with Patsy in the rain.

As though her mind had conjured it, a cup gently edged into her field of vision. Not quite the glass of booze in Cali's mind, but good enough because it contained some kind of steaming brown, creamy, liquid goodness. Best of all, it was held by that oh so familiar hand attached to a muscled forearm that led to broad shoulders and ended at a corded neck. Gentle waves of sandy-blond hair framed blue eyes soft with . . . what was that? Kindness? Empathy? Whatever the expression, it made her want to dissolve into tears and fold into the warm body bringing her this simple cup.

Cali pointed. "What's that?"

"Hot chocolate."

"Hot chocolate?"

"You got caught in the storm. You looked wet. And then you looked cold."

Cali had to focus on the cup. Her eyes were going to glass over and potentially leak. She didn't know the last time someone had taken the time to take care of her. To give her something without any strings attached. She hardened her racing heart. The tears were a result of the stress she was under, not his thoughtfulness, she reasoned. The hot chocolate simply made her feel nostalgic, not cherished. She gingerly wrapped her hand around the cup, grazing his fingers as he took them away to slide them into his pockets.

"But it's ninety degrees outside. And it's summer," she told the hot chocolate. "How did you even get this?"

Jory shrugged. "I asked the caterers to make it. Told them it was for you, and they scrambled to find what they could. They love you, by the way. Or at least they love feeding you. They had to melt some chocolate into the milk 'cause they didn't have any mix, but maybe that's better—more legit. You strike me as a legit hot chocolate kind of person."

Against her better judgment, Cali peered up, the leaking a serious threat now. "I am. I am that kind of person."

Jory nodded. They stared at each other, unable or uninterested in looking away.

Rebellion rose up in her. Why couldn't she have something with Jory? Her sister did it all the time, not to mention their mother. Cali never indulged in something potentially bad for her, ever. Always responsible, always the one making sure everyone was safe, secure. Couldn't she find some calm in the storm with this man, even just for a little while? She was strong, unlike her family. She could keep it in check.

Jory cleared his throat and gestured to the cup. "Have to keep you warm and functioning. Can't let you dissolve into pneumonia."

"Even though this is the martini shot," she noted.

Jory's mouth quirked with mischief. "Well, there might be some vodka in your hot chocolate."

The warmth from the cup seeping into her fingers spread to her chest. She mustered up her best coquette. "How scandalous, Mr. Blair."

"Indeed."

Jory lingered a moment longer, his smile turning tender, her own probably taking on goofy proportions.

Dan bellowed out, "Martini shot! Ready for camera!"

Then a second, higher-pitched, and much more slurred voice mimicked, "Ready for camera!"

Cali frowned in sync with Jory.

Oh God. Patsy.

"Places! Places! The show must go on! Save some of that martini for me!" Patsy started singing "There's No Business Like Show Business" at the top of her lungs.

Jory blew out a breath. "Sounds like someone else found the vodka."

The warmth in Cali's chest fled. "I have to get her out of here. She'll sing the whole song."

Frantically they searched, but while the sound of Patsy's Broadway tune grew closer, the intricate maze of the sets kept her hidden.

As Cali ran onto the set where they were shooting, she heard Dan muse, "She's pretty good."

Noël Stark

Paolo turned to Jory, curiosity crossing his features. "Is this episode a musical?" he asked.

Then, a crack snapped through the set as a flat toppled over to land right on top of him.

In place of the flat stood Patsy, half-empty bottle in hand, full of a sorority girl's confidence. "Oopsy!"

Sighing in defeat, Dan clicked his walkie. "Medic."

196

CHAPTER FIFTEEN

The door to his condo clicked shut. Jory was finally alone.

What a fucking week.

He sat down on his painfully white couch to rub his eyes in exhaustion, but abandoned the move when he felt something clumpy dig into his ribs. He leaned over to gain access to his utility vest pocket and fished out a slightly bruised banana. *What the hell?* He would never put any kind of fruit, let alone a banana in his pocket. Pockets were strange dark places that contained unhygienic things like coins and phones. They were not meant for food.

Cali.

The woman was relentless in her campaign to ply him with calories. Sneaking food into his pocket was a further infiltration of his autonomous personhood. He should be furious. He should be insulted.

Instead, he felt warm.

It was becoming obvious the woman put the needs of everyone above her own. He didn't think he was particularly special in that regard. What did make him feel special was how she'd reacted when he'd helped *her*. She'd held that hot chocolate like it had been a prized alien artifact brought through multiple and dangerous dimensions. It was just hot chocolate. But he'd felt as though he had given her the world.

He wanted to see that look on her face again. To make her understand she didn't have to carry the weight of everyone around her, that she could depend on someone else to carry the load. Thinking back on his own life, he'd been awash in support from the get-go. From his father when his mother died, from his aunts and uncles, who filled in the gaps made from her absence, from his grandmother endorsing his career, even though she'd proclaimed it was "common." They would undoubtedly be there for him through his health scare if he wanted that kind of attention, which he did not. They'd all been through enough.

But Cali was someone *he* could help, someone he could support. He could keep her out of his drama while taking some of hers away. He hadn't understood his need to be the one who bolstered, encouraged, and protected until strong, vibrant, and capable Cali Daniels held his hot chocolate like a precious gift.

He contemplated the banana in his hands. Even her choice of banana was considerate. Just this side of ripe—if a bit worse for wear from his pocket—it was exactly how he liked them. A shade greener and it would be too chalky. A shade yellower and it would be too mealy. He slowly peeled the banana as he mulled over the day with her. He'd had chemistry with other women, but this was some next-level shit. It must be the taboo of connecting on set, the possibility of being discovered, coupled with the freedom from any

Love, Camera, Action

attachments. She didn't want anything serious and neither did he which made for a sexy time, limited to the dangerous but no less exciting game they played. It couldn't go any further, though, which was freeing. A relief even.

A doorbell startled Jory from his thoughts. He had a doorbell? He supposed he must since he had a door, but why would anyone ring it? As if in answer to this very deep existential quandary, it rang again. Banana in hand, he rose from the couch, cautiously opened the door, and froze.

A forlorn and drained Cali stood there, all big eyes and pale skin, dressed in tight jeans and a teal T-shirt announcing, "Kevin's Birthday Cruise!"

Cali gestured to the banana. "That looks funnier than I thought it would."

He crooked an eyebrow. "You pictured me holding my banana?"

Cali started to smile but squashed it, gravely shaking her head in disappointment instead. "That was a terrible drunk uncle joke."

"Well, I have lots of drunk uncles, so it was only a matter of time."

She let a shy smile eke through this time, and he tentatively answered with one of his own. As the moment lengthened, so did the silence. Jory couldn't think what he was supposed to do next.

Luckily, Cali did. "Can I come in?"

"Oh yeah, of course. Yeah." Jory sheepishly moved aside.

She stepped into his immaculate condo and came to a stop at the kitchen island, hesitant. It was odd for her, and that uncomfortable urge rose up in him again, where he wanted to pull her into a hug to soothe away her fears, to feel her sigh and relax against his body.

He took up a position kitty-corner, putting the island between them. He sensed her unguarded fragility, her disquiet, and kept his distance so he wouldn't spook her. "How's your sister?"

"Asleep." Cali pulled a baby monitor out of her pocket and turned it on. Over the speaker a delicate snore drifted out, the light monitor rising and falling with each rumble. "She'll probably crash pretty hard for the next eight hours, but there's always a chance she'll wake up and go wander the streets for a party she can crash."

"You've done this before." He kept his features neutral but inwardly winced at the intensity of responsibility Cali had for her sister. That was something he never wanted to put on anyone. It was beyond unfair—selfish even.

"Couldn't handle waiting for her to wake up, so I bought this." She shook the monitor with a half-hearted wiggle.

Jory wanted so badly to raise his hand to her cheek, to give her some kind of respite. To hold her face and touch her hair as she nuzzled into his hand. His heart beat heavy at the fantasy, but he kept his hand at his side.

As though sensing his reticence, she lifted her eyes to his. They were filled with such sad resignation it made him livid.

"Do you know what decision fatigue is?" Cali said.

Jory was taken aback by the segue. He searched his mind for where he'd heard the term. "Something about Obama's suits?"

She smiled. "Sort of. Obama recognized that making too many decisions would drain his resources, leaving his executive function less capable to make appropriate choices.

Love, Camera, Action

So he made sure his suits were either navy blue or dark gray, making for one less decision in the day and therefore strengthening his self-regulation." Jory nodded but didn't quite understand what she was getting at. It must have shown, because she continued. "I'm having trouble with self-regulation because I've made too many decisions."

"So . . . you have limited executive function?"

Cali solemnly nodded.

He thought he was following her breadcrumbs, but he didn't want to get ahead of himself. "And now you don't want to make any more decisions?"

Cali shook her head.

He took a leap. "You want me to make the decisions for you?"

A nod.

"Wouldn't that put me in a position of taking advantage of your lack of executive function?" He could feel the familiar tightening of his cock, a common occurrence around this woman.

"Not if my last decision was to give you the power to make the decisions."

His heart clenched. Her melancholy eyes revealed the weight she carried, not only from the emotional turmoil over her sister and, from what he'd gathered, her mother, but the constant stress of giving guidance to a crew and cast on a troubled shoot. A shoot where, instead of being her ally, the DP had firmly set himself against her, tacitly allying himself with an executive producer who had never given her a chance. She looked at the end of her tether, and knowing he had been party to that made him nauseous.

He wanted to ease her troubles, to take away the pressure coursing through her. He knew somewhere in the back of his mind that this was where they had been heading, even on that first day, if he was being honest. He was hungry for it, for her. But he couldn't responsibly take that plunge until he knew they were on the same page, that there was a clear understanding. He knew what it meant to lose and wouldn't put someone else through the possibility of that.

"What about the one-and-done rule?" he asked.

"We haven't done this one."

"And when we're done, so will we be. This"—he motioned between them—"will be done. We will be done."

She nodded.

Could he actually have this? A deluge of desire overtook him, one he'd been holding back for weeks, denying the passion was even there, let alone raging beneath his tenuous control. People did this all the time, didn't they? Had illicit sex with people from work that they developed no deeper feelings for? An easy, hot arrangement between two adults who wanted to blow off steam?

He could do this. He was going to do this. And all the warning whispers and incredulous skepticism could fuck off.

Still, he had to be crystal clear. "You fully agree to this? You haven't been coerced in any way?"

Cali glanced down at an envelope sitting on the island, grabbed a pen and wrote *I, Cali Daniels, on the night of July 17, being of sound mind and body, consent to Jory Blair making all further decisions for me. I have not been coerced by him in any way unless I ask to be.*

Jory peered up from her messy cursive to search her exhausted face. "That letter is from my eighty-year-old great aunt."

"Oh. Sorry. Would she appreciate the sentiment?"

"Probably. She was very progressive in her day."

Love, Camera, Action

A tremulous smile pushed at her lips. She was nervous, he realized, her gaze lowered to his chest. Then she took a breath and bravely bared her neck to him just that little bit, just that submissive, little bit, reminding him he'd had no relief from the games that had crackled between them all day, or the past three weeks, really. He'd never seen her so still, and it filled him with awe that she was still for *him*. His blood flowed faster at the sight of her patiently waiting, while she fought to keep her breath even.

"Please, Jory. I want to forget who I am for a while."

His mind shut down and his body took over. He plunged his hands into her long auburn hair, turning the waves in the light to see the sparks of russet and copper. He tightened his grip, hard enough to pull at the roots and give her scalp that tingling sensation while forcing her head back to meet his eyes. Hers burned green, the dilated pupils usurping the brown as her breath quickened and her body relaxed into his hold.

Reveling in the power, he slowly brushed his lips across hers with the lightest kiss, despite wanting to crush himself against her. Her breath sighed out at the touch, her eyelashes brushing against his cheek as they lowered. He took leisurely sips of her mouth, the smallest nibbles to tease her, relishing her taste as she began to pull against his hold—trying to gain leverage.

He had to smile. Only a moment after explicitly handing over control, she was trying to claw it back, to direct the kiss and push into him. He backed off and held her firm as she squirmed in his grasp. "I'm making the decisions, right?"

Cali moaned in frustration but stilled into passivity again, waiting for his next move.

He hummed his approval. "That's good. That's very good."

He held her for a moment, teetering on the edge of what was about to happen. Her tenacious confidence was an incredible turn-on. He'd marveled over her ability to go toe to toe with him despite his hard-ass reputation, pushing him to be better. He was humbled by how openly she wanted him in this moment, needed him to take away the stresses of her outside world, even if it was just for tonight.

When he searched her face, so trusting and desperate for care, for oblivion, he didn't have much of a choice. He wanted this woman. And he swept in.

There was no teasing in this kiss. The pent-up energy he'd kept under wraps for days exploded and poured into her. All the hope he had for the future and all the fear he had in the present. And she took it all, with a strength that made him wonder who was caring for whom. She let him plunder her mouth, let him taste every crevice, plunging his tongue so deep she whimpered. He claimed every soft, hot space, showing her she was his now.

A thought surfaced—she tasted like a candy cane.

He pulled away from her lush mouth to rain kisses down her neck, breathing in the pomelo scent he recognized from the shampoo in his own condo welcome gift basket. "What did you just eat?"

"Sorry?" she breathed.

Jory lifted his head and saw eyes fogged with desire. She was all in, completely in his hands, and the power made him grunt like a caveman. "What did you just eat?"

"Oh. A mint protein bar and a diet cola."

"You taste like Christmas."

"Do you like Christmas?"

"I do on you."

Love, Camera, Action

He went back to her lips and swept his tongue inside her yuletide mouth while he bent her backward over his arm, giving her no choice but to take his onslaught. Her fingers squeezed his forearms as she battled to meet him stroke for stroke. He got the notion he could come from the ferocity of this kiss alone. Forcing himself to slow down, he matched the tempo of the strokes of his tongue to the grind of his hips against the beautiful valley between her legs. His attentions gained him a moan as she angled closer, searching for relief.

He released her mouth and stepped back, leaving her on wobbly legs. She stumbled from his sudden retreat, and he brought his hands to her hips to steady her. To steady them both.

"You with me, Cali?"

She blinked in an attempt to focus, and Jory was struck by how far she let herself go. *God, she's intense.* He'd never experienced someone give themselves over to the moment so completely. His relationships had always maintained that surface distance, whether they lasted months or a year. But somehow he knew more about this woman in a few weeks than everything he'd learned from his past relationships put together. Jory wondered what it would be like to be on the receiving end of her intensity all the time. In, and out, of the bedroom.

Jory shut the notion down and brought his hand up to cup her chin, digging his fingers in slightly so she remembered who was in charge. "You want to see what you do to me? What you've left me with this whole week? How I'd rather walk around with blue balls than come outside of your teasing pussy?"

Cali looked stunned with desire as her pupils blew her eyes black, but she managed a slight nod.

Jory raised an eyebrow in response. "Well, get to it, woman."

He was rewarded by a look of gleeful hunger on her face. Jory had to bite back a groan, so he could appear impassive and bored. He had a role to play, after all.

Cali obediently sank to her knees, heat climbing into her cheeks. Once settled, she waited for his next direction. There was a calm in her, an absence of the low-grade anxiety he hadn't known existed until she'd been given permission to put it away. The realization flooded him with a sudden sense of responsibility: he'd been given something precious with this exchange, and he had to be respectful. The feeling was foreign and slightly terrifying, and he realized how reined in he'd been with his other relationships. He felt himself letting go, giving himself over to what was building between them. He smoothed the hair from her forehead and tipped her chin.

"Take it out."

She unbuckled his belt with trembling fingers, pulling his zipper down with a slow reverence. Her face was rapturous, like she was unveiling some kind of magical talisman instead of peeling down his boxer briefs to set his dick free. She let out a gasp at the sight of his heavy cock, which did more for his ego than he liked to admit.

"You see what you do to me?" He gripped his shaft and gave it a pull. "And there's no relief from it."

Cali sulked. "I could have done something for you before."

"Do something for me now."

Cali exhaled, "Thank God." She opened up her mouth and took him deep. No teasing, no preamble, just all of him straight down.

Love, Camera, Action

"Holy fuck." Jory's knees buckled. Her suck was so strong her cheeks hollowed out, and that, combined with the flat of her tongue laving the base of his shaft as she pulled back, forced him to grip the edge of the kitchen island counter.

She pulled off with a pop and brought her hand up to replace her mouth, lazily sliding it back and forth while she peered up at him. "I've wanted to do that for weeks." She put her mouth on him again and charged on in relentless rhythm, gliding her hands along his cock with the wet she'd left behind.

She was exhaustive, finding every pressure point, every seam, every spot of pleasure as if this blow job was her dying wish. He threw his head back and groaned loud enough to be embarrassed if it didn't feel so fucking good. Hauling himself back from the edge of the abyss, he put what was left of his willpower into a stern command. "Enough."

Except she didn't listen. She doubled her efforts instead. Gritting his teeth, he wrapped his hand around her hair and pulled her firmly off him, her mouth releasing him with a gasp.

"What? Why?" She was all whiny pout.

He schooled his features. "Who's in charge here?"

"You are." *Begrudging, thy name is Calliope.*

He helped her from the floor, hoisting his khakis back up to rest on his hips—there was no putting his cock back in—and escorted her, with all the gravitas of a cotillion dance, to his snow-white couch.

He placed her at one armless end, where he unbuckled her belt and then went down on one knee to drift her jeans down her thighs. He brought one of her hands to his shoulder as he helped her out of each leg and then studied her as she stood in front of him in her red, boy-cut underwear. He ran his hands up and down her legs lightly, pleased when goose bumps rose on her skin. She sighed above him, letting her shoulders drop, just as he brought his hands to the back of her knees and jerked them forward, tumbling her back onto the couch. She let out a yelp of surprise.

He roughly pulled her butt to the edge, bringing her core in line with his face, and breathed in her scent—earth and fruit and tang all at once. "You smell fucking amazing."

He pulled her panties aside and dipped a finger into her, dragging through her soaking folds.

She sucked in her breath. "Oh geez."

He took his finger out and stuck it in his mouth, sucking it like a lollipop, groaning. "You're all essence of whatever the fuck ambrosia is."

"I only know ambrosia salad." Cali shuddered above him.

"You a fan of ambrosia salad?"

"It's hard to miss where I come from. It's the salad of the white-trash gods."

He breathed out a surprised chuckle. God she was funny. He spent most of his time on set trying not to laugh at her one-liners. Who knew why. Probably something about his misguided sense of control.

But jokes weren't part of this game. If she was cracking wise, she wasn't mindless with the desire Jory wanted to wring from her. He pulled down her panties in a rough move, and ran his fingers along her seam, dipping inside to circle her entrance then pushing deeper with a possessive thrust. She raised her head in a gasp, then dropped back down. He eased in and out, curling in the upthrust to catch that bundle of nerves from the inside.

She was so swollen, so tight. He'd go slow, which conveniently fit into his torturous plan. "Got to get you ready for me."

"I am so ready."

"No, you're not."

She looked up with a smirk. "You all that?"

Jory's inner Neanderthal rose to the surface, and he growled, "If you're lucky, you'll get it."

Cali couldn't think. She couldn't make a plan or formulate a decision. There was no responsibility to take, no doubt to stifle, no anxiety to extinguish. All she could do was *feel*. Jory had woven some crazy sorcery with his fingers inside her while his other hand claimed her breasts under "Kevin's Birthday Cruise."

She'd never been so vulnerable, so open, so out of control. So grateful.

Now she was messing up his expensive white couch, her knees splayed wide open for the enemy who was once the author of her troubles and now the catalyst for her amnesia, his expert fingers breaking apart her consciousness as he rubbed her G-spot.

And then he lowered his head.

He dragged the flat of his tongue over the length of her core, pressing hard, as though surveying it all before zeroing in on specifics. He lavished attention on her clit and then backed off, easing her away from the growing tension to focus on the inside of her sensitive lips. Then he did it again. And again. The more he circled, the more friction she wanted, and just when she was peaking, he backed off, leaving her to whine in frustration.

Cali never came from oral. The chatter in her brain wouldn't allow it, and so she was always self-conscious. The assumption that she should feel privileged a guy was going down on her, paired with the necessary passivity during the act, didn't jive well with her busy mind.

But Jory seemed to be in zero hurry. He tested and prodded and listened to her reactions, diving in and easing back, breathing as heavily as she did, as though her cunt were connected to his cock and what he was doing to her was mainly for him.

Then he started to talk, as if sensing her drift. "You're thinking."

Startled out of her fog, Cali came back to her body. "No, this is good. It's good." And it *was* good, but she *was* thinking and she cursed Jory for knowing as much.

"Think about how hard I'm going to fuck you once I decide you're wet enough for me." His filthy mouth banished her thoughts, and she felt herself get wetter, as though on his command. She moaned, wriggling in anticipation.

Jory smacked her flank. "Don't move. Or I'll only give you the tip." Cali shivered at the thought of him pushing into her, her body prepping for the cock she could still taste in her mouth—thick, long, hard—and she immediately stilled.

He swirled his fingers. "I'll fuck you so deep and slow."

"God, you're really good at dirty talk."

"That's not for you. I don't care how you feel."

Even though she doubted that was true, the pretense of it made her relax into his touch even more. She was so relieved she didn't need to *perform*, to prove she was enjoying every second. Making it about Jory gave her permission to relax enough to *actually* enjoy his mouth, his control over

Love, Camera, Action

her. To give herself up to him. The thought made her clit swell and her body tense, and she felt her body hurtling toward a cliff she almost never approached.

"Maybe I won't let you come now. Maybe I'll wait until you're face down in my pillows, begging for me to ram inside of you. When I fill every part of your swollen pussy and you milk me with it."

Her desire ratcheted up tighter as he lowered his mouth again. She was so far gone, she could only feel his hands working inside her and his tongue fluttering in a flurry of strokes—quick, quick, long, long, quick, quick, long, long— as her body climbed higher, winding like a top ready to spin off its string.

Despite herself, she shattered, keening as her release crackled through her body. He kept up his movements, fucking her with his hands while lapping up her wet as she pulsed and pulsed around him, all her tension rushing out in a whoosh that left her boneless.

Jory moaned in approval, his hands moving languorously, his tone stern. "You're in big trouble for not waiting for my cock. You've made me very unhappy."

"Sorry" was all she could eke out.

"Up."

What? How could she possibly get up? He'd killed her with his bossiness. She was dead from his mastery. How could he be so cruel to actually expect her to move?

She was about to tell him as much, but his eyes were black with hunger and hard with disapproval. There was also a spark of mischief there, like he was loving the game while worshipping her in the process. She felt an unexpected craving for him that had nothing to do with desire.

"Get up." He stood and pulled her up by her hands, using her momentum to hoist her over his shoulder in a fireman's hold.

Cali squealed, her blast of emotion forgotten. "What are you doing?"

All she got in response was a slap on her ass.

"Wait! I need the baby monitor." Cali hated to break for reality, but she couldn't let go of the ever-present responsibility.

"I never thought I'd hear that sentence tonight." But he changed directions so he could grab the monitor and continued on down the hall.

Suddenly she was bouncing on a bed in deep discombobulation, her world upside down. She pushed herself up on her elbows to watch him shove down his pants, revealing strong, thick thighs cording around to the lift of his ass that she could only see a hint of. Her focus was pulled back by the plain blue T-shirt rising up his body, his Pilates-toned body, followed by the roll of a condom over his incredible cock as he climbed her in predatorial grace.

His hands clasped the outside of her thighs to draw her legs up until her knees were beside her chest, leaving her open and exposed. "You have to make up for coming too soon."

His face was hard, his voice thick with want, and he took his cock in hand to slide through her sensitive core, rekindling the fire her orgasm had banked. Icy, controlled Jory was gone. In his place was a man she had only caught glimpses of, mostly when he was sparring with her. It made her wonder how much this man kept himself in check, how little he let himself out to run amok in the dangerous messiness of feelings.

Love, Camera, Action

With shaking hands, he notched himself at her opening and lowered his lids as he squeezed in. She'd been boneless a moment before. Now she clenched hard around him, angling her hips in a greedy grasp to pull him in deeper.

"This is all for you." She loved him inside her, craved it, but knew that it would be just that. She didn't want him to hold off to wait for her. "I won't come again."

"This is all for me. You're not allowed to come again." His tone was uncaring and selfish. Somehow it stoked her higher as he slid farther in, and she moaned out his name in surprise.

Jory ground his teeth as he seated himself fully, stopping for moment to take a long breath. Then he set a measured pace, his thrusts deepening along with his voice, "I'm going to make you very, very sorry you didn't listen to me."

A shuddering noise came out of him, and suddenly Cali wanted to shatter his steely reserve. There was something she was chasing, a need to see him unravel, to see his vulnerability only for her. Cali clawed through her fuck-drunk haze to taunt, "Fuck me harder. Don't hold back."

His eyes snapped to hers, full of challenge. "That's not for you to decide. I do what I want."

His fingers dug into her thighs as his hips quickened, determination on his face as he watched her response. She hadn't been lying; she never came twice. Hell, she was happy she had come once, but right now her body was calling her out. He changed his angle, and she felt the ridge of his length graze against that bundle of nerves. She whimpered at the intensity, and her body coiled again. He smirked through his grunts, sweat sheening his brow as she grasped him with every invasion. But when his triumphant gaze clashed with hers, his smirk stuttered. She got the overwhelming sense he could see everything in her—her failures, her faults, her regrets.

And it didn't matter.

"I see you. Don't." With the harsh order he brought his hand to her clit and rubbed. Soft at first, in direct opposition to what his cock was doing, then building in intensity. Her eyeballs literally rolled back at the sensation until she could barely remember to breathe.

His thrusts got wild, the slaps of his thighs ringing out in the room. He growled at her. "I told you, don't come. Even though you owe it to me, should give it all to me, because it's mine. Don't you dare come."

And then she exploded, screaming his name in a deafening rush and barely registering his quickening thrusts. His own roar filled her up, his head shooting back as he kept going, shuddering through his own eruption.

He collapsed on her, their chests heaving in tandem. She drank in the weight of him, as though his body kept Cali from flying out and losing herself, losing this, whatever *this* was. A sense of fulfillment stole over her, of rightness that came with his weight.

He rolled off, the absence of his body allowing her busy thoughts to intrude. They lay side by side, slowing their breaths.

The moment extended into an interminable silence, and the reality of what had happened soaked into her. This was their one, and now they were done. A sadness intruded that she couldn't name. He was obviously a sex god as well as a talented DP, and she should be grateful she'd gotten this time with him. She'd needed this release, and he had been happy enough to oblige, and now they could return to what

Love, Camera, Action

they were before. This was a good thing. She could cling to this moment from the safety of her memory.

She began to piece together the words so she could leave, definitively cutting off this unwanted glow and making sure he understood where they stood. The words were slow to come, though. He turned toward her, and she braced herself for the inevitable invitation to stay or the inanities of how amazing it had been—even though it really had—and she sorted through her mental Rolodex for her usual "out" lines. But nothing presented itself, and instead she slowly rolled her head to meet his eyes, wondering what she might find.

He was smiling. A boyish, self-satisfied smile that was open and relaxed. Her chest nearly burst. She ached to grab him, wrap her arms and legs around his body and never let go. She blinked the alien urge away, uneasy about exploring what it could mean, because, ultimately, it couldn't mean anything.

He pulled his hand up to rub his chest, like he was massaging his overextended heart. "I thought I told you not to come."

She shrugged. "I guess I can't take direction."

He rumbled out a chuckle, and she had to smile. She tried to reel it in, to be cool, but instead a giggle escaped through tight lips. Slow at first, released in little hiccups that made him break into a silly grin. Then all the tension and the fear of the last few weeks dissolved as the dam she'd erected to keep her distance shattered with a bark of laughter she couldn't hold back. He answered in kind, and they laughed together. They laughed until tears streamed down their faces.

CHAPTER SIXTEEN

Their laughter subsided, and Jory stilled beside Cali as she stared at the ceiling. The sound of tiny, muffled thumps on the sheets told her he was searching for her hand. When he found his mark, he linked his fingers with hers. An alien rush of satisfaction stole over her, and she fought back a sigh. She had to remember the ease she was feeling was the natural oxytocin running through her blood as a result of two incredible orgasms. Oxytocin led to unfounded notions of closeness and connection that would never survive when the sweat cooled. The urge to fuse her body with his so they could continue forward as one entity wasn't based on truth, no matter how attractive a prospect.

The afterglow winding its way around them would soon morph into plastic wrap determined to suffocate her. She'd watched her mother put herself in the hospital after her breakup with Rick, the most destructive of their mother's unhealthy relationships. Rick was one of those slick charmers most women could see a mile away for being a leech and a liar. But not their mom. To her, he'd been The One, in all his ponytailed, weed-selling, El Camino'd majesty. And despite Patsy's quick recoveries after each of her whirlwind romances, Cali had seen the cumulative effect they'd had on her. How every sliver of disappointment had driven deeper into her heart until the light that made her so unique faded. Cali wouldn't risk that kind of emotional breakdown over something as fickle as a man. If just because she was the only one able to pick up their pieces when her family fell apart.

Ignoring the voice pleading with her to take just a few breaths more in the safe cocoon Jory's presence had spun, she spoke. "That was pretty good."

Jory's head turned to her profile, and he said in dopey disbelief, "Pretty good? That was *pretty good?*"

His incredulous tone surprised her. She thought the sex was amazing, playful, exciting—and so, so hot. But she'd just assumed this would be his regular Friday night. Now she wondered if he didn't let go very often, and what he would be like if she stayed around long enough to blow through all that control.

Too bad she was about to leave. Yep, getting ready to leave. Any minute with the leaving. "Well, um, I'd never done that before."

"Had sex?"

Cali rolled her eyes. "No."

"Had a giant cock in your mouth?"

She huffed out a surprised laugh and followed it with exaggerated exasperation. "No."

Jory turned on his side and propped his head on his hand, with a sudden frown. "You've had someone bigger than me?"

Cali widened her eyes in mock innocence and cooed in a breathy, high voice, "Oh no. Yours was the biggest and most beautiful cock I've ever had in my life. Thank you for gifting it to me."

Jory snorted. "That's better."

Cali smiled but kept her eyes glued to the ceiling.

He nudged her. "What haven't you done before?"

"Come twice." Cali bit her lip, stupidly feeling shy and exposed.

"Oh, that. So you weren't trying to egg me on, that was real?"

"Well, I *was* trying to egg you on . . ."

"And were you pleased with the results?"

Cali turned and saw him fighting what appeared to be smug satisfaction. She narrowed her eyes, and he let the big conceited smile run rampant over his face.

She rolled her eyes again, and he laughed, settling on his back. "You think a lot. Like, a lot, a lot. At a million miles an hour. You need distraction to get off yourself."

"So you tricked me into coming again?" Cali's eyebrows shot up to her hairline.

He shrugged.

Cali returned her gaze to the safety of the ceiling, confusion and alarm intertwined. Jory seemed to have figured out something no one else had, not even her. He just instinctively knew, like it was nothing. Like it was obvious.

Maybe she hadn't had awesome orgasms in the past because they'd been mostly with acquaintances that were easily shuffled aside. She recognized there was more to explore in her own sexuality, but she hadn't gone there because of her rules. Meaningless flings were good to keep grasping men at bay, but they didn't lend themselves to a

Love, Camera, Action

deeper understanding of what her body was capable of. Perhaps it was time to amend her rules in favor of inner growth. God knew she had enough steam to locomote an old-timey train. She couldn't let that fester inside. It wouldn't be healthy, for her blood pressure or her chi or whatever.

An idea began to formulate at the edges of her mind that she didn't want to look at directly. But she could see its hand raised.

Jory cleared his throat and put on a casual tone that sounded out of character. "You have a boyfriend, girlfriend, or theyfriend back home?"

She stole a glance at him. "Who I'm casually cheating on with you?"

"Or you could be polyamorous."

Cali had to laugh at that, rising up on her own elbow to imitate his earlier pose. "I don't have the time to have one relationship let alone *many*. You?"

"No. No one at the moment." He spoke with an airiness that ran counter to the tension creeping into his body. "So yeah, no girlfriend or boyfriend or theyfriend. Hardly have time for friends really, just colleagues."

They nodded together as if this was just the way of things and they wouldn't have it any different. A heavy silence fell, and Cali felt the inklings of loneliness. His loneliness. Just his, for sure. Not hers, since she wasn't lonely.

Cali smiled impishly to chase away the feeling. "Have you had other colleagues with benefits? Although, I think there are HR rules about that."

"Yes." Jory sucked a breath through his teeth. "Many rules. Many, many rules."

"I won't tell anyone if you won't." Her smile deepened.

Cali thought she caught a glimpse of hurt in his eyes, but it was quickly replaced with faux deliberation. "Oh, I don't know. I thought I'd tell Howard and Melanie the only way I can control your flaky behavior is through my aforementioned giant cock."

"Flaky!"

"That's what you took from that?" His astonishment propelled him back up on his elbow.

"They think I'm flaky?" Cali heard the outrage in her voice and tried to dial herself back.

"No one thinks you're flaky."

"Howard thinks I'm flaky."

"Howard can be an asshole."

"And here I thought you two were such good friends."

Jory tensed. Cali knew the shot was childish. He'd apologized for discussing scenes behind her back, and there was that heartfelt vow to "do better," but she was feeling inexplicably vulnerable. The sense of powerlessness pushed her up, and she swung her legs over the edge of the bed to face away from him.

After a moment, she felt his hand on her back. Just resting at the base. Not rubbing or stroking, just still and strong and warm.

"Howard and I aren't friends," he assured her. "And I shouldn't have let him treat you like that. Those guys are from a different generation, have different values about what's right. But that doesn't mean any of it is okay."

"It's not your responsibility to stick up for me," Cali said defensively.

"No, but I should have stuck up for my own values."

She peered over her shoulder at him, searching for duplicity but only finding pained, self-recrimination.

Love, Camera, Action

Cali could see Jory trying to navigate his way through a world still steeped in toxic masculinity. And that was heartening. Still, she was on her own. As usual. "I need to make this work with Howard. It's like he's around whenever something bad happens."

"That's his special gift. It's too bad he wasn't around today." Cali shot him an incredulous look, and he backpedaled. "Not for your sister's big number, for the scenes before. That setup with Thalia in the church? I thought I was going to cry."

"That's because you were half out of your mind with a hard-on," Cali needled.

"Which you supplied," he shot back.

Cali smiled teasingly at him. His eyes were warm and playful. Her body wanted to lean into him, follow its own agenda to rekindle that hard-on for another round. She reeled it in and stayed on the topic of the set. "That scene was beautiful. She looked like her heart was breaking, even as her skin sizzled from the holy water."

"The camera caught one of the water droplets sparkling in the light."

"Then I grabbed your ass."

Jory blew out a breath. "And almost knocked me into the camera."

"Yeah, but I didn't," Cali pointed out.

"No, you didn't."

Now that she thought about it, they had worked together almost as one being that afternoon. There were times when they hadn't even spoken, just pointed and nodded when either had an idea or an adjustment. Their attention had been on something else—tormenting each other in a different way.

"Maybe that's the second orgasm," Cali said to herself.

"Sorry?" Jory frowned.

She didn't answer right away, finally turning her attention to that idea with the raised hand. It was an idea that had great risks but potentially great rewards. A possibility that firmly went against her one-and-done rules. Those rules were in place to keep things simple, but this situation called for a bit more nuance. It held some definite emotional dangers. He could catch feelings for her. She wouldn't for him, of course. But from everything she'd observed of Jory Blair, he didn't seem the head-over-heels type. And there was the obvious threat to their jobs.

Still, she approached with caution. "Every scene was good. Every scene after lunch, anyway. Remember the boardroom? It had an air of coldness that bordered on creepy."

"Paolo looked like he was going to murder the assistant."

"Did you see that?" She smacked his arm. "Your angle made him look like an assassin."

Deep satisfaction crossed his features. "Yeah, that was good."

"I think it was good because we were focused on each other."

Jory scrutinized her like she'd just arrived from the solar system Xarthon.

She playfully poked his chest. "You have to admit your shooting got markedly better."

"There's that left-handed compliment again." He grabbed her hand and yanked. She yelped as he pulled her on top of his chest.

Love, Camera, Action

"Listen! The crew is a mess when we're fighting, the work is bland when we're not, but it sings when we're . . . doing something else."

"Something else?" He raised a teasing eyebrow.

"Yeah," she hedged.

"You're a big girl. You can say it. The work sings after I finger-fuck you into oblivion."

Cali's skin heated and she buried her face in his chest.

Jory laughed. "Oh my God, you're blushing. You're so easy. Who knew the sex scene guru is actually embarrassed to talk about sex herself."

"I'm not embarrassed to talk about it!" she squeaked. "I'm just remembering what happened and having a physical response to the intensity of the situation. Perfectly normal."

"Perfectly normal," Jory mocked.

"Don't forget your hard-on."

Jory grimaced. "That wasn't great. I think Alison has our number. Michael definitely does."

"He does?" Cali's excitement began to deflate. No one could know if this was going to work.

"Yeah, he was ready to clock me when he thought I had ill intentions."

Cali guffawed. "Really? That's sweet." She quieted, the plan gaining definition in her mind. Cali searched out the baby monitor and listened for her sister's gentle snoring. The reminder of Patsy was a warning of how things could go so wrong. She spoke quietly, as if to herself. "We'd have to be careful."

"Careful about what?"

She scrunched her nose. "Are you still confused about what I'm suggesting?"

He took a moment to answer. "You're saying we should keep hooking up?"

"For the work," she clarified.

"For the work."

She felt his breathing grow shallow in his chest, and his body still. She'd watched him cycle through an idea from afar a dozen times on set when regarding a frame or an angle. Being this close, feeling his body coil, seeing his gaze intensify, embracing the power coursing through him was a singular sensation. One she would never forget.

His voice was husky when he asked, "What about your rules?"

It took her a moment to understand what he was talking about, wanting instead to lower her mouth and drink him down. "This would be one-and-done adjacent. I've never indulged in crazy monkey sex with a hot guy—"

"You think I'm hot?" His lip quirked.

"—in aid of the show."

"A sacrifice for art."

"Yes." She was giddy with the idea, yet she told herself to slow down. One thing had to be made clear so they both knew what to expect. "Just until the end of the shoot. That's the done part."

She felt a small shock go through his body as he tensed again. Or was that her? She held her breath, waiting for his decision, suddenly so invested in the answer.

He kept quiet for a long time. Long enough she began to suspect he wanted to back out, and to suspect she'd been foolish for making the suggestion. Mortification seeped in, along with something like disappointment.

"Okay."

She reared back, disbelieving. "Okay?"

Love, Camera, Action

He nodded slowly, his decision made, firm and unbreakable. "Okay."

"Okay." A rush of relief shot through her, as though she'd just avoided a terrible accident. A near miss with something she didn't want to define. She imagined instead how exciting it would be to work with Jory the way she'd always wanted to, in tandem toward the greater goal of making an unforgettable show. While getting the fringe benefit of many large and intense orgasms that would be healthy for her blood pressure or her chi or whatever.

She could totally keep a wrap on this and figured Jory could too. He was so controlled, letting loose would be good for him. And she couldn't wait to find ways to break through all that discipline just to see what would happen.

Jory raised a finger between them. "But once the shoot is over, so are we."

"Absolutely."

"And we keep it out of work. I don't want a PA stumbling in and ratting us out. I can't risk my reputation."

"Definitely, we'll keep it just at work." Cali stopped herself and shook her head. "I mean, after work. *After* work."

Jory nodded.

Cali nodded.

Then Jory stopped nodding. "And maybe at lunch."

CHAPTER SEVENTEEN

They did not keep it out of work. They didn't even keep it to lunch. They were all over the studio like a couple of teenagers. Even now Jory was running through possibilities of where they could go while he simultaneously assessed how much time they had between setups. Maybe thirty minutes?

Jory couldn't believe he was doing this. It was incredibly unprofessional and unbelievably dangerous and he just couldn't help himself. Apparently, neither could she. He felt a hysterical giggle burble up as he dragged a hand down his face to quell the emotion. They'd revisited some favorites—kissing behind the flats and fondling in the club bathroom. They'd discovered some new hideouts. Cali gave him a blow job behind Rafe's bedset, Jory went down on her in Anna's demon nest, and they fucked on the control panel of the CIA surveillance truck. They were always careful to be silent and return to the shoot from different directions.

Then they would meet up again after work and have the loudest, filthiest sex they could manage, as though all the

Love, Camera, Action

furtive, quiet fumbling during the day had only ramped up their interest in each other until it exploded behind Jory's condo's thick concrete walls.

Meanwhile, he was finding ways to make her life easier, so she could focus on the work. Lip biting was a clear indication her blood sugar was dropping, so he'd send over a PA with a selection of treats, both sweet and salty. Usually three were chosen, one to eat right away and two to put in her pockets for later. When she turned to see him watching her, she'd roll her eyes and shyly blush.

He set up a field trip for Patsy at the rare book library at Emory. MARBL leaned more toward African American history, but he thought it might be a welcome distraction from the Classics. When Cali asked him about it, he just shrugged and said he knew a guy. Which he did. The dean, to be specific, but he didn't tell her that.

The coup d'état came after he'd ripped her T-shirt off in the privacy of his condo, and then, when they lay spent on his bed, he casually tossed her a vintage Yosemite replacement T-shirt in all its burnt-orange glory. She squealed, "No way!" immediately modeling it while she straddled him.

Sometimes he thought the extra attention might give her the wrong idea, but it was no different from the support he gave when he coached Alison through a shot, or the letter of recommendation he gave Dan's daughter. He liked to help. It did not mean he was opening up the door to anything bigger. He would do it for anyone.

He couldn't deny that Cali's intuition had been right: their distracted collaboration was making onscreen magic. He'd never been so fluid with his creativity, so sure about what to do. The ideas and adjustments and insights flowed through them in every scene.

And it wasn't just them; the whole crew was inspired, working harder than ever before. They all made each scene, each shot, each frame the best it could be, the excitement palpable. Even Paolo and Thalia were on better terms and could be seen sharing a joke from time to time, much to their confusion.

Still, a sense of unease grew. He'd agreed to her deadline so they could make a firm break at the end of the shoot. What if she got more attached than she claimed? Every night she would return to her condo with a brisk formality, dragging herself out of bed once their breath slowed, never hinting at the possibility of staying over. Sometimes he would catch himself fantasizing what that would be like: falling asleep entangled in each other, blearily waking up to pull themselves together to get to set, discussing the day on the way over. That way lay destruction, and he was glad they both had their heads on straight. Even if it vaguely hurt every time she left.

It was just the sex fog talking. The fog that had made him forget about the test he'd rescheduled until he got a reminder call this morning. If he got his test today, he most likely wouldn't get the results until after she was gone. They could have this two-week vacation, and then he would face his uncertain future alone, the way it should be.

He shook himself to return to the task at hand. Where could they go? The diner was too open. The ice-cream parlor had a soda fountain counter that might work as a barrier, but it backed onto the set they were in next—so too close. What about the hell set? There were some stalagmites they could hide behind or hold onto, plus it bordered the south wall of the studio, so noise wouldn't be as big a worry. Jory

Love, Camera, Action

turned with focused determination to scout their location, and collided with Howard.

"Whoa there, Blair! You almost ran me over. You got a hot date or something?"

Jory took a minute to banish the irritation from his voice. "Howard. Yeah, I was just about to go check on whether my fish-eye lens was appropriate for the next setup. Excuse me."

Howard held out his hands. "Hold up, hold up. I just need a minute of your time. You can spare a second for your showrunner, can't you?"

"Sure. Of course. Yes. Of course." Jory began the calculations required to bail on this conversation.

"I've been watching the footage, and I'm very impressed." Howard had dropped his voice. "*Very* impressed."

"Oh, great. Thanks, Howard."

"I mean, you're really taking this episode to the next level. I'd heard about the Blair magic, but this is something else."

Jory bristled at the assumption. "Well, Cali has been incredible to work with."

Howard snorted. "That's gracious of you. The generous collaborator to the end."

Jory got the impression Howard thought this new energy was all him. He wanted Cali's efforts to be recognized, but if he was too over the top with his praise, would it blow their cover? He was so sick of trying to manage this guy. "No, really. She's terrific. We're all working very well with her."

"And that's what makes you such a great DP. You can make anything work." Howard slapped Jory's shoulder.

"Listen. I have something percolating for you that could go at any moment. I can't say anything yet, but if it happens, it's going to move fast, so keep your wits about you."

Jory's phone buzzed in his back pocket. He almost dropped it while scrambling to pull it out. "That's great, Howard. Let's talk. Sorry, I've got to take this." Jory lifted his phone to his ear and was already on the move. "Hello?"

"Hi, Jor. Did I catch you at a bad time? I didn't think you'd answer."

Relief flooded him at the sound of his father's calm, warm voice. "I'm surprised you found the time to call during your busy wedding-planning schedule," Jory teased.

Jory was happy his father had found Astrid. He'd gone through so much with Jory's mom and then raising Jory on his own. He knew his father had been lonely despite assuring Jory he was fine. Then he met Astrid and never looked back. He deserved to be with someone healthy, someone who had a chance of living as long as he did. Jory knew rationally that anyone could die at any moment, but he knew when the odds were stacked against a person.

Like the odds were stacked against him.

"I gotta say, I'm loving it. She's really pulling out the bells and whistles. It's turning into a three-day event."

"Not like Mom."

"God, no. You're mother liked things quiet, which was fine by me. I liked things with her."

His father would know what to do with Howard and this job. But as Jory walked to the neighboring set, where he could have some quiet in the CEO office where he and Cali had had their first argument, a completely different question came out.

Love, Camera, Action

"Listen, Dad, how did you know that you wanted to be with Mom?"

"Uh . . . well," he stammered. "That's out of the blue. Why do you ask?"

"I've just been thinking about her lately." Jory stopped at the desk, staring out the fake windows, where a brick wall now stood, the faux backdrop of Central Park stripped away. "About you and her before she got sick."

Jory's dad cleared his throat. "Oh. Well. It wasn't some lightning bolt or anything. We started out in the standard way, talking and dating and that sort of thing. And then we were just . . . a part of each other's lives." His father took a moment, sifting through his memory. "It's strange, now that I think back on it. There was no real decision made. It just became obvious we would continue on together. Even when I proposed, it felt like a mutual decision. We didn't think about being together, we just . . . were together, as easy and as integral as breathing."

Jory was struck by the simplicity of that. No grand gesture, no hurdle to overcome. He wondered why he hadn't asked before. When he was younger, he'd ask his dad what kind of pets she'd had as a girl, where she'd taught his dad how to ski, what their first wedding had been like. But not the beginning. "So Mom was all in?"

"We both were." His dad paused. "But Astrid was like a bolt out of the sky. Bam! I had no choice but to fall in love. She was all in too." He chuckled. "Is this coming from somewhere? Have you met someone?"

Through the opening of the set, Jory could see Dan talking on the phone, laughing, loud and hearty. Jory knew he was talking to his wife, and clearly she'd just said something outrageous because Dan's eyes were watering. Jory's throat started to close as emotion welled up. "No, no. I guess I'm just worried."

"About the test?"

"Yeah."

"Whatever happens, we'll deal with it."

Jory never doubted his father would be there for him and yet wished that wouldn't be the case. If not for Jory's grandmother, his father would've bankrupted them with their spontaneous vacations in his mom's last year, along with her medical bills. His father had stayed by his mother's side for months while she quietly slipped away. Jory didn't want that for his father again.

"It was so hard, Dad." Jory's voice caught.

"It was. It was." His father sighed through the phone. "I wish I'd kept some of that away from you. You didn't deserve that as a young boy."

"It's okay."

"I'm not sure it was."

Jory went quiet while the silence on the other end stretched, both men deep in the past.

His father cleared a throat full of memories. "I'm not sure if this is the right time to ask, but have you gone for your test yet?"

"I'm going today. We finish early."

"Good. Good. Thanks, son." His father exhaled in what sounded like relief.

"I don't want to worry you."

"I'll worry if I want."

Jory huffed out a laugh.

They said their goodbyes, and Jory tossed the phone on the desk with a clatter. He stared at the brick wall, wondering if he should bash his head against it.

Love, Camera, Action

Suddenly, arms snaked around his belly, making him jump.

"Easy, boy." Cali whispered in his ear as hands went to his belt. "I have some ideas about you and this desk, and we only have fifteen."

Her thumbs slid below his waistband, scraping his sensitive skin and firing his body up, but his heart wouldn't let him go there. He stilled her busy fingers and turned in the circle of her arms. "I need a minute."

Cali rested her limbs in a low-slung hug across his hips. "You okay?"

Jory relaxed in the hold, draping his arms over hers and linking his hands behind her back. He took a moment to soak in the comfort, how right she felt, even as he acknowledged how fragile this time was. "Yeah, yeah. Just talking to my dad."

Cali's body tensed. "Oh. Parents. Yeah. Always tricky." She gave him a squeeze and began to draw away, when her brow furrowed. He felt something slide out of his back pocket that she brought up between them. The small yellow film cartridge. "What's this?"

"Oh right. I forgot about that." The last of his energy seeped out of his body. He injected a rueful playfulness he didn't feel. "These games are making me forget everything." Like who he was.

She leaned back so she could investigate the film more closely, turning it over in her hands. She was still close enough to smell, and he breathed her in quietly so she wouldn't notice. "You shooting something on Super 8?"

Jory flushed, like he'd just been caught in an obsession with scrapbooking. He reached to take it back. "It's just a thing I'm working on."

She kept the cartridge away, ignoring his grasping hand. "It's old. Like, decades."

"I found it in a camera I got at a pawnshop."

"You collect cameras?"

"I collect film."

"Like, found film?" Her eyes finally met his, wide with surprise.

Jory nodded warily. "I collect lost footage, home movies that have been forgotten or thrown out." He shrugged to feign his indifference. "I'm not sure what I'm going to do with them all yet. I keep waiting for inspiration to strike."

"Well, surprise, surprise. A little side project, eh?" She regarded him with open curiosity. He felt exposed, but now he didn't care. He wanted her to know. "Rescuing moments of people's lives from oblivion. You're like a superhero."

Jory had never thought of it that way, but her reverence lit up the untouched safety centers in his brain. What would happen if he opened up to her a little more about his fears? What if he allowed himself to hope, maybe just a little?

It was impossible. She had enough on her plate with her messed-up family.

Cali waved the cartridge. "What's on this one?"

He focused back on the film. "Not sure. I have to send it to a processing lab in LA or New York. It's too old for them to do it here."

"You don't need to send it away. I can develop it for you tonight, if you want."

Jory started. "You can?"

"Sure. It won't look as pristine as a lab's, but maybe that's not what you're looking for."

Love, Camera, Action

It wasn't what he was looking for. He was looking for real and messy and chaotic. And now he'd found it, he was determined to let it slip away.

"I'll get the stuff," she continued, "and we'll do it after work."

"Um, well, tonight's a bit complicated. I have this medical test after work. Although I can skip it. Why don't I skip it?"

He moved to pull her back, but she stepped away and crossed her arms. A definite matron vibe flowed over her. "Should you skip it?"

"Yeah, it's fine." Jory waved her worry away.

"What's it for?" Her worry wasn't going anywhere.

"Are you always so forward in your demand for medical information?" he deflected.

"I know when people are trying to pass something off as nothing when it's actually something, and something that needs to be dealt with now rather than letting it fester until it becomes something huge."

"Uh . . . give me a second to figure that one out," he teased. But he was stalling. Could he tell her? Would his admission bring her closer or push her away? He had vowed to make things easier for her, not add to her already full buffet of responsibilities. But it didn't seem like she was going to let him get away with dismissing it, or her. "First of all, it's not a big deal—just a precautionary thing. I have to get an endoscopy to make sure a growth that showed up on an earlier scan is benign."

"Geez. That's not stressful at all," she quipped.

He chuffed out a laugh at her sarcasm. "Yeah, well, last year my dad asked me to get tested for this thing called Lynch syndrome." He raced through the details to get it over with. "My mom died from stomach cancer and sometimes it's hereditary. So when I got tested, it turns out I have the syndrome."

"Go on," she nudged.

He looked past her shoulder. "It doesn't mean I have cancer or will get cancer, just that the chances are higher. So when they scanned me, they found a growth, and they just want to make sure it's nothing to worry about."

She took a moment before she spoke, delivering her words in gentle but matter-of-fact tones, her lips inches away. "I had this friend whose mom didn't get this growth in her breast checked out for years because she was scared of doctors, even though her boob had grown the size of a watermelon. Like huge. And purple. My friend forced her to go to the hospital, and she had stage-four breast cancer."

Jory leaned back in shock. "Why would you tell me that story?"

She pulled him toward her again. "Because she still beat it. So, good-news story. And you'll get yours looked at before it ever becomes a problem, even though it's probably nothing. The moral is, it's better to know." Tenderness filled her features. She was always joking or sassy or fiery. This was new, and he wanted to bathe in it. She bridged the small space between them to softly kiss his lips. "I'll take you so you don't chicken out."

"I'm not a chicken," he argued while he let her kiss him.

"Then I'll drive you home because you'll be doped up, yes?"

He nodded reluctantly and she brushed his lips with her own. "And then we'll process the film. Easy peasy."

Cali deepened the kiss, and he grunted grumpily as he joined in. The kiss stayed sweet and slow, with none of the

Love, Camera, Action

frenetic energy they usually shared. The type of kiss normally earned from years of practice. He felt a pain in his chest, which he reasoned was from the film cartridge squashed between them rather than something deeper he didn't want to admit to. He hoped the tremor in his lips would be mistaken for nervousness about the test and not the real fear—the inevitability of losing her.

CHAPTER EIGHTEEN

"The fish tank is a nice touch," Cali mused. "We should take a pic for Set Dec for our doctor's waiting room."

"The burbling would infuriate Sound," Jory muttered.

"Right, of course. Crap."

Cali took in the posh clinic and couldn't shake the feeling they were still at the studio. Her experiences with doctor's offices were from the national health-care school of interior design: gray, utilitarian, and Brutalist. Doctor's offices had occupied no small portion of Cali's childhood. Whether it was renewing her mom's prescriptions or finding a different doctor in order to double them, or taking Patsy to the pediatrician when their mom wasn't around. She didn't remember ever going for herself, but did remember what it felt like to wait in those purgatorial spaces while bracing for news.

This place didn't feel like a doctor's office at all. It had hardwood floors softened with bespoke rugs and Regency side tables snuggled between wingback chairs, all enveloped

Love, Camera, Action

by calming classical music and the smell of lavender. "Why is this office so fancy?"

Jory glanced up from his intake form. "Is it?"

Cali took in his sheltered innocence and sighed. He was *so* from money. "I come from the land of socialized medicine. We don't have exotic fish tanks in our doctor's offices. And I've seen my fair share of doctor's offices."

Jory buried his face in his intake form. "Nice furniture doesn't mean they can help you."

"I think here, the fancier the office, the better the care."

"When you're dying, you're dying."

Cali went quiet and took a quick assessment of Jory's state of mind. She was a master at judging a person's mood when they were teetering at the edge of crisis, and Jory showed all the signs: a bleak quality in his voice, fingers gripping the pen until his knuckles turned white, his other hand about to snap the clipboard in two. He finished the form with an agitated scribble and shot out of his chair to dump it on the desk, then jammed his hands in his pockets and sat back down.

Jory clearly had bad memories of doctor's offices too, but he wasn't about to 'fess up about it. Cali's quick triage told her she had better keep his mind off things, or he would bolt.

She stood up and walked calmly to the complimentary green tea service. She'd read in a book once that the simple act of holding a cup of tea gave people suffering from trauma a sense of calm they couldn't get from medication. Something about keeping the hot liquid balanced on the delicate saucer. The book was set in early 1900s Halifax, when they had actual china, but this clinic's chichi recycled paper cups with a bamboo print would have to do.

She prepared two cups and brought them over, offering him one.

"Oh, no thanks."

"I'm not going back over there. It's too far."

"You have it."

"I have my own. Take the tea."

He rolled his eyes and took the cup as she sat back down. He wrapped two hands around it like it was a pole tethering him from being blown away in a tornado. But after a moment of staring into its golden-green depths, he began to calm.

She should be the one panicking. Here she was, in another doctor's office, supporting someone—who wasn't a family member—through possible disaster. For some reason however, this felt less loaded. Maybe it was because Jory was so put together the rest of the time that watching him be vulnerable was a relief. Plus, she couldn't leave him. She knew what it meant to face uncertain news alone.

And when facing uncertain news, it was always best to distract. "Sometimes when you're dying, you're dying. But in my experience, dying can be a slippery thing—literally."

Jory gave her the side-eye. "What does that even mean?"

Cali traced her finger around the cup's rim. "One Christmas Eve I had to get my mom to the hospital pretty fast."

"On Christmas Eve? Why?" Jory swiveled as much as the wingback chair would allow.

She squinted at the ceiling to recall the spark of that night's circumstances. "Oh, she'd had a bad night with her boyfriend Rick and decided to teach him a lesson by swallowing a bunch of pills."

Jory took a deep inhale. "You say that like it's no big deal."

Love, Camera, Action

"Well, there was a certain"—Cali tipped her head to the side—"I wouldn't say regularity to it, but let's just say I had plans in place."

"Why are all your stories so flippantly dark?"

"It's the northern sensibility, but never mind about that." She dismissed him with a wave. "That's not part of the story." She put her tea down and turned in her own wingback chair, scooching it closer to his, the scraping sound eliciting a disapproving glower from the carefully groomed receptionist. Cali swung a leg over the arm and let it rest on Jory's hard thigh. She was never prepared for the jolt that came when touching him, and she shivered as the charge washed over her skin. She knew she was being inappropriate, but the contact would ground him. She was rewarded by the relaxing of his shoulders as he shook his head over her low-class antics in this high-class doctor's office. "This night, my usual backups weren't around because, well, it was Christmas Eve, and it was snowing like crazy, so it would take forever for someone to come, so Patsy and I got her into the car and I drove."

Jory interrupted with what he probably assumed was a logical question. "Why didn't you call an ambulance?"

"Didn't want to get into child services paperwork." Cali felt the echoes of dread in remembering how afraid she was. That she would lose Patsy to foster care along with the delicate security Cali had built at home. She wiped the cloud from her memory.

"Child services? But you drove."

"I was fourteen, and Patsy was ten. We wanted to avoid contact with authority as much as possible. Stop distracting me."

This was usually the point in the story where the other person said something like, "You were fourteen?" or "Weren't you scared?" or "How did you do it?" Jory stayed silent, listening without judgment, patiently waiting for the tale to unfold. He was hard to hook, but when he was in, the story was the most important thing in the world to him. His focus was on her now, not the test, and she'd have to keep him here.

"I'd been watching my mom drive for a while, cataloguing how it all worked and in what sequence to prep for this type of eventuality. Plus, my mom had just bought a 1980 Camaro, which was totally stupid considering our money situation, but a super-cool car, and I was itching to drive it. Buuuuuut watching someone drive and actually driving are two different things."

"You don't say," he said dryly.

"Right? Driving in a snowstorm is next level, and driving a *Camaro* in a snowstorm is approaching boss." Jory's brow furrowed, so she explained: "The rear-wheel drive makes it easy to fishtail, as well as to get stuck in snow. It was not a smart purchase."

She took his curled free hand, opened it, and began tracing his fingers. She marveled over their contours, the rough spots, the softness of the skin in between, the strength that lay dormant as the tension seeped out of them. She lowered her voice to an intimate murmur, setting the scene. "It was actually a really beautiful night. Perfect white-Christmas snow, heavy and soft. The kind that mutes everything, making the world so, so quiet. But it's also a little wet, which means it's hard to drive through, and as it gets colder, it lays a bed of ice underneath you can't necessarily see. But, you know, *needs must* and all that."

Cali remembered Patsy in the rearview mirror, wide-eyed and scared, running her hands through their mom's hair, telling her it was going to be okay. Cali had checked to

Love, Camera, Action

make sure their mom was lying on her side so she wouldn't choke on anything coming up, but Patsy had already maneuvered her into position, despite how small she herself was.

"So there I was, hands gripped on the steering wheel, back straight"—Cali sat forward in her chair to demonstrate, bringing her hands up to an imaginary wheel but keeping her leg on his to maintain their connection—"barely moving, windshield wipers on high, and driving about thirty an hour."

"That fast?" Jory exclaimed.

"Oh, thirty *kilometers*, I mean. So, eighteen miles? Ish? The snow plows hadn't gone through our neighborhood yet, and some woman was out cross-country skiing down the sidewalk. She was going faster than we were."

Jory's jaw dropped. "Someone was skiing down the sidewalk? Is that common?"

Cali shrugged. "People do it, but it's not a usual mode of transportation, no. Anyway, Patsy was starting to freak out in the back, so I turned on the radio so she could sing. As you know, she loves to sing."

"What was the song?"

Cali stopped at that, fondness creeping into her chest. No one had asked that before, and to Cali, it was an important detail. "'Love Shack.'"

"Nice." He nodded with appreciation. An image of Jory singing along to the classic when he was alone in his car filled her mind. She tried not to smile at how cute he was.

"Yeah, we were really belting it out. And then I could see the hospital and felt this rush of accomplishment that I'd done it and started singing even louder. But the hospital was up on this hill"—Cali demonstrated the steep angle with her hand—"and when we stopped at the light, we started sliding back. Patsy was shouting my name, and I could feel I was losing control of the car, and the radio was blaring, and I jammed on the gas and the wheels spun and spun, and we slid back farther and farther."

Cali was fully on the edge of her chair now, arms waving in description, features mimicking her panic. Jory's mouth gaped, his attention only on her. "And I was trying to remember what to do, when the wheels caught on something and shot us forward, through the red light." Cali slapped her hands to show their forward thrust. "The car swerved with the momentum, and my sister was screaming, and I was screaming at her to shut up, and Mom was groaning, and the car started spinning, and I literally let go of the wheel and did this." Cali slapped her hands over her eyes.

"Oh my God."

"And we whirled and screamed and whirled and screamed, and then . . . we stopped." Cali went quiet, keeping her hands over her face for dramatic effect. "And I looked out"—Cali peeked through her fingers—"and we'd landed right into a parking spot nearest the ER."

Jory snorted out a laugh of disbelief. "Fools and drunks."

"Sorry?"

"My dad always says, 'God protects fools and drunks.'"

"Well, he was protecting both that night. It was the best parking job I've ever executed."

Jory laughed louder and Cali smiled at the sight, thinking his joy was something she could watch for a long time. "So just remember, when I drive you home, you're going with a woman who's got mad skills."

He grinned. "Oh, I know you've got mad skills."

Love, Camera, Action

Cali pursed her lips and leaned back, feeling shy and proud at the same time.

He coughed out the last laugh and settled. "Was she okay?"

"Who?"

"Your mom."

"Oh, right." Cali tried to remember where she was in the story. "Well, all the spinning made her puke. On my sister, which Patsy obviously wasn't happy about, but all the pills came up, so we ended up not having to go in. I drove us back home and threw them both in the bathtub."

Jory went quiet. The silence stretched as she watched him turn the story over in his mind. Cali glanced away, self-conscious, thinking about that night. How she'd since turned the incident into a cocktail-party story to amuse people over her colorful upbringing. But at the time, she'd been petrified. "I don't usually tell that part of the story." Then, quickly switching gears, "Oh, they have candy," she exclaimed.

Cali stood up and walked to the reception desk counter, ignoring the receptionist's cool regard, and grabbed the bowl. She offered it to Jory, who started to say something and then changed his mind, instead taking a candied ginger. She grabbed one before returning the bowl and sitting back down. She watched him roll the candy in his mouth while she crunched hers.

"How is your sister?" he asked softly.

"She's alright. This particular relationship meltdown has hit her hard. She's been quiet and sober, which is odd."

They both stared at his hands, which were loosely linked. "What does your sister think you're doing when you're not there? You know, when we're . . ."

"She knows we're hooking up."

Jory's shoulders stiffened. "Does she wonder if you'll break your rule to keep things casual?"

"No. She knows how stubborn I am. I've spent too many years cleaning up my mom and sister after their relationships fall apart. They go all in." She turned to Jory in time to see him flinch. "And afterward, there's nothing left."

"Mr. Blair?" A nurse appeared in the doorway, and Jory looked up at her in surprise, as though just remembering where he was and why.

Cali felt a sense of accomplishment at having distracted him for so long. She'd distract him again with something more physical later. For now she gave him an easy smile of support. "Get in there, tiger. You'll do great. And when you come back, I'll have another candy waiting."

Jory stayed in place for a moment and then leaned over and whispered in her ear, "Thank you." He squeezed her hand and straightened to follow the nurse inside.

Cali felt strangely flustered. She'd never been thanked for the circus tricks she pulled to get someone through a hard time. Mostly they went unnoticed, but Jory somehow saw them and was grateful. The smile drifted from Cali's face as she sat back to wait, the familiar sense of dread washing over her. How her life might change with the outcome of this visit, not only in regard to Jory's health but also in what they were starting to mean to each other. She wondered if maybe she shouldn't have come with Jory. Maybe she should have just dropped him off at the office and waited outside in the car to make sure he didn't skip out. But the thought of leaving him alone was inconceivable.

Love, Camera, Action

And as she settled into the bougie chairs to wait, the thought of not leaving him alone, in general, wasn't *horrible*. Maybe it wasn't so much a feeling of dread this time over the outcome of the doctor's visit, but the possibility of not seeing him once her job was done. She rolled it around in her mind, in her body, searching for the impulse to flee or destroy, and instead found the strangest hope that an actual relationship wasn't impossible. It didn't have to be fraught with heartache. She could want more.

She could be safe.

An hour later, an orderly wheeled a doped-up Jory out the front door of the clinic, where Cali collected the keys to the Jeep from the valet. Nope, this was definitely not socialized medicine. While Cali climbed in, the orderly helped a disgruntled Jory, who was ineffectually fighting him every step, into the car.

Once firmly buckled in, Cali put the car in gear—a stick no less, how manly—and drove them to their condos. She glanced over at Jory, whose head was listing to the side, his eyes trying to focus in between battles for consciousness.

"You okay there, sugar?" she asked. She couldn't help but smile. It was quite a sight to see Jory incapacitated.

He turned his eyes to her and heaved out a heavy sigh. "You're so pretty. You look so good driving this car. You could drive me in a snowstorm anytime."

"I'll put that on my résumé. *Jory Blair says Cali Daniels can drive him in a snowstorm anytime.*"

He huffed out a laugh, and Cali returned her focus to the road. "You're always doing that," he mumbled.

"Doing what?" She changed lanes to get away from a piece of tire in the road. "Why are there always shredded bits of tire on the shoulders of Atlanta highways? Do cars just spontaneously lose chunks of rubber as they drive along?"

"You're always deflecting compliments. And you take care of everybody. Who takes care of *you*?"

Cali shot a look at him. He looked deep in thought but was probably just drowsy from the sedative. "Maybe if you had more snowstorms in Southern California, you'd have to look after people too," she joked.

"No snowstorms. Storms on the ocean, though. Colossal gales across a vast abyss." His lids drifted closed. "Your eyes are like the ocean when it storms, churning green and brown."

"Sounds gross."

"No. No. It's wild, majestic, terrifying, and beautiful. I've imagined your eyes changing color as you watch the shifting ocean."

"From what I hear the ocean's mostly blue."

Jory's eyes startled open. "What? You've never seen the ocean?"

"Nope."

Jory lifted a hand to her hair, where he pet her clumsily. "That's the saddest thing I've ever heard."

"I don't know if it's the *saddest* thing."

"You'll come to my beach house." Cali glanced over, and he was staring at her intently, resolve in his eyes. "I want you to see. The storms, the colors."

Cali turned back to the road.

"It's my favorite place in the world," he slurred. "I've thought about you so many times there, your hair whipping in the wind, you laughing at the force of it."

Cali wondered what it would be like to go to Jory's beach house and stare at the ocean. To take something for herself,

Love, Camera, Action

to be with someone who didn't want anything from her, who actually brought ease and a healthy kind of excitement to her life. Someone who brought her inspiration and awe.

"I'd take you there now if I didn't . . . if I wasn't . . ."

Cali waited for him to finish his sentence but when she looked back over at him, he was asleep.

CHAPTER NINETEEN

Jory watched Cali mix together a concoction of instant coffee, vitamin C powder, and something called "washing soda" in a plastic bottle, while he passed his fingers over the film cartridge in a light-tight bag. The bag was to make sure he could transfer the fragile film to a Paterson tank without fear of overexposing it and losing the images forever. Once in the Paterson tank—a long conical holder with a screw lid and a tube down the middle—the unprocessed film would be bathed in the chemicals necessary to reveal the images.

It was a delicate process. One steeped in nostalgia. Not only because the last time he had transferred film by touch was in college, or that no one used film anymore, instead shooting everything on digital; the metaphoric import of transferring memories from the precarious medium of unexposed film to something hardier always humbled him.

With his hands buried deep in the bag, he used only his sense of touch to guide him. He was struck by the

Love, Camera, Action

just-remembered tactile connection to the material he cast his images on, like a blacksmith putting his brute strength aside in order to fashion a silver clasp for a delicate necklace. As he carefully coaxed the film from its box to transplant it to the tank, Jory stole glances at Cali, who was focused on her brew with witchlike intent.

Her hair was up in a thoughtless ponytail, and her cheek had a smudge of white washing soda on it. He felt like he was back in his college dorm after scoring with one of the girls in the poli sci department, prepping a homemade bong while arguing about the state of feminism.

Cali poured water into the mixture that would reveal the hidden images he'd foraged, going through this process for his benefit. Working quietly together in the softness of night gave him a strange sense of remembrance, as though they had done it for years. Jory pictured coming home to her at the end of the day, or her to him, or meeting up together. Making some easy pasta dish that she would coo over, since it was clear she wouldn't be cooking. Then, after debating over a movie, instead of having fast, hungry sex, taking their time to truly get lost in each other.

Listening to her talk about her mom and sister's relationships, unknowingly using his father's phrase "all in" had been a kick to the gut. Whereas his father described the act of loving a person as one of commitment and joy, Cali saw it as requiring a sacrifice of self, a vulnerability that couldn't be borne. No wonder she had negative views about romantic love. She'd had no positive examples of what love could be, what it could build. Instead, she'd only witnessed what it could tear down, what it could take.

She peered over at him. "This mixture gives the film a kind of a gold tinge—are you good with that?"

"Sure. Where did you learn how to do this?"

Cali screwed the cap on the bottle, to shake the ingredients together. "When I started out, I shot as much film as I could get my hands on—expired film, leftover ends from other productions—and I'd rope in whoever I could to shoot whatever project I was working on. When I couldn't find anyone, I'd do it."

Jory raised a skeptical eyebrow. "You can shoot?"

Cali smiled ruefully. "Not like you, but I can set up a frame." She held the bubbling mixture up to her eyes to gauge its progress. "I mostly shot digital because it was cheaper, but I wanted to learn how to work with film. I could never afford a processing lab, so I figured out how to do it myself."

Jory couldn't imagine what Cali had struggled through to learn her craft. Directing a film was an expensive endeavor that involved a lot of people. If you had to do it yourself, it was murder—the scrounging, the pulling of favors, the trial and error. DIY was an exhausting way to learn but often taught you lessons you never got in school. It was also a far cry from the resources he'd had at his top-notch institutions, where he'd learned the game of politics just as much as technical insight.

Jory finished transferring the film, unzipped the bag, and handed the tank to Cali. "Why didn't you go to school?"

Cali placed the tank on the counter and slowly poured the mixture through the opening at the top. Her answer was as measured as her pour. "I was going to. Had been accepted to my school of choice, picked all my classes, sourced all my books. I had a little education fund my dad set up for me before he left. It wasn't much. Enough to get me through the first year, but when it came time to pay for everything, I found out my mom was behind in the mortgage payments. Like, way behind. I paid the mortgage instead."

Jory choked. "Why?"

Cali shrugged, like it was ancient history. Like she hadn't given away her future for a mother who couldn't look after her. "It was either pay for that or find an apartment for her and Patsy, who was thirteen at the time, and it ended up being the same amount of money. So I paid the mortgage."

She finished pouring in the chemicals and screwed the lid on the tank. She held it up and slowly upended it. The liquid washed over the film, like water softly flowing over rocks, while awareness of Cali flowed over Jory. She'd had so little support, so little care, yet she'd risen above the life that had been laid out for her, to break into a business, into an art form, that had little interest in those without money or connections. He marveled at her tenacity and was furious no one had helped.

"What happened to the money for the mortgage payments?"

"Uh . . . It might have been Rick, the boyfriend who was the reason she took the pills. He came back after that incident, weaseling his way in to pitch some scheme about a fish finder for crabs." Cali put on a serious voice. "You see, a fish finder works by radar bouncing off the fish's bladder, but there's nothing to bounce off for crabs because they don't have bladders. Which seems weird because wouldn't the radar bounce off its shell? Apparently not, and Rick was on the ground floor of something that could find crab. It was going to be big." Cali widened her eyes in mock reverence before returning her focus to the tank, upending it again and putting her ear to the side to listen if the liquid was dispersing properly. "He kind of disappeared after that, probably along with her money."

Jory couldn't imagine the betrayal Cali must have felt. To have spent the time pouring over course catalogs, dreaming of the people she'd meet and collaborate with, imagining what exciting things she'd learn. To have all that possibility ripped away the moment before it came to fruition must have been heartbreaking.

Cali sighed. "So, 'cause of that, along with having to work to keep everyone's wheels turning, school was put on the back burner long enough for me to forget about it. What time is it?"

Jory blinked at the sudden switch of subject. He glanced at the microwave clock. "Eleven fifteen."

Cali nodded and kept up the slow end-over-end wash of the film in the tank, the soothing sound filling up the chasm between them. Then she wiped her forehead with her forearm on an upward sweep. "When did you start shooting? I'm sure it was before going to UCLA and AFI."

Jory raised an accusing eyebrow. "You IMDb'ing me or something?"

"Among other cyberstalkery things."

"Really?" Knowing Cali was a fan gave him a ping of boyish satisfaction.

"I probably shouldn't tell you this." She narrowed her eyes. "Lest your ego climb to even greater heights, but I've always had a huge crush on your work."

"Until you found out what an asshole I was?"

Cali smiled teasingly. She checked the clock again and then dumped the mixture from the tank into the sink. She presented her profile, topped by the loose ponytail, which slouched forward giving her the softness of a Victorian cameo.

Love, Camera, Action

She really was beautiful in a completely unconscious way. As though she never gave her looks a second thought, ignoring them because there were other more important things to worry about. Her skin glowed with an olive undertone, her neck long and graceful that led to shoulders that carried so much emotional weight. Her arms were strong and toned without being sculpted and, at the moment, framed her perfect breasts: large, full, and round. The breasts of a fertility goddess, generous and inviting.

His mind skittered to the future and how it balanced on a phone call that would arrive after she'd gone. Suddenly he felt Cali's grounding hand on his arm. When he tipped his head to hers, her features were full of concern, but her voice was all command. "Don't worry about the test. It's out in the ether now. Enjoy this moment with me."

He stared at her, his lungs filling as he inhaled a breath and slowly let it out. She raised a hand to his cheek with such tenderness, he trembled, and then she nudged him. "Tell me how you started shooting."

He blinked the tremors away. "Right. Uh, well, I was always stealing my mom's point-and-shoot to take pictures of bugs and sunsets and artfully arranged garbage. She got mad at me because there was never any film left in it for her, so she got me a camcorder. I filmed people mostly after that."

"How old were you?" Cali's focus was back on the tank as she turned on the tap and rinsed the film inside.

"Twelve."

Cali poured the stop bath into the tank. "What was the first thing you recorded with your camcorder?"

"My parents' wedding." Cali's brows shot up in surprise. Jory clarified. "Well, their vow renewal ceremony."

"Oh. What did you shoot?"

"It was on the beach. So . . ." He thought back. "Bare feet on sand, my grandmother's hat blown into the water. My parents, backlit by the sunset."

"Sounds beautiful." She spoke as if "Idyllic Wedding" was a mythical place that only existed for others. "How old were they? They seem a bit young for a renewal ceremony."

Jory shifted his gaze away from her and turned his back to the sink to lean against it. "Well, my mom had just been diagnosed with stomach cancer, so they wanted a pick-me-up I guess." Jory mused on how the memory invaded his thoughts at the oddest moments, while setting up a lens, on a location scout, during an actor's close-up. How it had informed every choice he'd made since. "She died eighteen months later."

"God, you were so young," Cali whispered. He concentrated on the sound of the stop bath flowing around the film, sounding like the ocean on that beautiful but heart-wrenching day. Cali broke him from the memory. "Is worry over your test why you don't eat?"

It took a moment to remember where he was. "I eat," he said defensively.

"Barely."

Jory considered evading but knew she wouldn't be fooled by his brush-offs. He cleared his throat, forcing himself to be honest. "Well, partly. It was from me fasting for the test, which I would then cancel. I've also been stricter with my diet in general."

"Hence the diet calendar. Sorry for making fun of you," she said sheepishly.

Jory paused; their exchange after getting take-out burgers at Spiral seemed like decades ago. "I had one before this,

Love, Camera, Action

just not as intense, so you weren't wrong. But sometimes I think I don't eat because I don't want to make it worse. Like I'm starving the possibility of cancer by starving myself. I know it doesn't make any sense."

Cali spoke softly, her attention on the tank. "It makes sense. I think how we eat reflects our base emotional state. I constantly shove food in my pockets because I'm afraid I won't be able to find anything later, even though I haven't had that issue for years."

Jory became self-conscious of his own troubles weighing her down. He walked over to the cupboard to get them each a glass of water, while Cali continued to upend the tank. Jory followed the swoop of her arms as she dumped the stop bath into the sink.

"Anyway. At the renewal ceremony, my grandmother kept trying to take the camera away, saying"—Jory put on his grandmother's old-money New Hampshire accent—"*'Put thaht down, dahling. It is an inappropriate medium meant only for the mahsses.'*"

Cali smiled but stayed quiet.

"I wouldn't take the camera away from my face." Jory remembered the relief he'd experienced having the barrier of the lens to hide behind. To have that separation between him and what was happening while being able to control what he filmed and how beautiful he could make it. But also using it as a way to document the time his family had had together that was all too short.

"Do you ever watch the footage?"

"Sometimes. The three of us would watch it together before she passed away, laughing. My dad hasn't seen it since. I would watch it in secret when I was missing her."

Cali quietly watched him, and he stilled under her regard. "Well, bless your mom for giving the world such beautiful images."

The kitchen went silent other than the gentle sloshing of the rinse in the tank. No one had expressed that to him, although he thought of it every day—his mother's unfailing faith in him. How she intuitively gave him his love of the lens and what it could capture. The emotions it could bestow.

His eyes misted and he tried to blink away the tears as Cali poured out the fixer. He had the urge to grab a camera to put some separation between him and his vulnerabilities—and her. He stayed where he was instead.

"It's ready." She ran the tap over the film, the bubbles washing away in the sink. "Let's see what we've got." And she dumped the processed film out.

Jory took the few steps to stand beside her, hip to hip. A strange wave of something like sentimentality washed over him. There must be a German word for feeling the loss of something you've never had. He savored what was happening between them, turning the numinous moment over in his mind, as Cali turned the film in her hands, memorizing it for a rainy day.

She carefully brought the wet film up to the light, spooling it through her fingers and squinting at the tiny images. Jory didn't look at the film, but at Cali who was all grace, strength, and passion.

"It's a kids' birthday party." She brought it closer to her eyes. "Maybe late '70s. Wow."

Her face glowed with unadulterated delight, a surprised laugh escaping her lips. And an unexpected despair coursed

Love, Camera, Action

through him, because he'd done what he vowed not to, and fallen in love with her.

Cali marveled at the sepia-toned balloons and individual frames of riotous, singing children surrounding one little girl standing poised over glowing candles. Hands threading through the film, Cali watched the infinitesimal changes take place until the candles were blown out and everyone was clapping, a gap-toothed grin beaming out of the birthday girl. A wave of gratitude shot through her that Jory had saved this moment from oblivion.

As the film flowed over her fingers, the image suddenly changed to a modern one—a man staring in a bathroom mirror, camera in hand as he shot out the rest of the reel. *Jory.* His image was tiny, but she was able to discern his expression. He stared into the lens, expression empty and desolate at first to be slowly replaced with a curious smile and a longing gaze, as though he were yearning for something just out of his grasp.

When she turned, his face held that same look of longing, a mix of reverent, mournful hopelessness she didn't understand. And was desperate to banish.

She let the film slide into the sink as she brought her hands to his cheeks, smoothing the lines of worry with her thumbs. He relaxed under her fingers and his eyes drifted closed. She reached up to kiss each lid, his long sigh drifting over her lips. She followed that sigh and kissed him, slow and soft.

The frenetic energy that had always coursed between them was gone, replaced by something quiet and solid.

Something Cali had never experienced and was dangerously thirsty for. She would be out of his life in two more weeks, back in Toronto with her sister while he stayed here in Atlanta. That should be a relief to her—an easy end with clear markers. Instead, it made her chest tighten with a vague sense of impotent fury.

The thought was too overwhelming, too large for her mind and soul to contemplate, so she decided to suffocate her feelings by swamping his. Deepening the kiss, she vowed she would give him everything in this moment while she committed what was between them to memory for when she was gone and her heart was safely stowed again.

But he had other ideas.

He met her commitment with his own, enveloping her with steadfastness and comfort until she was warm and soft, her thirst slaked by him, her desperation held and then dispersed.

He slid his hands down her sides and gripped her hips to hoist her up onto the kitchen island. She yelped in surprise and then laughed into his mouth.

He smiled against her as he ran hands under her shirt, cupping her breasts and thumbing her nipples. She groaned into him, her kiss turning sloppy as her focus scattered at the intensity of his touch. Pulling her shirt off, he dipped his head and sucked on the dusky nipple tightened to a peak. She gasped as he pulled harder, then laved his tongue across to soothe the heat that rose there.

Cali sank her fingers through his hair, scraping her nails along his scalp while bending her head to his neck, where she bit him along the tendon that extended to his shoulder. He growled, and she took a lungful of his now familiar some-kind-of-tree scent. A pang shot through her as she realized she'd

Love, Camera, Action

soon be without his smell. Without him. She wanted just a little bit longer. Couldn't she have just a little bit longer?

The overwhelming need to get closer made them awkward and clumsy as he struggled to pull his shirt off. She lifted her hips to shimmy off her pants and underwear in one move and then toed his boxer briefs off with her feet. Her hands rubbed over him while he sheathed his cock with shaking hands, breathing deep to calm himself. He brought his thumb up and spread tears she didn't know she'd shed over her cheeks. Exploring their feel on her face, nurturing her with them, nurturing himself. And when his blue eyes drew hers, dark with desire and something else she couldn't name, he slid home.

Cali's passage pulled him in greedily, and she gasped at the fullness of him. Then she let out a long, deep moan as she relaxed around his cock, grasping him with her legs so he couldn't move, relishing the rightness. She kept her eyes on his as she brushed his hair back and gently kissed his lips. He let out a faint whimper at the contact, and his forehead fell against hers, fusing them together.

They stayed that way, forehead to forehead, their breaths matched—his in with her out, her out with his in—as though each propelled life into the other, until he began to thrust, their bodies falling into a natural sync. A final release not the end goal, but this exchange, this connection that somehow transcended sex. And for the first time in her life, the more she gave, the more she got.

They climbed together toward their peak, slow and relentless, and when he reached between them to push her over the edge, he followed as she pulsed around him.

As their breathing slowed and Cali's heart returned to normal, she felt the urge to pull Jory into her arms and hold him. His eyes were still closed, eyelashes delicate and long against his cheeks, his breath in tandem with hers. Giving this up, giving *him* up in two weeks suddenly seemed like a preposterous idea. She'd never been in a relationship before and certainly didn't have any good examples of what a healthy one was, but what if she tried? What if she changed her rule and was brave?

He'd proved he could take care of himself. He'd shown he didn't need her to look after him, and even took pains to look after her. He listened to her ideas, coaxed out and then banished her insecurities, sat with her stories, and didn't ask obvious questions. He had his baggage, for sure. He'd been deeply affected by his mother's death and was still healing from it. But she had lots of experience dealing with oversized baggage. She'd been hefting it since she was five.

She knew he felt something too. He'd all but admitted it in the car when his defenses were down. Could she take the risk and hope that maybe she could find a man who could actually be counted on?

"God, I'm afraid," he whispered. A confession, a discovery, a humiliation. So quiet she almost didn't hear him.

But she did. Her heart melted through her chest and melded with his. "Afraid of what?"

He stilled. And when he opened his crystalline blue eyes, the desolation she'd seen on that film had returned, clear and bottomless. No hint of yearning or curiosity, just bleak hopelessness, solidifying into a cold decision.

"I'm afraid . . . we have to talk."

He pulled away from her, looking at the floor. Which was where her heart must have landed.

"Uh-oh." Cali closed her legs and slid off the counter. "Sounds serious. Give me a second to get my underwear on."

Love, Camera, Action

Blood rushed to her head, and she had to hold on to the counter to steady herself, on her own, with no help from him. As she looked around for her underwear, the excuses came.

"I think our focus is drifting from our original agreement."

"Our focus."

"I've been thinking about this for a while. You were right, our . . . hookups . . . made the work better, but it's become too dangerous for me."

"You've been thinking about this for a while."

"Yes."

"'Cause it kind of seemed like you thought of it just now, and you were about to say something else entirely. Which would be fine, since that was pretty intense." As she circled the island, a scrap of red appeared just past a corner. At least she could have this conversation without her ass hanging out.

"It was intense, too intense for what we agreed on."

Cali hated how her knees shook as she pulled her underwear up her legs. "So we should take a step back. Cool things down. Find our focus." She lengthened out the syllables on that last one, rancor dripping off her tongue.

"I do. Think that. Don't you?" he asked warily.

"Yeah, sure. Sure." Cali looked around for the rest of her clothes, still unable to look at him, but knowing he hadn't moved from his spot. "Totally get that. Totally . . . get that." She spied her pants by the couch. Wow, she'd really flung them. "I'm assuming you want to take back your invitation to your beach house as well?"

"My beach house?"

She almost laughed at the alarm in his voice and couldn't help taunting him. "On the way back. You invited me to

263

your beach house so you could watch my eyes change with the color of the ocean." She straightened with her pants in her hand, looking at him now with accusation. "Don't worry—you were doped up. I didn't think it was real."

Although she had. She had thought it was real. She'd begun to think it was all real.

"I can't go anyway." Cali pushed one leg in her pants and then the other, wondering how she'd never noticed how painful getting dressed was. She struggled into her hoodie and grabbed her bag. "There's a lot of stuff going on with my sister, and I have this gig back in Toronto that will probably start as soon as we're done."

"Well, that's good then. Yeah, I couldn't bring you to the beach house anyway because . . . um . . ."

"The plumbing's out? It's all booked up with the rest of your family? The moon is at the wrong angle? Again, totally get it." She couldn't help sounding bitter. She *was* bitter. She gestured to the sink. "Make sure you get that film on a spool as soon as you can. You don't want it to crimp anywhere," she said as she pulled on her shoes. "It has to dry first. Don't put wet film on a spool."

"Okay." His voice was quiet, lifeless. Her traitorous heart went out to him. He looked so lost, like he was losing his best friend, like he was losing himself.

It didn't matter. She couldn't, wouldn't help him. "Clothespins are best. I should have thought to buy them."

"It's fine."

"Drape it over the shower stall maybe." She moved to the door.

"Okay."

"Okay." She took a scan of the room, making sure she hadn't left anything.

264

Love, Camera, Action

"Don't worry," he said gently. "You have everything."

She saw his emptiness, his walls slamming up. She slammed up her own. "I'll see you Monday."

She opened up the door and slid out, closing it behind her. She started down the hall at a normal pace and then gradually picked up speed until she broke out into a run.

CHAPTER TWENTY

Jory was fighting to breathe.

At first he thought it was the thick, muggy soup that made up the Atlanta atmosphere at three o'clock on a July afternoon. Made worse, of course, by the black cloth tent erected for the on-location Video Village that trapped all that stagnant air inside. The hot air made hotter by Howard constantly undermining Cali's authority with comments like, "I'm not sure that's what the script intended" and "Do we really need that moment?" and "Make sure Thalia doesn't look so butch."

Then Jory thought he couldn't breathe because he was worried over his test results. They wouldn't come back for a couple of weeks, plenty of time to work himself up into an existential lather. But funnily enough, he couldn't bring himself to care.

The real reason Jory couldn't breathe was that the gray had returned and had brought along newcomers, charcoal

Love, Camera, Action

and black. Because when Cali closed the door of his condo, she took all the color with her, along with the oxygen.

His entire being expanded when he and Cali made love—a term he'd cringed over before realizing it was an actual thing—and he'd broke it off with her before his misery expanded to the point where he would drag her down with him.

He'd imagined he'd feel some kind of sanctimonious rightness, a martyr-like serenity. He couldn't be so selfish as to bring someone into his world when he might be leaving it soon. His mother had been completely healthy when she got her diagnosis, glowing even. And within eighteen months she was gone. What kind of monster would put someone through that, knowing fully what it meant? What his father had gone through . . . And even if Jory wasn't sick now, it would always be hanging over their heads like the Sword of Damocles, a future full of the threat of pain and disease.

Instead of feeling righteous, he only felt shame over acting like an asshole to the woman he loved. And he had been an asshole, just not the type of asshole she'd thought. Although she hadn't looked at him like he was an asshole. She looked like he'd broken her heart.

And now she was freezing him out while they baked in the Atlanta heat, shooting this stupid action scene.

Jory could objectively recognize the postapocalyptic action sequence shot outside a dilapidated factory with rusted crossbeams and crumbling concrete walls awash in the blinding light of the Atlanta summer looked amazing. Paolo's character Rafe had finally caught on that Thalia's character Anna was stealing his soul piece by piece, and they were beating the crap out of each other as a result. It was like they were dueling on the sun.

Patsy had come to set to watch the sequence. Cali hadn't lied about her sister being in rough shape. She huddled in the back row in one of the directors' chairs, somehow not asphyxiating in a hoodie and loose jeans, and wearing a baseball cap and sunglasses. She had the air of a starlet feigning anonymity rather than a washed-up academic.

Patsy spent most of her time glaring at Howard, then shooting Cali glances, which went ignored. Soon those glances found their way to him. She would shake her head and mouth, "*Who is this dick?*" and "*What a dick!*" and "*Can I drop kick this dick?*" Jory solemnly nodded his ascent.

Meanwhile, Howard kept going, blissfully unaware of his delicate position as Patsy readied her drop kick behind him.

"I'm not sure why we're spending so much time on these close-ups," Howard drawled.

Jory watched Cali physically tamp down an irritated sigh, most likely to formulate an underserved response about the importance of character in an action scene.

Jory couldn't take Howard's passive insults anymore and shot out of his chair. "I'm going to set up that Steadicam shot Cali asked for," he announced. Disregarding her look of surprise, he leveled a glowering stare at Howard. "I want to make sure we capture these incredible performances Cali's been getting. Aren't they incredible, Howard?" Before Howard could sputter, Jory strode away.

Cali hadn't asked for a Steadicam shot, but now that Jory had said it, he realized it was what the scene needed. It would capture the grueling and chaotic essence of the fight.

Love, Camera, Action

It would also get him out of that black-tented hell. Not that he could truly escape hell. He was in his own personal version of it that followed him wherever he went.

Cali had said they were temporary, said she didn't do relationships. She was as stubborn in her ideas about love as she was about her ideas on set. She would be fine.

Yet his gaze kept drifting to her, wishing he'd played Friday night differently. Wishing they were still running off for trysts behind the sets. Still making beautiful images frame by frame in inspired harmony. Instead of feeling the distance between them slowly killing him, not the possible cancer.

While he waited for Alison to set up the camera, a ding resonated from his pocket. He swore at himself. He should have shut his phone off so it wouldn't ruin a take, but he'd been making stupid mistakes all day. When he wrestled the phone out of his pocket to turn it off, he saw the text was from his father and that there was a photo attached. Hoping for any kind of a balm to soothe what was becoming the worst day of his life, he opened the message.

Hey, Jor. Was watching some old footage and had to send you this screenshot. Before you ask, Astrid showed me how to do it. She's a wonder. It's from one of your old videos. I've watched them over and over, and I don't think I ever thanked you for taking them. We had such great times, the three of us together. I'm thankful for every second. Even the hard stuff. Love you.

Attached was a chaotic selfie of Jory, his father, and his mom.

Jory remembered the moment with crystal clarity. It hadn't been taken during a grand gesture like the renewal ceremony or the trip to Iceland or at the stadium during the Lakers finals that somehow his dad got tickets for. It was in his mom's hospice room, when she still had the strength to laugh. His dad had had enough of Jory hiding behind the lens, so he good-naturedly wrestled him for the camera. As they both fell on the bed, all three of them howled with laughter, and the camera caught the moment.

Now Jory *really* couldn't breathe.

He thought his father had never watched his videos, that they were too painful. Instead, his father had relived the joy and the pain of their lives together, relishing every moment, never turning away from what was hard, because that would mean turning his back on what was good. And he'd had the courage to try again with someone new, someone different, someone he loved just as deeply. Despite the danger of losing love again.

Jory realized he was grateful he'd had that time too. He wouldn't give up a moment he'd spent with his mother, no matter how awful it had been, because they had been together. And love was bigger than that.

Jory's hands shook as he texted back a short message, doubtful he could do much else. *Have you got any more?*

Jory blurrily caught sight of Thalia quietly talking herself through the choreography while Paolo moved through it with his body, bouncing with pure joy. Jory's own body felt stretched to the breaking point, and he pulled his shirt away from his neck, positive it was tightening around him. He focused on Alison nervously changing the lens, then fumbling it out of her hands and chasing it as it fell to the ground and rolled away.

"Alison! Be careful!" Jory barked. "That lens is worth more than your weekly rate."

Love, Camera, Action

"Sorry, sorry." She bent over to retrieve the wobbling lens but quickly straightened, stealing a glance at Video Village. She awkwardly changed the angle of her body and bent over with her butt aimed toward the building instead.

Jory winced. Alison didn't deserve his mood. He had to stop letting his emotions get in the way of looking after his crew. He should instead be figuring out why she was on edge, as though she wanted to hide. Usually she was so measured in her movements, her presence calm and exacting, but today she was a mess. Jory peered over his shoulder in the direction of Alison's skittered looks but only saw Cali emerging from Video Village, marching toward him on a mission. Each purposeful, annoyed, devastating stride another blow to his heart.

In self-defense, he turned his back on her to face Alison, who had pocketed the lens and floundered with the balance of the camera. He took the bottom of the post from her and gentled his tone. "Sorry, Alison. I shouldn't have snapped. The heat is getting to me."

She focused hard on the camera, hastily wiping away the sweat on her brow with the back of her hand. "The heat's pretty intense."

"I got it." Jory steadied the rig. "Why don't you go clean up that lens in the truck?"

Alison gave him a shaky nod and left as Cali took her place. He kept his attention on finishing the setup but could see in his periphery that the area under her eyes had a faint blue tinge that spoke of sleepless nights and heavy decisions. He fought the urge to abandon the camera and ease whatever worries lurked there.

"I didn't ask for a Steadicam shot." Irritation laced Cali's voice.

Jory clicked the buckles into place on the vest that would stabilize the gear. "You shouldn't let Howard talk to you like that."

"So you swooped in to save me?"

He attached the arm to the bottom of his vest. If he looked at her while she was indignant, he'd just marvel over how passion brought out the green of her eyes or how the blazing sun glinted off her hair, or something else he'd keenly missed in the fifty-five hours they'd spent apart. "Someone needed to say something."

"I appreciate that your version of saying something is to give me an unwarranted compliment while delivering Howard a veiled admonishment." She widened her stance. "But maybe you should think about what it does to my position when someone intimates to the showrunner that the director *needs* saving, as though she has no ability to look after her crew, the shoot, or herself."

She was right. She couldn't afford to appear weak with Howard around, even for a moment, but he crumpled, knowing she didn't want his help. He steadied the shake in his voice. "Where do you want me?"

Cali mumbled under her breath something that sounded suspiciously like "far, far away." Then Dan pulled her aside to discuss the next shot.

Another ding from his phone brought him back, and Jory opened the link his father had sent without thinking.

Hundreds of tiny thumbnails filled the screen. Pictures of his mom, his dad, them all together. All the moments before his mom was diagnosed and all the moments leading up to her death. But as he scrolled through, the pictures continued. Shots of him and his dad on camping trips on their own, family reunions at the beach house, Jory

Love, Camera, Action

laughing after his grandmother indignantly slapped his hand away from the turkey. He watched himself grow, his family grow, year after year, continuing on.

They'd all managed to have lives after the tragedy that had marked them so deeply. And although they hadn't denied the sadness in their lives, hadn't denied they felt his mother's absence every day, they also weren't afraid to feel joy again. To feel hope. As Jory thumbed through the pictures, he felt another absence there, someone he kept expecting to see, someone who should be there, but wasn't.

Cali.

A tear landed on the screen, covering a picture of his sardonic face. He'd been hiding from his life just like that tear obscured him now. Hiding from the best thing that had happened to him in years—not to save Cali from pain, although that was definitely a part of it, but to save himself.

He didn't want to be obscured anymore. He didn't want to feel her absence in his pictures.

He wiped the tear from his phone and the others from his face. He *had* to tell her how he felt, even if he'd fucked it up too much already. Even if she didn't want him anymore or had never wanted him in the first place. All his worries washed away as the future opened to him. A future where he wouldn't be shackled by the unknown, where he could build a life in hope instead of against fear, where he could follow the spark of joy in his work he'd found again with Cali. And the spark of love that could transcend death.

"Blair!"

Howard lurched over from Video Village toward him. Jory cast a plea to the heavens. Could he not get some respite today? Or at least from this guy? Jory busied himself with the camera, already turning his thoughts on how to fix this tangle with Cali. Howard hoisted his pants up over his girth as he approached, patches of dark sweat pooling on his gray polo shirt. "Listen, this heat is killing me, but I wanted to talk to you before I left. I showed Jeff some footage of what you've been doing on this latest episode in spite of this lame duck director."

Jory's fuse burned bright and short. "I'm telling you, Howard—"

"I know, I know. You're doing it together. Whatever. Jeff was blown away and thinks you just need one credit. So I'll do the paperwork tomorrow, and we'll be all set. Keep a lid on it and get through today."

"Keep a lid on what? Paperwork for what?" Maybe he could convince Cali to start fresh, to acknowledge what was between them, to drop the rules.

Howard lowered his voice. "I'm giving an episode to you."

"You are? That's great." He'd have to be honest with her about his fears about his health, about his test, which was terrifying in itself, but he had to start somewhere. And maybe he could find out what her fears were.

"So you'll be taking over tomorrow. Just keep it on the QT."

"Tomorrow?" Jory snapped his focus back to Howard just as he felt the camera fall. He scrambled to grab it and saved it just in time, hoisting it back on the stand.

"Yep. I just have to square it with Legal about why I'm getting rid of Cali, and you'll be in. Shouldn't take too long. Just keep it all going until then, and we'll be golden."

Love, Camera, Action

Howard slapped Jory on the side of the arm and pulled his phone out of his pocket, lifting it to his ear. "Murray! Where the fuck have you been, you dickwad?" Howard laughed and lumbered away toward the camera trucks.

Jory stepped forward to follow, but the gear pulled him back. What just happened? He didn't want this episode. He didn't want to take Cali's job from her. But now it was clear this was what Howard had been angling for the whole time. And Jory should have known. Off in the distance, thunder rumbled, announcing his impending doom.

He was sick to his stomach as he realized what he'd done. He'd kept his relationship with Howard quiet to protect Cali, but also to foster the connection so Howard would get him a director's gig. When Cali found out, there would be no other way to interpret the situation except that he'd been gunning for her job from the start. Using her, manipulating her. She would rightfully leave him to face a future without the woman he loved. A future filled with the knowledge that she would always believe he had used her to better his career. That he proved her rule. That love was a lie.

Fuck that. *Fuck that.* He needed to do something, something drastic because there *was* no future without her.

Thunder rumbled again as an idea began to take form. An idea that was insane, that destroyed everything he had built for himself, but one that felt so right, he couldn't ignore it.

He walked toward set with purpose, barely noticing the weight of the camera, a manic rightness fueling his conviction.

One of Cali's superhero traits was projecting that she had it all together when she really did not. And today, she did not. Was not together. In any way. At all.

Working alongside Jory after that disastrous whatever—could you call it a breakup? A cool down? An end to . . . ?—that was between them was a special kind of agony she hadn't known existed. She'd finally let her guard down with someone, and the resulting affair had exemplified her long-held views that relationships were emotional traps for needy women. She should be glad he'd showed his true colors before she'd embarrassed herself.

She wasn't glad. She was hurt. And very angry.

Luckily—in a way—she didn't have time to dwell on it since Patsy had broken down and locked herself in the bathroom with another bottle of vodka. She'd cried for hours until Cali had forced the door open in time to hold Patsy's hair back while she puked. After dumping the remaining vodka down the sink, Cali was on watch. And now she was here trying to direct this action scene with Howard needling her every move.

She just wanted to focus on her job so she could disappear inside the work. Cali loved action scenes. Loved, loved, *loved* them. The balletic choreography that made a fight feel messy and brutal and awkward filled her with giddy excitement. Paolo had at least six inches on Thalia, but Cali and the stunt coordinator had designed the choreography so Thalia could use Paolo's size against him—Thalia's ingenuity winning out over Paolo's strength.

The actors moved through their choreography with studied ferocity while Jory's new Steadicam shots brought a

Love, Camera, Action

frenetic energy Cali hadn't seen in his shooting before. He moved like a man possessed, ducking and weaving to get close-ups and messy angles as he captured the desperate blows and fevered grunts between the actors. It was exciting, but his intensity sparked a deep unease in her—as though she were watching, powerless, a tsunami's inevitable approach miles from the shore she was standing on.

Focus on the scene.

The thunder that had made its presence known off in the distance was getting closer, and Dan sent a wary glance at the dark clouds gathering for the afternoon storm.

She was about to call an end to the day when Jory jogged over despite the weight of his camera. "I want to go again."

Cali frowned. "We've got it."

"I want one more."

Dan eyed the disappearing sun with an anxiety that mirrored Cali's. "I don't like those clouds."

Jory turned his determined gaze on Dan. "Strike the rest of the cameras, and I'll shoot alone."

"We have to pull down the lights and all the other gear."

"I don't need them. We go verité, as real as possible."

Cali paused. "That raw look goes against the aesthetic of the show."

"I'm trying something fresh," Jory insisted.

She frowned at him. He was practically vibrating with manic energy. Why was he pushing so hard? She just wanted to get done with the day so she wouldn't have to see his stupid, annoying, lovely face. "We really don't need it. We could end early."

"Are you happy with this scene?" Jory challenged.

Cali knew her answer would be her undoing. "It's fine."

"I thought so. Just me, no other cameras. One more."
Jory stalked away without waiting for an answer.

A little voice inside sent a warning. This wasn't cool and
collected Jory. This was something else. Dan heaved a beleaguered sigh and shouted orders for the rest of the crew to
pack up and get ahead of the storm.

Cali turned to the actors who were trying to control
their breathing from the exertion. "How are you two? Do
you have one more in you?"

Paolo punched the air. "Hell yeah!"

Thalia gave a curt nod.

Without waiting for Cali's go-ahead, Jory positioned
himself and impatiently swirled his finger in the interna-
tional sign of "let's go again," without so much as looking
her way.

The mounting wind whipped Cali's hair into her face.
She testily pushed it back. The crew scurried around them,
tearing everything down to get the equipment and themselves inside. Soon it was just the five of them standing at
the ready as the storm threatened.

Dan hollered. "We gotta go."

Cali nodded the scene forward. "Action!"

Thalia and Paolo burst into movement. Thalia delivered
a flurry of jabs against Paolo's ribs that caused him to stag-
ger back from the force. She took advantage of his confusion to deliver a roundhouse kick. His head snapped to the
left, his body following it, sending him reeling into the wall.
Jory danced in and out, capturing their expressions, their
fists, their feet—all the same as before.

Frustration erupted over Jory's features, and he growled
at Paolo. "Is that all you got? Is this all you're good for?
You're a man. Prove it."

Love, Camera, Action

Cali stared. This was the first time she'd heard Jory give Paolo a direction outside of where to stand. But this wasn't direction, it was manipulation. Jory was using Paolo's insecurities against him, and knowing Paolo's penchant for interpreting direction in unpredictable ways, it was a disastrous call. Before she could give a counter-direction, Paolo feinted where he should have blocked, ducked when he should have punched, and pulled Thalia in for a blistering kiss.

It was electric, it was sizzling, and it was completely inappropriate.

Jory grinned like a man possessed.

Thalia pushed Paolo away with a furious scream that was answered by a bolt of lightning and clap of thunder so loud it seemed to come from her vengeful roar.

Torrential sheets of rain poured down.

Thalia launched herself at Paolo like the demon she was—landing real blows. Paolo staggered under the onslaught, barely keeping her at bay until he had no choice but to parry her moves, strike for strike as his own fury boiled to the surface. Jory captured every electrifying second with a dangerous grace that was terrifying in its intensity.

When lightning cracked a second time, Cali came to her senses. Not only were her actors assaulting each other, Jory was a walking lightning rod.

"Cut! Cut! Cut!" Cali shouted as Thalia rained down shot after shot, Paolo fending her off while Jory dodged around them, the scene continuing on with a life of its own.

"Jory!" Cali screamed into the wind.

His eyes flicked up to hers but shot away—ignoring her.

"Jory! Cut!" Another bolt shook the ground. Cali jumped in front of the camera and pulled the actors apart. "Stop!"

"Get out of the frame!" Jory yelled.

As though coming out of a daze, Paolo's eyes cleared, and he dropped his hands just as Thalia exploded a wicked fast jab to his face. Paolo stumbled back and his hands flew to his nose, already spurting blood. Thalia wound up for another shot, but Cali held her back.

Thalia screamed at Paolo, "Don't touch me! Don't you ever touch me!" She shook Cali off and blasted away, Paolo watching her retreat with anguish on his face. His shoulders slumped and he trudged in the opposite direction.

Dan clicked his walkie and shouted over the wind, "Medic!" He sent a murderous look at Cali and Jory and then jogged after Paolo.

Seething with rage, Cali rounded on Jory. "What. The fuck. Was that?"

Jory jerked the camera off its arm and shoved it onto its balancing post. "You ruined it!" A PA swooped in and quickly collected the rig, racing to pull the camera out of the rain, leaving Jory and Cali alone.

"Ruined what? Getting electrocuted?"

"Oh, come on! Do you honestly think we were going to get hit by lightning?" Jory's face was hard, the rain running down each contour, giving him the air of an unconquerable warrior.

"We're in an open space, in an electrical storm, and you're strapped to a metal conductor, so, yeah."

"We were capturing gold."

"There are rules for a reason," she gritted out.

"Always the rules with you." Frustration boiled to the surface of his features. "Did you see what they were doing? The actors were there, in the dream, *in* the characters. They weren't Paolo and Thalia. They were Anna and Rafe in the rawest moment I've been able to capture between the two of them. And suddenly you're afraid."

"You put the actors' safety at risk! Your own! Dan's!"

"I notice *you're* not on that list."

"I don't matter." She winced at the slip.

"Whoa, what did you say?"

"It doesn't matter. *It* doesn't matter." Panic replaced anger as her throat began to close. "You can't make people feel unsafe."

Suddenly all his mania fled, swapped with a look of dawning understanding. "Cali—"

No. No. That was not how this was going down. "I don't take risks that push actors in a way that's emotionally manipulative. I don't take risks that goad a man into assaulting his costar, when that costar probably has PTSD from past experiences and then assaults him back."

"Cali, stop—"

"I don't risk my DP shooting in a lightning storm, while he thinks putting everyone in a dangerous position is the best way to get a good scene."

"No, you're afraid when things are out of your control. When they're messy," he shouted above the wind. "I'm trying to take a risk for *this*." He motioned between them.

"It's too late!" she cried.

Shock bloomed across his face. "Because people don't deserve second chances? Because people don't get freaked out? Because taking a risk is so hard for you? You make up rules to keep other people away so you don't have to risk anything, and sacrifice yourself for your sister and your mother under the guise that they can't look after themselves. But you need them needing you so you don't have to live your own life."

"All I do is take risks!" She began to shake. "How do you think I got here? It wasn't because I grew up in LA and went to AFI and had my ride paid for." She saw the hurt in Jory's eyes but couldn't stop herself from unsheathing her claws. "You are the great DP with the rising career, but you've been putting yourself away, slice by slice, in bitter resignation for years because you think that's the job. For what? Some beautiful, empty shots with no soul? To pander to producers you barely respect?"

"Cali, this isn't about the job anymore."

Cali knew it wasn't about the job anymore, but she couldn't separate her hurt from what had just happened on set, they seemed so horrifically entwined. "I'm the one who's been risking myself on this show to get magic, not you. But when I take a risk, it's foolish, and when you take one, it's genius. Howard should fire me already and get you to direct!"

Jory stilled, his jaw slack.

And Cali knew. She knew. "Howard wants to fire me and hire you."

Jory shook his head. "Cali that's not—"

"When did Howard ask you?" Cali stepped back from him, her chest collapsing in on itself. "Was it before we . . . ?"

"No, my God no. I mean. Well . . ." Jory stammered. She had never heard Jory stammer.

"It was. Wow. That's. Oh my God." Cali put her hands on her thighs and leaned over. She was going to be sick.

"No. No! It's not what you think." Jory stepped toward her.

She put a hand up. "I'm fine. That's fine. You'll be perfect for it. I can go back home to look after all those people who I need to need me, and you can stay here and get the

Love, Camera, Action

future that's coming to you. I'm sure you and Howard will be very happy."

Jory lurched back, stunned, but Cali didn't care. He'd lied to her all the time she'd been struggling to make things work. She turned her back and stumbled through the rain, leaving the postapocalyptic set behind, knowing it was her world that had been blown apart.

CHAPTER TWENTY-ONE

Cali barely slept. Dread had become the life force flowing through her, mixed with a heady dose of fear, self-recrimination, and unworthiness.

After the shoot finished, Cali went to check in on Thalia while Dan looked in on Paolo. The third AD, stationed outside Thalia's trailer, let Cali know that she wasn't seeing anyone, and if Cali wanted to pass on any information, she would have to do so through Thalia's management. As Cali trudged to her car, a text from Dan told her that while Paolo's nose was a bit swollen, he was already recovering. Jory was staying with him while the medic looked Paolo over. She wished she could have seen the actors, to assure herself they were truly alright. But as light began to seep through her lush, heavy curtains, she realized she might never see them again.

She would be fired today. Not just fired off the show, but fired from the business. Once the stain of being let go from one show seeped into your reputation, it followed you to

Love, Camera, Action

every interview, every connection. The business was gossipy and news traveled fast. She'd be on a plane back to Toronto with nothing to show for her hard work except a big black mark.

She would return to work in obscurity—if obscurity would have her—and struggle to keep her family afloat and her sanity intact. But she had lost something greater than a "break," greater than a job or her career. She'd lost hope she could have someone of her own to care for, who would care for her. Somewhere deep down she'd believed she could have her "One." She didn't realize she'd even had that hope until it had been smashed to pieces, and now her One was done, revealed for the big lie it was.

She curled into a ball on her bed, her king-sized, Egyptian cotton–sheeted bed, and sifted through every exchange between her and Jory. Had he been lying all along? Maybe he had been working both sides, gaining advantage from her mistakes while taking credit for her successes. He never had come clean with Paolo. Maybe he had been pitting the star against her so Jory could come in and save the day, impressing Howard with his ability to manage the talent and clean up after the newbie director.

As tidy a story that would make, it didn't ring true. She knew her reasoning was off, but it was hard to be rational when she felt so betrayed. Now she had to get up and go to work and pretend nothing had happened. Pretend the hammer wasn't about to come down, pretend her career hadn't been destroyed, pretend her heart hadn't turned to ash.

Cali dragged herself out of bed and began to dress, pulling on clothes like a suit of armor: her most comfortable yet stylish jeans, a red zip-up that taunted "Bring it" over the heart, and her sturdy Blundstone boots. She wouldn't be accused of cowardice on her walk to the gallows. She would go to set early to prepare her day and direct the best scenes of her life, while meeting her fate with as much dignity as she could muster. Joan of Arc approaching the stake. Alone.

When she walked out of her room, she saw a light on in the kitchen. Patsy sat huddled over a mug at the island, staring into the middle distance. Usually Cali would put her own needs away to meet Patsy's, cheer her up, listen to her woes, curse the latest man—no matter the cost to herself.

For the first time, Cali saw the unfairness of being the strong one, the one who made all the decisions, all the sacrifices. Maybe Jory was right. That she'd allowed it. That she took care of others because it was safer than taking care of herself. She was tired of being a martyr. Tired of giving everything she had for other people's drama. She deserved her own.

"I can't do this anymore."

Patsy pulled back from the abyss and turned dark, dull eyes to Cali.

"This." Cali motioned between them. "This thing we do. I don't want to be the responsible one anymore. I love you and I'm worried for you and I'm sorry you're going through a shit time, but I'm having my own shit time. I need you to look after yourself."

Patsy stayed quiet. And that pissed Cali off. Why was she always the one who did all the work? Cali would fill in the silence with chatter until she ended up helping again. Telling herself it was fine and she could do this one thing, she could carry everyone, she was strong. Well, she wouldn't do it. Cali blew out a breath and stepped away to leave.

Love, Camera, Action

"You're really good at this," Patsy murmured.

Cali blinked. "Sorry?"

"You're really good at this. Being a director."

What now? "Pats, come on. Focus on what I'm saying." Cali felt her anger rise. "I can't support you anymore. I can't be the one who picks up your pieces as you destroy yourself over and over. I have my own pieces to pick up, and there are pieces, Patsy. There are pieces all over the place." Cali flung her arms around to underline the multitude of fictional pieces. "And I want to be able to pick them up. Or, God forbid, have someone else pick them up. I am so done with everyone else's pieces!"

Patsy stared at her in silence for a moment, then gave a slow nod. "You should be done." Patsy's gaze turned hard. "And you shouldn't stop directing."

"I never said—"

Patsy cut Cali off with a sharp glance. She knew there was trouble. Patsy always knew.

Cali's shoulders sank and she rubbed her face. "They're going to fire me today."

"Really?"

"Yes."

Patsy paused, thinking. "But they haven't fired you yet."

"No, not yet."

Patsy nodded. "I don't know what's going on with your fuckwit boss or that grumpy hot guy, but they should be helping you. You're a goddamn treasure."

"They don't—" Cali stuttered to a stop. "What grumpy hot guy?"

"The camera guy. The one you've been sleeping with. Your stuff is always good, but with that guy it's breathtaking. There's a chemistry between you that's hard to ignore."

Cali's mind raced through all the moments she and Jory had created that would now live forever in the television universe. Then, those moments on set when she'd catch him watching her direct the actors, respect and warmth in his eyes. How joy burst in her chest when he laughed. That his kiss felt like the home she'd never had.

"I don't want you to be like me," Patsy said.

Cali shook her head to bring herself back to the present. "It's not your fault things go wrong."

"It is, actually." Patsy grew quiet, introspective. "I've been lying, mostly to myself. I know you think I get dumped. That men dump me because I'm too intense, that I want too much. But . . ." Patsy huffed out a blast of air, looking for courage. "It's me that dumps them. I end it. Always. Because they don't have what I'm searching for."

Cali couldn't understand what Patsy was saying. For years Patsy had been crying over lost relationships, drinking herself to sleep in weeklong binges, losing time at work and at school. But now that Cali thought back on it, Patsy never told her what had happened outside of saying, *It's over.* "Why did you let me think you were the one dumped?"

"Because you have firm ideas about the nonexistence of love. And I didn't want to face what the real problem was." Patsy voice was watery. "I had love once. Real true love, and I threw it away because I didn't believe in it. I was afraid he would leave me, so I left him. And I've been searching for that same love ever since."

Cali forced herself to be still despite her warring emotions—anger over being deceived, guilt for not knowing, shame over her own stubbornness. "Who was he?" Cali murmured.

"Colin."

288

Love, Camera, Action

"The colleague you left your program over? Who cheated on his wife with you?"

"Yes, the colleague, but he didn't cheat with me. We first met when he was the TA for my third-year Classics course. We were together for six months, and I broke it off before he left to do his PhD. He came back into my life last month, a fully tenured professor, filling in for someone who left my dissertation board. When I saw him, I realized I'd never stopped loving him. But he has a wife and a baby and a cottage." Patsy stared into her coffee mug. "He's perfectly happy without me. And I've wasted all this time searching for what I had with him."

Cali couldn't believe it. Her sister had hidden this from her because she believed Cali wouldn't understand. But holy hell, did she understand. Cali had kept herself away from relationships so she wouldn't get hurt, and Patsy had thrown herself into them because she *had*. But at least Patsy had tried. Cali hadn't even done that. And worse, Cali was in the process of throwing away the very thing Patsy so desperately searched for.

Patsy raised desolate eyes to Cali. "You have to trust something will go right instead of looking for what might go wrong."

Cali's nose tingled. "The grumpy hot guy is not what he seems."

Patsy cast an assessing gaze over Cali and considered her for a long time before she nodded. "We rarely are. Just don't be like me. Don't push love away because you're afraid you'll lose it. Or you will."

Inconvenient and embarrassing tears threatened to fall. Cali tried to force them back, but one escaped.

Patsy watched the tear slide down her cheek. "Crybaby."

Cali laughed, but it only caused more tears to flee.

Patsy held out a take-out napkin. "One seed at a time, okay?"

Cali took it and scratched the tears away with the rough paper. "One seed at a time."

Patsy placed a hand to her sister's cheek, and Cali covered it with her own to soak in its warmth. Patsy whispered, "You do so much and you get so little. I'm ashamed for having done that to you."

Cali squeezed her eyes tighter.

Patsy gave Cali a pat. "Now go show those assholes who they're losing."

"You're not coming?" Cali blew her nose.

"Nah, thought I'd try to get back in my program. With a different dissertation board."

"Okay." Cali let out a tremulous breath. "Let me know if you need anything."

"No." Patsy smiled. "I won't."

As Cali walked through the studio, a sense of eerie calm stole over her. She wondered when they would fire her. If they'd strike when she first came in or at the end of the day. It all seemed unimportant in the light of Patsy's confession. For years, Cali had believed her sister was a victim. That she needed the fairytale of true love like their mother to endorse her existence. Instead, Patsy was slowly destroying herself because she'd had the real thing and had thrown it away, victimizing the men instead.

Love, Camera, Action

If Cali had misperceived what was going on all this time with her sister, what else had she gotten wrong? *Who* else had she gotten wrong? Her world had shifted, and she wasn't entirely sure she was unhappy about it.

But first seed first. No matter how heartbroken she was over Jory, she wanted to leave this set with a sense of accomplishment. Right off the top of the day, Cali had to direct the season's biggest scene with a confidence she could no longer fake—the scene where the main characters fall in love. If this was going to be her last kick at the can, she would make it unforgettable, one seed at time.

She'd been mulling over this scene from the moment she'd read the script, turning it in her mind, weighing various ways to shoot the exchanges between the two characters, how their bodies would touch, the sounds they would make, the delivery of their lines. The options she'd come up with felt flat now. Inauthentic and immature. Perhaps in the face of her own changing feelings, she recognized her ideas about love had been merely that—ideas. She hadn't been thinking with her heart, because perhaps she had never understood the nature of love. She'd seen, from the outside, how it destroyed, but not how it built from within. How love made you giddy and unsure, bereft when it proved false, but ultimately left you . . . better.

The scene was back in Paolo/Rafe's bedroom, a mirror to the sex scene Cali had directed her first day. A day from forever ago. Cali felt like a different woman, no longer the naive hopeful who had flirted with the idea she could stretch herself as a director with the help of a seemingly cold, gorgeous, and talented DP.

Cali blinked hard to focus back on the task at hand.

In the script, Paolo/Rafe again wakes up with Thalia/ Anna above him, but instead of the interaction heating up into a sexy romp, they connect on a deeper level as the first inklings of love spark between them.

Sex scenes were easy compared to love scenes. Love required a delicate hand to hold an audience captive, to humble them as they witnessed two people take a leap of faith. Anything with soft music or easy glides or—that word again—"cliché" concepts, could make the moment a cheese fest worthy of a groan. But if you didn't delve into the emotion their connection would come off staged and empty. Now she had to design the perfect love scene when her own heart was breaking, when her actors were on the verge of charging each other with assault, with the crew knowing she was a dead woman walking, alongside a duplicitous DP who would usurp her place. A DP she was in love with.

Cali's eyes stung.

Shuffling sounds that could only belong to Dan approached. "You're here early."

"I wanted to get a jump on the day." Cali met him with what she hoped was the definition of Brave Face.

"Good idea." Dan shifted his gaze. "Um . . . Howard wants to see you in his office after this scene."

Cali nodded. Her hour of execution had been set.

Dan gave her a thoughtful look. "Jory crossed some boundaries yesterday. The union might want to know what happened. Or Melanie."

Dan was handing her a chance to turn the tables in her favor. If she reported Jory for a breach of protocol by endangering the cast and themselves, she could have a case against being fired. Even as she entertained the idea, sharp pangs

Love, Camera, Action

ricocheted around her belly. She supposed those were love pangs. She couldn't betray Jory like that, even though it was his fault. *Ugh.* This love thing wouldn't even allow her proper revenge. What a drag.

Cali waved a hand. "No, it's okay. I had it out with him."

Dan considered her, and Cali straightened under his assessment. Dan had definite dad energy, and she soaked it in, hoping for his approval. He smiled and said enigmatically, "Keep an open mind. Fortunes can change on a dime in this business."

Then he walked away. It was sweet of him to give her some hope when she knew there was none. She was not the type hope worked for.

One seed at a time.

Her first seed was Thalia.

Cali padded down the long main hall that intersected the perpendicular offshoots to the other departments—Wardrobe, Props, Administration. The departments were hushed, populated only by the lowliest of assistants hoping to be noticed for their early arrivals. The quiet rhythm of her steps helped her think, to reflect on her sister's words. That she should trust, she shouldn't let love go, shouldn't be afraid to be left. Even Dan had said her fate could change on a dime.

Perhaps she'd been wrong about Jory. She hadn't given him a chance to explain. Perhaps his face had filled with his version of horror because she'd gotten the wrong idea, instead of with guilt over having been caught. Maybe there was some logical reason he was taking her job, like some vengeful goblin was holding his long-lost twin captive and only Jory could save him by betraying an innocent maiden.

Or maybe there was a more mundane explanation. A tiny tendril of hope wove its way through her heart.

Howard's door opened at the end of the hall, and out stepped the subject of her thoughts. Cali slowed to a stop and watched Jory click the door shut, a smile on his face. A *triumphant* smile.

So, the first explanation, then. Just betrayal. She ducked away before he could see her, moving deeper into the maze of the production hallways to avoid him, training her ears for any sound of hurried steps or the call of her name—any sliver of an indication he was chasing her down, trying to explain, to set things right. But there wasn't one footfall, not one exclamation or shuffle behind her.

As she walked through the liminal space of long hallways and closed doors, she expected her devastation to be complete, but instead found that the tendril of hope hadn't quite turned to dust. It stubbornly remained, a daisy growing out of concrete. With Jory, Cali had discovered she could have something she'd always thought wasn't meant for her. She'd never entertained the possibility of having a partner who could share her burdens and joys simply because she'd assumed she would be alone. She'd never seen an example of how someone could be helpful, not only because the men in her mother's and sister's lives were so useless, but also because her mother and sister had never truly helped her either.

But she'd shared something with Jory, even if it was only for a few short weeks. They'd worked together in the bedroom and on set, and in the quiet moments in between. Cali even felt at times she could be the weak one, because Jory was there to take over, to make sure everything was alright. There had been an ease, a safety in being with him,

Love, Camera, Action

as well as an excitement that they were building something greater than what each of them could build on their own.

Her heart was breaking, for sure. Trampled into the ground and oozing out life force. But it was still beating. And now she knew love could be more than a sap on someone's strength, that it could create something new. Which meant Cali could find it again with someone else. Maybe not immediately, but someday. And that was cause for hope.

She just wished it could have been with Jory.

Cali took her bearings and discovered she'd found her way to her destination, the door to Makeup. Wiping another errant tear that had somehow managed to escape, she took a deep breath and opened the door, strode past the line of mirrors, and sat in a chair beside Thalia.

Thalia's hair stylist pulled out a roller, artfully manipulating a wave into a disheveled mess while Thalia's eyes met Cali's in the mirror with a cold vengeance. "I am very angry."

Cali held her stare. "You should be."

Thalia leaned forward, pulling the stylist with her, squeezing lotion from a pump onto her hands and slapping them together to beat the moisture in. "That's twice he's forced himself on me, and I won't tolerate it."

"You shouldn't."

Thalia straightened, pushing the stylist back. "I'm going to report him to the actor's union."

"He's already reported himself."

Thalia's head snapped toward Cali, sending rollers and clips flying around the room. The stylist muttered, "Aw man . . ." and began picking them up.

Cali held Thalia's gaze with open candor. "He turned himself in for disciplinary action. He's taking full responsibility."

Thalia's jaw dropped. "Oh."

Cali let the moment breathe. She needed Thalia on board with her this morning, and that meant complete transparency. Transparency was a risk, but there was no other way with a woman like her. "What I'm about to offer might not hold any weight in the next few hours because my position here is . . . on shaky ground. But I will back you up in regard to what I've witnessed between you and Paolo."

Thalia studied her warily, as though she hadn't expected any support, and now that she'd gotten some, wasn't sure what to do with it.

Cali continued. "That said, I don't think Paolo is the type of man who is either predatory or entitled. Just so we're clear, I'm not a fan of the unconscious sexism excuse. At this point everyone should realize when they're being misogynistic assholes. But I feel Paolo falls under the category of a guy trying to learn a new way to be."

A darkness gathered in Thalia's eyes that was frankly terrifying. Cali understood why she'd landed the role of the demon, because Cali had the idea she was about to get incinerated. Still, she forged on. "Teaching him that new way is not your job, nor is it mine. He has to learn that himself. But I do think his responsible act of holding himself accountable and doing it quickly shouldn't be ignored."

Thalia spoke in a quiet, threatening voice. "Are you telling me this so I'll be a good little girl and do the love scene today?"

"My job is to deliver this episode for as long as they allow me to do that. So yes, I have a vested interest in you continuing to work with Paolo. If you think he deserves another chance, then I would make sure you are safe so the job gets done. But despite my horse in this race, if you can't abide him, then you shouldn't do the scene. Screw

Love, Camera, Action

everything and everyone else. Your safety and self-worth are more important."

The hair stylist popped up from the floor, looking at Cali like she'd just told a toddler to cross the freeway. Cali ignored her. She knew giving Thalia an out was a risk. Some producers made sure actors felt they had little power—they were easier to control that way. Cali thought, if she instead *gave* Thalia the power, and she chose Cali's way, then Thalia would be in, one hundred percent. Of course, if Thalia took that power and walked away, Cali was fucked.

Thalia's eyelids fluttered in shock. "Are you saying I don't have to do the scene?"

Cali nodded.

"I couldn't do that."

"Of course you could. It might be too much to ask you to rise above what happened with Paolo. That is not a dare," Cali underlined, pointing a finger at her. "If you want to back out, I'm sure you can find something in your contract that allows you to legally refuse to continue, and you should call your agent right now and find out if that's possible."

Thalia frowned. Cali waited, fighting the urge to fill the void.

The stylist brought up her brush and asked quietly, "Should I keep going?"

Thalia considered her own reflection in the mirror. "I'm a professional."

"One of the best I've worked with," Cali affirmed.

"So. Director. What should I do?"

Cali wasn't sure if Thalia was challenging her or sincerely asking the question. She decided it was both. "Look for the man you're acting with who was brave enough to admit he was wrong and humble enough to take responsibility."

Thalia fell silent, her lips pressed together. Then she straightened. "If he makes one move off script, I'm walking."

"Deal." Cali nodded to the stylist to keep on with the artful dishevelment. The stylist let out a relieved sigh.

Cali got up from her chair to leave, but Thalia stopped her with a hand on her arm. "You're one of the best directors I've worked with. And I've worked with a lot. Whatever goes down, I'll always say that."

Humbled, and misty (again—ugh!), Cali nodded. "Thank you."

She closed the Makeup door behind her and leaned against it, silently appealing to the TV gods for some grace to get through this morning. *One seed at a time.*

She pushed away from the door and collided into Paolo. They swayed under the impact, and Cali grabbed his elbows to steady them. "Whoa! You okay? I don't want you to take another trip to the medic."

Paolo instantly went red. "Oh, hi, Cali," he said and fumbled toward the Makeup door.

Cali put up her hands. "That's not a great idea. She's pretty angry."

He tried to shoulder through. "I need to clear things up between us."

Cali sidestepped to block him. "Now is not the time."

Paolo's face fell. "This is all my fault."

He collapsed hard against the wall, eyes down, posture defeated.

Cali gingerly mirrored his pose. "I know you're more comfortable with Jory, but do you mind if I share an observation with you?"

Love, Camera, Action

Paolo's eyes rose to hers, and Cali held her breath at the storm of emotions she saw there: guilt, hope, fear, vulnerability. This man was full to the brim, and no one had tapped into it, least of all him.

Cali wanted to hit this scene out of the park for herself, but also to show Paolo what he could do. That he *was* an actor and, with a little help, could be a skilled one. "I think you care deeply about what you're doing on this show. I see you striving to do good work, but you haven't found your way yet."

Paolo's lips parted, as though he'd been caught out. "I do want to be good. They don't think I can."

"Who?" Cali knew but wanted Paolo to say it.

"The crew. The producers." Paolo studied his feet. "Thalia."

Cali nodded. Thalia was the real problem. Not the crew or the producers. Paolo wanted Thalia to respect him. "I think you have to stop thinking about what's good and start doing what's true. You're not an actor who works from here." Cali tapped her temple. "Acting for you is doing. It's listening. Find an action to focus on that will free you up to really listen, and the authentic Paolo will come out."

Paolo stilled. A serenity washed over him in direct opposition to his usual frenetic energy. This shy, quiet person was probably closer to who the real Paolo was. He was breathtaking.

Cali continued, "You won't be able to fix what's happened between you and Thalia before this scene. So here's a trick that will hopefully work for your acting and keep her safe."

Paolo peered at her with hopeful eyes.

Cali drew an imaginary line between her heart and his with her hand. "Pretend there's a rope that connects your heart to hers. The tighter the rope pulls, the more it hurts, so you have to keep close. You want to touch her, but it burns when you do."

Torment seeped into Paolo's gaze. "That's what I feel anyway."

Cali could only nod. Who knew the two of them would be pining for people who didn't want them? Paolo was in deep and she was loathe to leave him drowning alone. She let her own torment leak out, her voice hitching. "Listen to that emotion, as painful as it is. Feel the emptiness, the futility. Feel the hopelessness and the regret. But remember the love too. What did you say before? 'You relish that pain since it means you exist.'"

Paolo nodded at her in understanding, a compatriot.

"Do that." Cali smiled and turned to go, then stopped herself. "Just to clarify, don't touch her skin and be all like, 'Ah! It burns!' or make hissing sounds and blow on your fingers. Be manly about it. Take the pain."

Paolo gave her a wry look. "I got it."

Cali started to step away, when Paolo's voice pulled her back, "I know it's Jory who thinks I can't act. Not you."

"Oh?" She tried to hide her shock.

"I kind of got it before, but Jory set me straight. I was dumb, thinking I should play the game by sidling up to the guy who would be here the longest. I should have gone with the person who believed in me."

Jory had set him straight? When? Why? It didn't make sense. He should never have undermined an actor's trust in him. Maybe she had gotten it wrong. Maybe she'd jumped to conclusions about Jory's intentions—again. God, this trust thing was brutal. Cali felt that stupid tendril of hope grow bigger.

Love, Camera, Action

"We cool?" Paolo put out his fist. Cali awkwardly bumped it.

He sheepishly smiled and walked away, hands in his pockets, head down.

Cali slowly turned to take in the last, long hallway in front of her. She blew out a breath and quietly walked to set for her final seed.

CHAPTER TWENTY-TWO

Jory stepped onto the Paolo/Rafe bedroom set with a powerful sense of déjà vu. The set decs were placing the "proper" amount of pillows allowable for a man on the bed, and Brandon was attaching a mic to the headboard. The light Jory had fixed that first day Cali arrived was out again. He grabbed a ladder to fix it, remembering how much color she'd brought to his life, and that's when the true panic set in. What if he was too late or hadn't gone far enough or had destroyed everything?

Phase two of his plan had been set in motion and phase three—the begging portion of the plan—was to go into effect the moment he saw her. Phase one—forcing the actors to fight for real while shooting in a storm in order for him to appear unhinged and negligent—had been completed. The hope being Howard would be forced to fire him instead of Cali.

The truth was he *had* been unhinged. The thought of losing Cali over some half-cocked idea of advancing his career had sent him into banana land. Given what he'd done to her, she might not even want to be with him, but he couldn't leave

Love, Camera, Action

her unprotected. Sabotaging himself was all he could come up with on the fly. He forgot to factor in the *actual* danger.

But when he'd gone to Howard's office this morning, Howard had fluffed the incident off like it was no big deal. So, Jory quit. When he closed the office door behind him, he thought he'd experience some form of horror, of desolation. After all, he had just decimated his world. Instead, an unrealized tension sloughed off his body, a veil pulled away to reveal the world as it truly was—shiny and new and full of promise. And he couldn't stop smiling about it.

And that made him angry.

He had been duped by ambition and prestige, unknowingly paying for it with tiny slices of his soul he'd handed over bit by bit, just like Cali had said. He hadn't really wanted to direct. He'd wanted control. Control in hopes of gaining a sense of security by giving away his creativity and spontaneity. A devil's bargain.

Just like he was trying to control how others responded to his health, controlling himself, controlling what had been blossoming between Cali and him, which was about as possible as controlling a thunderstorm. Regardless of how she would react to his gesture, he'd done the right thing. Now he would have to accept whatever Cali and Fate had decided.

Light fixed, he descended the ladder and checked his frame in the monitor. Dan eased up beside him. "You good?"

Meeting the gaze of this man he had so much respect for was harder than expected. Jory had endangered the safety of the cast and crew. True, he had been suffering under an emotional storm of his own, but it hadn't been his best moment. "Other than trying not to implode over my own negligence, I'm fine. Why?"

"Because you look somewhere between wet bread and coprolite."

"What's coprolite?"

"Fossilized dinosaur poop. My son wants to be a paleontologist."

"How could I look like wet bread and fossilized shit?"

"Something about your hair."

Jory huffed out a laugh. "Has anyone told you that you have all the unnerving qualities of a magical crone?"

Dan snorted. "I can't say I've heard that one, but I'll take it." Dan took Jory's measure, while Jory fought the urge to wince under its weight. "Cali didn't say anything, you know. About you making us into human lightning rods. And she asked me not to say anything either, although I should."

"Yeah, you should. Don't worry, I took care of it."

Dan's eyebrows went up. "All of it?"

Jory was afraid to ask. "What's 'all of it?'"

Dan indicated the monitor. Cali walked onto set and Jory's breath hitched. God he loved her. The way she commanded authority with an easy air rather than an iron fist. How everyone greeted her with a friendly deference that she held with humble hands. She was keeping up a magnificent front seeing as how she thought this was her last day, that her career was in tatters and the person she had trusted had betrayed her. Most people would be a quivering mess, but she commanded the set like she wouldn't give it up until it was pried from her fingers.

Still, her eyes were flat. He'd never seen her eyes flat. They were always sparkling, rolling, hardening, scheming, laughing . . . but never flat. Jory hated himself for being the author of that change, and his chest filled with grief over the

Love, Camera, Action

loss of the woman he'd met weeks earlier. The woman who was full of fire and intelligence and rebellion.

A punch to his arm knocked Jory out of his reverie. "Ow."

"*She* is all of it." Dan pointed at the screen.

"Oh." Jory focused back on the monitor. "Yes, she is."

"There's more to life than a good shot," Dan said.

"I'm learning that."

"Learn faster. Scene's up." Dan strode away.

Cali's husky voice floated over the flats. "Jory, Dan, can you join us?"

This was it. Although plan A had consisted of multiple phases, there was no plan B. Unless plan B was dissolving into a pool of regret and living out the rest of his life as—as what? A teacher, he supposed. That outcome wouldn't be good for anybody.

Jory followed Dan onto set, where Thalia and Paolo stood at opposite ends of the room. Paolo was still for once, dressed in a robe, leaning against a flat with his attention trained on the floor. Thalia was ostensibly ignoring him, her leather-clad demon self focused on Cali, but Jory got the impression her every nerve ending was attuned to Paolo.

Standing by the bed, Cali spoke with the new intimacy coach. Cali had argued for the necessity of a coach for every sex scene, no matter how big or small, and had won. Howard had probably smelled a lawsuit, but it was a victory for Cali, nonetheless.

She turned to the crew and everyone quietened. "I'm looking for a little bit of help here."

Jory's eyebrows shot up in surprise. He had heard Cali ask for people's opinions, but only when she had a clear idea of what she wanted already. Using the word "help" seemed to be alien to her, like she was trying it out for the first time. The crew, however, appeared rudderless . . . unclear of how to move forward. They weren't used to being asked direct questions, especially from directors who were supposed to rule like benevolent dictators.

Cali continued. "The last time we were in this bedroom, there was a clear battle for sexual dominance between our characters. But now, after all that's passed, they have developed an emotional connection. In this scene, they make a silent vow to each other to move through this hell together, because, as we know from future episodes, it will literally be hell."

Cali paused for a second, taking in the cast and crew as though for the last time. Her eyes landed on his. "But there has also been treachery."

Jory felt the gravity of her accusation. He couldn't run away to his camera, his lens, and put it between them. He had to pull himself up by the scruff of his neck and be in this now, or he'd lose her.

"A deception between them they must overcome if they are to move forward. So how do we visually communicate a balancing of power as they develop a deepening trust? How do we show what it means to hand over vulnerability to let love in?"

When he'd planned phase three of winning Cali back, he'd prepared an impassioned speech about how he'd gone wrong and what he would do to regain her trust. If it was space she needed, he'd give her space. If it was support, he'd find the myriad ways to do that and be glad of it. Somehow he sensed this was the weakest part of his plan, and if he'd learned anything from her, it was that plans change. She needed images rather than words—one frame better than a thousand promises.

Love, Camera, Action

"I have an idea that might help." He'd used her word "help," to offer an olive branch. Once he'd said it, he realized that was all he ever wanted to do for her—to help. The knowledge that he might be too late overwhelmed him.

Cali paused for a nanosecond and then stepped back, giving him the floor. "Please."

Jory took a tentative step forward. Paolo looked at him like he was a fraud, which Jory suspected was true, while Thalia gave the distinct impression she would tear him apart if he made one misstep. He hadn't been this unsure of his position in years. It was strangely exciting.

"There's a tantric pose called yab-yum that might be appropriate."

Dan's mouth tweaked up. "Go on."

"It's not really a sexual pose. It's more about intimacy." Jory made his tone deferential, referring to the coach. "Do you mind if I position the actors?"

The intimacy coach silently checked in with Thalia, who delivered a curt nod, and then Paolo, who gave a hesitant one. Jory motioned to Paolo. "Paolo is on the bottom again, with Thalia straddling, just like in the scene before. But this time, when you wake Paolo, you sit up cross-legged." Paolo sat on the bed, crossing his legs, his head lowered in mute respect.

Jory continued, "Thalia stays on top but sits in the hollow of Paolo's legs and wraps her legs around his hips."

Gingerly, Thalia got on top of Paolo. She checked where his hands were—by his side, clutching the sheets. She settled in, leaning away from him while he remained still as a stone.

"If it's alright with Thalia, Paolo should put his hands on her hips."

Paolo peered up through his lashes at Thalia who had become suddenly shy. She nodded, and he rested his hands lightly on her hips, a sigh escaping at the contact.

Jory was struck by how sweet their awkward politeness was, and wondered how Cali had managed to get them to this point when yesterday they'd been about to kill each other. "This position is about aligning your chakras, or energy centers, to each other's. Most importantly your third eye, which you connect by touching foreheads. Go ahead."

With the delicacy of a lunar landing, Thalia and Paolo touched each other's forehead, both of them squeezing their eyes shut on contact.

"And then breathe," Jory said, his voice roughening at the sight of the two warring actors in such a vulnerable position. "On Thalia's out breath, Paolo you breathe in, and on his out, Thalia, you breathe in."

Their breaths stuttered at first, but they eventually found a rhythm together. Jory stole a glance at Cali, who blinked as she took in the scene.

Did she remember? They'd been in the same position when they'd last made love—an act of instinctual surrender. He had been hers in that moment, but she had also been his: to protect and honor and . . . help. Either she wouldn't get it and he was wrong about what they'd shared, or she would comprehend that she held his heart in her hands. His blood raced at the thought, his head light with the possibility of it.

Jory cleared the emotion from his throat. "Yeah, so, it's a position that uses the third eye to attune to each other's souls. The breaths you share symbolize you are one, separate but together."

Love, Camera, Action

The set was silent, enraptured by Paolo and Thalia's synchronized breaths.

Cali walked up to the actors and gently placed a hand on Thalia's and Paolo's shoulders. "You guys good with this?"

Their eyes opened, as if coming out of a shared dream, Paolo pulling back and Thalia blinking herself awake. They nodded to Cali while disentangling themselves, looking everywhere but at each other.

Cali addressed the crew a bit too brightly. "That's it. That's what the scene needs. Thank you, Jory."

He could tell she was rattled, even through her shuttered gaze. His nerves were vibrating, but he told himself to be patient.

Cali clapped her hands. "Let's shoot."

She marched past him. The little spark from pleasing her dimmed as he followed her to their seats in front of the monitors. They sat in their chairs and quietly watched the crew do finals, bodies rigid, focus trained ahead. Jory should call the writers on the show because this was a form of hell he was pretty sure they had yet to explore.

"Action."

Jory watched the monitor. He didn't check the frame or judge the angle. Instead, he let himself get swept away by the moment. A moment he and Cali had created together. Thalia rode Paolo through his nightmare, and when he woke, he jolted with a gasp—all exactly the same as the scene before. But this time, they regarded each other in wary trepidation. Thalia inched back as if to leave, but Paolo swiftly sat up, stilling her with hands on her hips, wincing at the contact like he had been burned. When Thalia saw his agonized expression she softened, leaning into him. She brought her hand to Paolo's face to soothe his pain, which only made him wince more. But he didn't shy away; he bore her touch. Eyes brimming with care, Thalia lowered her forehead to his, and they began to breathe together in silence.

It was fucking gold.

Cali and Jory leaned in to watch, drawn to each other as they were drawn to the screen. He could feel her heat, smell her scent, and their breaths synced in tandem with Thalia's and Paolo's. This was where he wanted to be for the rest of his life, beside her, making magic on screen. Making magic with each other.

"What did you say to them?" Jory murmured.

She shrugged. "I just helped reveal what they were already feeling."

Thalia and Paolo were practically motionless but for their breathing, unaware of the crew or the camera, only intent on each other. Giving and receiving with open hearts.

"That's love." Her voice shook.

Jory tore his attention from the screen to see Cali awash in humbled awe. "That's love," he agreed.

In his periphery, Jory saw Thalia and Paolo change the angle of their connection so they could kiss, soft and sweet. Cali whispered, "They're not supposed to kiss." She turned to him, eyes glassy. "They're going off script. They're not supposed to kiss."

Jory couldn't let this moment pass. "I need to tell you something."

"It's okay. I think you'll be great."

"I can't—wait. What?"

"You're going to be a great director." Cali's eyes started to mist, and his heart combusted like celluloid in the sun.

Love, Camera, Action

"No. Wait. That's not—"

Cali exploded out of her chair, squeaking out, "Cut! Moving on!" And she bolted into the maze of the back sets.

Jory jumped out of his own chair, past the monitors where Thalia and Paolo were still kissing, and chased after her, not knowing where she was going until Cali opened up a door to the set for a supply closet. She growled out her frustration and wheeled around, but Jory blocked her escape. Her alarmed eyes darted for a way past as Jory grabbed her elbow and hauled her inside the closet. "You think I took the job?"

Cali pulled her elbow out of his grip and crossed her arms. "It's a good opportunity, and you proved your capability back there on the set."

Jory narrowed his eyes. "Did you open the scene up to the floor because you wanted to give me a chance to prove myself?"

"Not at all. I honestly needed the help."

"You needed the help?"

"I needed the help! I wasn't sure how to move the scene forward," she ground out.

"You weren't taking care of me? Because my happiness is not your responsibility, Cali. Especially since you think I took your job!"

She gritted her teeth. "I opened up the scene because I still believe in collaboration, even if it's with someone I have an ever deepening conflict with. I'm also taking care of the cast and crew so there will be an easier transition when they have to weather yet another change in leadership. It's better they have my blessing so it's easier on them. And you did take my job! I saw you coming out of Howard's office all triumphant and pleased with yourself."

"You saw me come out . . . ?" He flinched, then shook the tangent away. "I was smiling because I *was* pleased with myself. But not for the reason you think, and that's beside the point. You"—he pointed at her in accusation—"should be getting help because you're fucking amazing at what you do, and you're a good person, and you're special. Everyone should be helping you so you can spread more of you around. You shouldn't be helping me!"

"What was I supposed to do? Rant and rave and call you names and beat your chest with my fists?" Cali threw her hands up in exasperation.

"That would be a start." He nodded vigorously.

"You're an asshole." She squared off, drawing herself up like an angry cat. "You made my life hell on set because you were gunning for my job. You slept with me while you were stabbing me in the back."

"Yeah. That's it. Say that."

"You made me care for you when you're a big liar."

"Yeah, that's right." He drew back. "Wait, you care for me?"

But Cali was on a roll. She jabbed her finger into his chest with every point she made. "I've been trying so hard to trust you, to get over my own crap and give us a chance, and then you go and put our safety at risk for a terrible idea!"

Jory's carefully planned speech went out the window as his desperation spilled forth. "It was terrible, and I'm sorry. I wasn't in my right mind because I have a lot of baggage around sickness and cancer and people taking care of me. I watched my mother die and then had to live through all my pain and my father's and my family's, and I didn't want to put anyone I cared about through that."

Love, Camera, Action

"That is so"—Cali's face scrunched—"stupid."

"Thanks."

"You don't even know if you're sick. And if you are, you want to stop people from caring for you because you don't want to give them pain, so you give them pain by not letting them care for you?"

His shoulders deflated. "Well, when you say it like that."

"And the logical step is to put on a metal camera in a thunderstorm while emotionally manipulating the actors until they beat each other up?"

"Howard told me he wanted to replace you with me right before the scene, and yes, I had let him know I wanted to direct, but never to your detriment, and I had to think of something that would get me fired without you knowing so you wouldn't be linked to me. And endangering everyone was all I could come up with!"

Cali paused, perplexed. "I can't help but believe you because that's so preposterous."

"I know!" He moaned. "I'm new at this." He was desperate to touch her, his heart disintegrating to ashes because she thought so badly of him. "I couldn't take your job. Do you honestly think I would take your job? Especially after everything that happened between us?"

"I saw you come out of Howard's office. With a smile on your face!" she accused again.

"I went into his office to quit."

Her jaw dropped. "What?"

Suddenly, their little supply closet world shuddered as the door smashed open.

"What the fuck is going on in here?"

CHAPTER TWENTY-THREE

Cali wasn't sure she could take much more excitement, and her threshold was high. She was positive she had just heard Jory say he had quit and hadn't taken her job—that he'd been, in fact, trying to get fired. Her senses were at peak awareness with his proximity, and his smell invaded her brain, making her endorphins surge. The affection and outrage in his eyes stopped her breath. She had to admit, she had no idea what was going on.

And then there was Howard. Whose face was very red and whose finger was pointing at Jory. "You pathetic moron. I knew you could only have done something *that* stupid for pussy."

Jory put himself between Cali and Howard. "Excuse me?"

Cali tried to edge around Jory, but even though the supply closet set wasn't really the size of a closet, because a camera had to shoot in it, the room wasn't large either. After a few tries at being delicate, she pushed Jory out of the way. "Something stupid like what?"

Love, Camera, Action

Howard turned to her, his shoulders scraping against the shelving of the faux closet, toppling the paper towels stacked there onto his head. He batted them away with wild hands, voice filled with contempt. "Don't think you're safe just because you manipulated this dumbass into notions of nobility."

"What notions of nobility?" Cali skipped over the obvious insults.

"I'll have you both blackballed from any production in the English-speaking world by the end of the day. And the non-English-speaking world by the end of the week!"

"For what?" she gritted out. Cali's dam of patience for this megalomaniac was cracking.

"I've already quit!" Jory growled through clenched teeth.

Cali turned to him. "You keep saying that."

Jory kept his attention on Howard. "And I called Jeff Cummings to withdraw my name from consideration and put Cali forward for the job. He doesn't have a high opinion of you, by the way. Seems that he thinks you're an asshole and was all too ready to hear about an up-and-coming female director."

Cali was still not following the plot. "You know Jeff Cummings?"

"I do now."

Howard wedged himself between them. "I'll have you both escorted off set for gross negligence."

Cali was on the edge of enough. Jory apparently believed in her—was taking a bullet, which had always been her thing. To have someone support her when it disadvantaged their own path was a heady feeling. To not have to act alone, to be part of a front, gave her a strength and clarity of mind that broke through all her doubt and self-sacrifice. And this guy, this *showrunner* was threatening him. Trust was definitely a skill she'd have to work on, but protectiveness was something she knew well. She grew to mama-bear size.

"How have we shown gross negligence, hmm, Howard? By turning your mediocre show into gold? By staying on budget and bringing out the best in your crew while you swan around making arbitrary decisions that make no sense? By moving this story into the new world while we suffer under your old-boy attitudes?" Cali closed in on him. "I am so *sick* of being second-guessed by fuckwits who are holding onto their white-middle-aged-man privilege by their fingernails. I am so *tired* of being told what's right by men who are terrible at their jobs while I do all the work and they get the accolades."

"I *own* this business," Howard roared.

Cali's spine elongated. She was on fire and she was going to ride it until she went supernova. "You are a dinosaur, and the big meteor is coming. I *saved* you by coming in here. You should be on your knees in gratitude. Instead, you're trying to fire me and my DP, who is a fucking genius, because you're a petulant little boy."

"Someone's getting fired." A fourth voice cut through the closet with all the authority of a deity.

Everyone looked over and saw Melanie, insinuating herself into their tight circle and somehow holding all the power.

Howard tried to back up but took a shelf corner to the head. "Thank you, Melanie." He said, rubbing his temple.

Melanie spoke in a measured tone, "Don't thank me, Howard. Jory can't be fired without extensive evidence of gross misconduct."

"I put the cast and crew in danger," Jory barked out. "I should be fired."

Love, Camera, Action

"And you will get sanctioned." Melanie addressed Jory dryly. "The circumstances do not call for termination because no one is filing a complaint. You stopped the shoot in a timely manner, and you've had an exemplary record up until this point. But consider yourself warned."

"It doesn't matter. I quit."

"You can't quit without a two-episode notice."

"Oh. Oh yeah." Jory rubbed the back of his neck, elbowing Howard in the ear. "I forgot about that."

"And since Cali is delivering some of the best work of this season, firing her could result in a wrongful dismissal suit," Melanie stated matter-of-factly. "Not to mention, firing the only female director would be terrible optics in light of the showrunner's removal from the series because of the impending sexual harassment claim made by Alison Whitall. Howard, it is you who is fired."

The supply closet went silent. Everyone's attention turned to the man whose face had just drained of all color.

"That little tease is bringing a harassment suit against me?" Howard spat. "I'd like to see her try."

Suddenly there was a crack of wood and their supply-closet world swayed. Jory had Howard by the throat up against the wall with a violence Cali had never seen. The flat pulled at its anchors and bowed, groaning under Jory and Howard's weight.

"You creeped on my camera assistant, you fucking asshole? I. Will. End. You." Jory pushed Howard, making the set undulate with every accented shove.

Howard ineffectively pulled at Jory's arms to catch his breath.

Melanie raised her voice, "That's enough, Jory! I do not have the energy for an assault case."

Jory stared at him with sightless eyes as Howard continued to squirm.

Cali placed a hand on Jory's back and felt heat pumping through his shirt. "Jory, stop."

Jory took a breath and gave Howard one final shove. "I will bankroll any lawsuit Alison mounts against you and personally search for other women you have gone after."

"Of which I'm sure there are many," Cali added.

Melanie stepped aside as well as she could. "Frederick?"

Outside the supply closet stood a mountainous enforcer in a dark suit. "Mr. Fox. If you would follow me?"

"This will never stick." Howard tried to straighten himself while glaring at all of them. "I will take each and every one of you down."

Melanie gave him a smile that sent shivers down Cali's spine. "I look forward to it."

Frederick stepped aside to allow Howard to pass, leaving the three of them alone in the supply closet.

Melanie blew out a breath, the only evidence she was even marginally upset, and turned to Jory and Cali. "I trust you'll be moving on to the next scene? Time ticks." She brought her phone up to her ear and stepped out of the closet. "Jeff, how lovely to hear from you."

Cali tried to make sense of it all. Jory didn't want her job. He'd quit. Sacrificed himself for her. And then talked her up to Jeff Cummings. *Jeff Cummings!* She still had her job. Jory still had his job. And Howard was facing a lawsuit. She should say something but could only come up with: "What the fuck were you doing quitting?"

Jory turned to her, still flushed from pushing around Howard, shaking out his hands and rolling his shoulders. "That's the first thing you want to say?"

Love, Camera, Action

"Yes. Why would you quit?" she demanded.

"Because it wasn't right that you were being taken off the show. Because I didn't want to get a shot at directing by usurping you. Because it tore me apart when you thought I had betrayed you like those men who messed up your mom and your sister."

"Turns out my sister was the messer-upper."

"What?"

"It doesn't matter." Cali dismissed the tangent, more interested in Jory's anguished face.

"Because you're not the only one who gets to make sacrifices," he added in a wry tone.

"I don't love making sacrifices," Cali said petulantly.

"No, but you've gotten used to it." There was an earnest quality to his voice when he spoke again. "The production needs you. This *business* needs you. Your voice and your heart and your fire." He swallowed. "*I* need you."

Cali opened her mouth to speak, but no sound came out. She may have swooned a bit, because Jory shot his hands to her elbows to steady her. "Not in the way that I become a burden like all your other responsibilities," he continued. "I don't want to be looked after."

"Too bad—you might have to be."

"I don't want that for you."

"But don't you see how much you help me? I've never had someone support me like you do, and you should let me do the same. I have no real-world experience with this, but I understand that's what a relationship is supposed to be."

"I'll try to get over my debilitating fear of bringing those I love down around me if you get over your need for people needing you. Let me be your supplicant, your man behind the great woman, your muse. And if you don't want that . . ." He examined the floor. "Well, I'll honor your decision."

Jory stilled, waiting for an answer. Emotion rose up in Cali with such a force she worried she would spontaneously combust until she was nothing but a puddle of goo on the floor of this pretend supply closet. But maybe from that goo she could rise, formed into a new person. One who could trust, who could depend on someone who wouldn't let her down or make her life an obstacle course. Become a new person with *this* person. This beautiful, caring man who had somehow become *her* person.

Jory searched her face with a ferocity that spoke of hope and conviction and vulnerability. Cali forced herself to speak. "You'll be my muse?"

"Yes."

"You'll be still while I film you?"

"Absolutely."

"You'll lie across a chaise lounge with a rose between your teeth and a delicate flush to your cheeks?"

His beautiful mouth tweaked ever so slightly. "I'm exceptional at delicately flushing."

Her mouth tweaked back. "And you'll turn to absinthe when I throw you over for a younger, comelier DP?"

"After I break his, her, or their neck, yes," he growled.

Cali had run out of jokes, out of parries. It was time to be brave, but she was still so very afraid. She swallowed hard. "And you'll love me back?"

His mouth opened in surprise as he squeezed her elbows, disbelief softening his features. He brought her closer and barely made a sound as he asked, "You love me?"

Cali nodded and dug her nails into his forearms so she could be understood, in all her raw fear and fragility.

Love, Camera, Action

Jory's eyes filled with a surety she would never tire of seeing. "Then I will love you back. I will *really*, really love you back."

Jory pulled her to him, but something nagged at her mind, a loophole unclosed, and she pulled away. "Wait. Does that mean you don't love me now, but you plan to?"

Jory blinked. "Uh . . . No, no. I love you *now*. I was just going along with the whole muse thing. I love you now. Right now."

"Okay," she breathed out. "I love you too."

He cocked an eyebrow. "Can I kiss you now?"

She didn't wait to answer, claiming him for herself. Their lips met with urgency and tenderness, and all the hope and pain they could share as they went forward together. It was a kiss laced with a love fully acknowledged in the light of day in a dark supply closet. A kiss that tasted of new beginnings, of old ways dying, and the promise of something neither could anticipate. And they tasted it again and again.

In the periphery of Cali's consciousness, she heard a throat clear, and then clear again. Then a third time, accompanied by a harrumph. Jory pulled back, and in a daze she turned toward the intruder.

Dan stood in the doorway, a smug look on his face. "Finally. Scene's up."

EPILOGUE

Two weeks later

Man, the woman could eat. Jory had made Cali a pasta carbonara with double the bacon and triple the cheese, and from the moment the aroma of the rich sauce met her senses, she breathed it in and lowered her lids in complete satisfaction in a way he was becoming very familiar with, in and out of the kitchen.

He'd got the call that the growth was benign. It was a huge relief that came with a caveat: he'd have to be extra vigilant with check-ins so the doctors could keep tabs on him, and monitor any possibility of change. Cali had jumped in with the ferocity of a war-time nurse, which Jory combatted by promising he'd be on top of it. She calmed down, but it didn't stop her from making sure he took care of himself.

On *The Demon*, they'd made it through the final scenes in harmony when they collaborated and in discord when

Love, Camera, Action

they'd pushed each other. At night they'd taken the edge off when they took turns running their own private show.

Now, sitting at his kitchen island after a rigorous bout of "taking the edge off," they leisurely ate as Patsy's light snores rumbled through the baby monitor.

"She got a new dissertation board," Cali said hopefully, although Jory knew she was worried. He hated the uncertainty that so often took root in Cali's countenance, but he had found a new satisfaction when he helped her alleviate it. Her fears weren't gone, and probably never would be, which was something he'd have to learn to live with. But he had patience and determination.

"When does she present?"

"Day after we get back to Toronto."

Jory winced. He knew Cali had to go back, but it didn't make his worry over her leaving any less. This air of uncertainty was also something he was learning to deal with, to understand that a separation didn't have to mean forever. He reminded himself that Melanie had already asked Cali to come back and shoot the season finale, and even better, he was going up to Toronto next weekend when production took a short hiatus while the studio decided who would replace Howard.

Then, after a week at the beach house, followed by his father and Astrid's wedding, he and Cali would start a gig together—on Jeff Cummings's new show. Jeff had decided to take them both on as a team, locking them in for the whole series after seeing early cuts of their work on *The Demon*. With a little luck, a gig like that could go on for years. Not only that, Jeff had brought Patsy on as a Classics expert since the series was an updated retelling of the Greek myths. Jory guessed more snoring through baby monitors was in his future.

"What should I bring up to Toronto?" he asked.

Cali regarded him quizzically. "What do you mean?"

"What kind of clothes?"

"It's summer."

"Yeah, but it's Canada."

"Oh." Cali shrugged. "Bring a coat, a hat, and some mitts. You know, summer wear."

"Really?"

"No, not really." She shook her head. "It'll be thirty-five degrees."

"That's freezing!"

Cali's eyebrows furrowed in confusion and then understanding dawned. "Sorry, it's ninety-five degrees in your draconian way of gauging temperature."

Jory put on a guttural Canadian accent. "Sohrrey. Sohh-hhrey. You're so cute."

Cali pushed up nonexistent sleeves, readying for a fight. "Canadians are not cute. And 'sahrry' isn't any better. Sahrry. Sahrry!"

Jory stood up from his chair, threw his napkin down in mock outrage, and stalked her around the kitchen island. Cali squeaked with excitement and jumped from her stool. "Sahrry! Sahrry!" She bolted for the living room, but he easily tackled her on his now favorite couch.

He was about to assail her with his mouth when his thigh connected with something hard in her pocket. Guilt flooded her features, for what he didn't know. So, he tickled her. "What's in your pocket?"

"Nothing! Nothing! Stop!" she squealed.

"Are you hiding some hard-boxed contraband?"

She gasped for breath and jerked around as she tried to keep his hands away. It didn't take him long to pull out a brand-new cartridge of Super 8 film. Cali stilled under him.

Love, Camera, Action

"What's this?" Jory rattled the cartridge.

Cali bit her lip while she tried to shrug it off but was clearly nervous at how he would react. "I thought you could start shooting your own memories."

Jory's nose started to burn. Cali looked like she was worried her gift had been a bad choice. As if anything so considerate could go wrong.

He kissed her soundly. When he felt her relax, he whispered, "Thank you" against her trembling lips.

Jory sat up, swinging his feet over the edge of the couch to grab the camera from the table. Cali pushed herself up to sit beside him. Jory felt a sudden *rightness* in the moment, like he and Cali were always supposed to sit together like this, loading film in a camera, breathless in anticipation of what they could make together.

Guiding the cartridge into place, Jory snapped the camera shut and swung it toward Cali, his new favorite subject.

What he saw through the eyepiece shocked him: Cali's face filling with alarm.

"No, no, no." She waved her hands in front of her as she sprang from the couch.

Jory lowered the camera. "Wait. Are you . . . camera shy?"

"No, no. Not at all," Cali lied. "I just prefer to be behind the camera."

Jory stood up and slowly advanced on her as though she were a skittish fawn and he was the big bad wolf. "But who else would I film, if not you?"

Cali backed away. Her eyes darted from side to side, searching for escape. "I don't know, the couch?"

"The couch doesn't blush as well as you do." Jory raised the camera back to his eye and pushed "Record," the satisfying whirr of the film vibrating through the camera.

Noël Stark

Cali put her hands out to ward him off. "Come on! Stop it! Seriously!" And she bolted for the bedroom with a screech.

He chuckled, feeling alive and playful and so in love as he followed her. "Don't run in there—or this is going to be a much different kind of movie."

ACKNOWLEDGMENTS

This book took a long time to write, in a lot of strange places, during a lot of stolen moments – on the bus to work, at work when I should have been working, in the back seats of cars coming home from work. On stationary bikes and in pumpkin patches, in the dark after bedtime and in the early morning to owls hooting outside my West Hollywood apartment. I'm still amazed it has made it into the world. And there are a lot of people to thank for that.

In order of appearance: To my sister Denise who introduced me to romance novels. To Ross for believing I could write one. To Jeanne De Vita who I met through a workshop at The Ripped Bodice and who gave me that vital first push. To Ashley James who checked in, week after week, to make sure the dreaded first draft was on track. To Amy Schiffman who, along with Stefanie Huie, while mentoring me on a completely different project, took on the beginnings of this one and gave me the confidence to continue.

To the talented, kind and generous Kelly Siskind, my class of '21 Pitch Wars mentor, who loved that first draft enough to wrestle it into shape. I am so, so, so grateful for her. To the Pitch Wars community and Brenda LaPointe Drake who, through their relentless volunteerism and belief in new authors not only helped me but encouraged hundreds of writers to realize their dreams over the ten years that Pitch Wars was active.

To Jonathan Rosen at the Seymour Agency who believed in this book, and to Cole Lanahan for picking up the torch and bringing it home.

To Jess Verdi at Alcove for the vulnerability and openheartedness she brought to the edit and for her steadfast encouragement when I was swimming in doubt. To the rest of the team at Alcove: Matt Martz, Martin Biro, Thai Fantauzzi Perez, Rebecca Nelson, Dulce Botello, Mikaela Bender, Stephanie Manova, Megan Matti, Doug White, Cassidy Graham and Monica Manzo. And to Kristen Solecki for her gorgeous and sassy cover.

To Amy, Emma, Annette and Scott for reading various drafts, giving integral input and being excellent cheerleaders. To my parents, Don and Diane, to the Andersons, and to the Naivelt community for their continual support.

And, as always, to my son Jude and my step kids Emma, Declan and Ben, who are constant sources of wonder and joy.